STOLEN KISSES

"Och, Rosamund, dinna fash yersel'. 'Twas but an innocent wee kiss, from a mon to his bride. Admit it! Ye've been wondering, too. And ye wanted it as much as I did."

"The devil I wanted it, sir," she retorted. "And as for it being innocent—it was no more innocent than *you*, milord."

He chuckled to himself, thoughtfully touching his lips where the taste of her still lingered. She didn't want his kisses—but she hadn't said she disliked them any more than she'd lifted his hand off her breast in the night.

"Sassenach?" he called after her.

She paused in the doorway, glaring daggers at him. "What now?"

He ran the tip of his tongue over his lips and winked. "I like the taste of ye. I like it verra much."

She blushed. "Devil take you, McLeod!"

STOLEN

Penelope Neri

LEISURE BOOKS NEW YORK CITY

A LEISURE BOOK®

January 2002

Published by

Dorchester Publishing Co., Inc.
276 Fifth Avenue
New York, NY 10001

ISBN 0-8439-4371-8

Visit us on the web at www.dorchesterpub.com.

"What's in a name? That which we call a rose,
By any other name would smell as sweet;"
—*Romeo and Juliet,* Act II, Scene 2.

Chapter One

The tinkle of breaking glass echoed in Drummond's ears as he crawled over the windowsill into Riverside House. Yet, there was no outcry from below. No shout of alarm that signaled discovery.

Releasing the breath he was holding, he straightened and looked about him. His lip curled in contempt. Even here, in his harlot's love nest, the "Butcher" lived like the prince he was, God rot him. Such fine trappings were a far cry from the leaking croft-houses his countrymen called home.

The shadowed bedchamber was draped in blue damask, patterned with gold crowns. A pastel mural of lewd centaurs and naked nymphs romped across the ceiling. The high bed was draped in white velvet. The Turkey carpet felt like clabbered cream beneath his boots.

Leaving His Grace's chamber, he edged down the upper gallery, listening at each paneled door he came to, before moving on to the next.

Halfway down the gallery, he froze. He could hear a woman's voice within the next chamber. Arabella's, surely?

A muscle throbbed at his temple as he drew the pistol from his belt. His hand shook from the fever as he cocked the hammer, but with an iron will, he steadied it.

Tonight he would not falter. Tonight he was a righter of wrongs. An avenging angel.

And because of him and the vow he had made, tonight Arabella would die.

Rosamund bit her lip, sick to her belly with misgiving as she looked down at the emerald earbobs in her hand.

Known as the Eyes of the Tiger, the jewels were worth a sultan's ransom. But once she took them and left Riverside House, there would be no going back. Her life would never be the same again.

From this evening forth, she would be a thief. No better than the thieves and pickpockets who cluttered the steps of St. Paul's, or the cutpurses of Mayfair. Even if no one else ever found out what she'd done, *she* would know. Could she live with herself, with that knowledge, day in and day out, for the rest of her life? She swallowed. What choice did she have?

She stared at her reflection in the looking glass before her. The slender, brown-haired young woman who stared defiantly back at her had once been mistress of a modest house in Sadler's Wells. She had worn gowns of good if not excellent quality, and attended Miss Pennington's Academy for Young Ladies. More importantly, she had liked the person she saw reflected in her mirror. Had admired her for her high principles, her tenacity, her kindness and her honesty.

Ah, yes. Especially her honesty.

Her mind made up, Rose set her jaw and lifted her chin a little higher. She had been wrong about one thing. She still had a choice. Indeed, choices were all she had left! Well, then, Devil take Tom Wainwright and his crafty plans. She wouldn't do it, so there! She'd return the jewels to the coffer and leave Riverside House the way she'd entered it—by the casement window.

Like the legendary phoenix that Miss Pennington had spoken of—a bird that had risen from the ashes of its own ruin—she and Jim would rise up in the world again someday, without resorting to thievery.

Selecting a powdered wig from the wig stand, she tucked her own hair beneath it and pulled it on, patting the stiff curls.

"So there!" she told her reflection, sticking out

her tongue. She smiled, feeling ever so much better now that her mind was made up. "All I have to do now is make a clean escape," she muttered. "And how, pray, shall I do that? By door— or by window?"

A loud, metallic "click" answered her.

Hands half in, half out of the jewel chest before her, she stiffened, frozen in place.

Someone was standing behind her!

Her heart in her mouth, she waited for a cruel hand to clamp over her shoulder. An arm to choke her by the neck.

"One squeak, and ye're dead where ye stand, lass," a gruff voice threatened.

Too frightened to face the man, she brought her chin up and stared at the mirror before her.

Her eyes met his in the looking glass—and a cold pair they were, too. Gray and hard as flint, and deepset beneath brows like slashes of ink on paper. His long, disheveled hair was the glossy blue-black of coal.

In truth, everything about him spelled darkness and danger.

"Turn around, ye wee bitch!"

Dropping the emeralds down her bodice, she did so. Her heart slammed against her ribs like a frantic sparrow, caught in a snare. She needed time. Time to think what to do.

"Please, sir, let me exp—"

"Quiet, or I'll cut out your tongue!"

She gulped over the knot of terror in her

throat. She had no doubt he'd do as he threatened. Those empty eyes made her skin crawl. He would not balk at murder.

Oh, Jim, forgive me, she prayed silently. *Please, please forgive me. . . .*

Drummond swayed as he hooked an arm around the lassie's white throat. He drew her back, cradling her golden-brown head against his chest, for all the world like a lover, he thought with a mocking smile.

The moment he'd dreamed of was here. Each day since the battle, he'd imagined taking this woman's life. Indeed, it was all that had kept him going on the difficult journey south. And now she was here, and completely at his mercy. Arabella Slater. "Butcher" Cumberland's pampered mistress. His whore. The woman the fat duke loved more than anyone—except himself.

His grip on the pistol slackened a fraction. The bluidy fever. It was making him lightheaded, weakening his resolve.

"Your life, madam, for those taken," he rasped in the woman's ear. "A poor exchange, aye? But one that will serve, if it breaks the Butcher's heart."

Jamming the pistol's long snout under the soft swell of her breast, he ground out, "For Cameron, and Dunmor! Hold fast!"

His finger curled tenderly, almost lovingly, around the flintlock's trigger, and squeezed.

He closed his eyes, steeling himself for the recoil, the deafening explosion.

Instead, his finger froze.

Seconds passed on leaden wings. Minutes seemed hours.

Nothing.

Fire, damn ye! he ordered himself silently. *Do it, mon! Ye call yourself the McLeod? Then what are ye waiting for? Do it, do it now!*

I canna, came his answer. *God help me, I'm no' His Grace, to kill in cold blood, without reason or rhyme.*

For Cameron, then. Do it for Cam . . .

But he could not.

The bedchamber tilted about him. Blackness crowded in. He blinked hard to clear his vision and collect his scattered thoughts.

Damn the fever that smoldered inside him like a damp fuse. Clammy sweat trickled down his spine. Vengeance, killing, murder—they were the last things on his mind!

He could feel the woman's labored breath on his hand. Her small breasts heaved against his forearm. Her rump rode snugly against his thighs.

A perverse part of him ached to take the woman in his arms. To tumble her and with their coupling, spit in the face of death.

Damn her for being so *alive*, so warm, so vibrantly female that he could not kill her. Or rather, could not kill her *now* . . .

He'd take her with him, to the ship, he decided. And later, when he'd recovered his spleen, he'd kill her. What difference would a day make? Several days?

None at all, for nothing could bring them back.

Dropping to one knee, the man opened an armoire drawer and withdrew a stocking. Setting aside the pistol, he reached for her wrist. "Your hand. Give it here."

She kicked out. Her bare foot caught him full in the nose, before he could jerk aside.

He yelped in surprise, dropped the pistol and toppled sideways, all balance lost. With another kick, she sent his weapon skittering across the floorboards, and dived for the door.

But, agile as a cat, despite his size, the brute was on her in a wink. Pistol in hand, he blocked her path to freedom, his expression murderous now.

"Ye'll pay for that, ye slippery wee eel!" he threatened through clenched teeth. Blood streamed from his nose. His pewter eyes glittered. "By God, ye'll pay!"

She backed away until she could feel the hard edge of the vanity table at her back. "Who are you?" she demanded, her voice breaking as she looked up at him.

"Laird Drummond McLeod, at your service, my lady." He inclined his dark head, his gallantry mocking her. "The seventh and last McLeod of the McLeods of Dunmor, thanks to the butchering whoreson ye take to your bed!"

He drew himself up to his full height, several inches over six feet.

"You have lost me, milord," she said in her best Miss Pennington's voice. It was no lie, not really. She *was* confused. Who was he? And more importantly, who did he think *she* was? Reaching behind her, she clawed for the porcelain powder box she'd seen there. "I have no idea who you are talking about, sir. Explain yourself, pray."

He snorted. "Ye ken bluidy well who ye are, mada—"

She flung the powder box at him. It struck him full in the face, the rim splitting his lip.

The bowl crashed to the floorboards, shattering into translucent shards. Wig powder billowed over her, over him, over the chamber, coating bedposts, canopy, chamber pot and armoire in white.

While he struggled with his streaming eyes, she ducked behind a dressing screen. Tugging at the doorknob in the small door behind it, she begged, "Oh, please, don't be locked, not now. Come on, come on! *Open!*"

But it would not.

Still half-blinded by powder, he lurched toward her, cursing in a foreign tongue. Grabbing hold of her lace-trimmed sleeve, he hauled her out from behind the folding screen. The worn fabric tore as he did so.

"Got ye, ye slippery besom. Ye'll no' escape me that easily." He spat powder from his mouth. "I've come too bluidy far t'lose ye now."

"Please, let me go, sir," she demanded. Tugging at her arm, she tried to wriggle free of his numbing hold. "I did nothing wrong. Nothing at all, I swear it."

She flung around and looked him full in the eye, a picture—she hoped—of innocence. "Honestly, sir," she pleaded. "You arrived too soon. Let me go, and I'll put it all back—I'll do whatever yer want," she offered.

Suddenly she uttered a loud grunt, and then stomped hard on the brute's foot. She followed it up with a knee to the middle that doubled him over. But before she could squirm past him, he caught her by the waist.

"Yield," he ground out, waving the pistol in her face as he dragged her up against him. "Yield, or I'll blow your blasted head off, right now. And this time, so help me God, I willna balk."

He was white about the lips. His brow was sweaty, too. All in all, there was a desperate air about him that boded ill for her chances.

"All right, gov'na. You win. I'll come quietly," she promised. She eyed the horse-pistol in his fist. "Just promise you won't shoot me."

His scowl darkened. "I'll promise ye nothing. Now walk, milady. We've a rendezvous to keep."

With a faint nod, she led the way from the chamber without further protest.

There would be other chances to escape between here and Newgate, she told herself as she stumbled down the gallery. Tom was out there somewhere, waiting for her. She would bide her time—and pray her captor dropped his guard.

Chapter Two

He and the woman had climbed back down the oak tree when Drummond heard Andy's shrill whistle. It was the signal to break for the river with all possible haste.

Grasping Arabella's wrist, he ran, hauling her after him, keeping low so the hedges would hide them from passersby.

A damp and murky twilight cloaked the city of London now. Hugging the shadows, he dragged Arabella down to the wooden jetty, where his cousin waited with a rowboat, ready to cast off.

Andy's eyes widened in amazement when he saw him. No wonder. He could imagine what he must look like, thanks to the drizzle and the

Penelope Neri

blood, which had carved furrows in the powder that coated his face.

His cousin's exclamation confirmed it.

"Sweet Mother of God!" Andy whispered. "Is it you, Drum?"

"Who do you think it is, ye bluidy fool?" He scowled. "His Holiness, the Pope? Why did ye whistle me up?"

"Someone called out the guard," Andy explained. "And then I . . ." His voice trailed away as the wench stepped out from behind the hedge. "Sweet Jesus! Tell me that isna the lassie." His jaw dropped as necklaces, earbobs and gold chains showered to the jetty from beneath the woman's skirts.

"It isna the lassie. Satisfied?" He was in no mood for more of Andy's lectures.

Lifting Arabella into the rowboat, he planted her on the crosspiece. "Move so much as a muscle," he told her, "and I'll clout ye."

"Devil take you," she shot back. "I'll move if I wish."

"Why, mon. *Why?*" Andy moaned. "Are ye so blessed eager to get us hanged, is that it?"

"Never mind that. Who sounded the alarm?" he demanded as he untied the line and sprang aboard the craft.

It rocked wildly, almost spilling both him and the girl into the drink.

"A man. Strange, that. I saw him by the hedgerows, after ye went in through the window. He waited for a bit, then ran off."

"He saw me, then?"

"That's the odd part. I dinna think so. But soon after, the place was crawling with guards. Then candles and lamps were lit in one chamber after the other. The bastards were searching the house, Drum. Another blessed minute, they would have had you!"

A quick glance confirmed Andy's story, puzzling though it was. Riverside House was ablaze with light. The reflections of the lighted windows swam like square moons in the oily black Thames.

Thank God, no guards were searching the grounds yet. They'd have time to get well away, before the hue and cry moved outdoors.

"What the devil were ye thinking of?" Andy hissed as he took up his position facing Drummond. His pale, freckled face was aghast in the gloom. "Ye said ye meant to kill the lass—not elope wi' her!"

"I do." He licked his cracked, dry lips. "I will," he swore grimly, yet he could not meet his cousin's eyes.

"Then why didn't ye?" Andy challenged

"There's been a wee change in plans. I'll explain later. For now, *row*, blast ye!"

The dark lout's rowing quickly moved the rowboat out into deeper water.

Behind them, Riverside House reared up from the water-meadow like a—a mausoleum, Rosamund thought. She wetted her dry lips. The good Lord knew, it had almost proved *her* coffin! And still might.

She slipped a finger between the frayed neck of her gown and her throat, and swallowed. Although the ominous snout of the pistol was no longer lodged beneath her breast, she could readily imagine the hangman's noose about her throat.

She bit her lip, fighting angry tears. *That treacherous sod! That wretched turncoat!* If what the freckled one said was true, then Tom had betrayed her! She gnawed at her lower lip. She never should have agreed to this. Not in a million years. Nothing—not even the Eyes of the Tiger— was worth hanging for, as she'd be hanged.

"Trust me," Tom had said as they'd stood outside Riverside House that afternoon.

"I do," she'd whispered, tucking up her skirts for the climb. It was no lie. She'd trusted Tom to be waiting at the bottom of the tree when she shinned back down. Trusted him to pocket the loot, too. But beyond that, she hadn't trusted him an inch. He was a handsome cove, but crooked as Bent Street.

In eerie silence, save for the splash of oars cutting water and the labored breathing of the oarsman, the rowboat moved steadily, surely toward the Pool of London.

They glided on a black looking glass, cloaked by drifting fog and the silvery mist that rose off the Thames.

She was adrift with a brace of madmen—and foreign madmen, at that. Trapped in a nightmare from which she could not awaken.

The taproom of the Golden Swan where she'd served ale last night seemed as distant as a dream. A hazy memory drawn from someone else's life. She hugged herself about the arms.

"Cold, are ye?" the oarsman observed, eyeing her with callous contempt.

"What do you care?" she demanded, scowling.

"I dinna give a damn," he jeered. "There are others far colder than you in your fine fur cloaks, Arabella. Brave laddies who lie in cold, dark graves. Fallen Highlanders whose blood cries out for vengeance."

She frowned. He'd called her Arabella more than once. That, and the way they'd left Riverside House by window and tree, rather than by any door, kindled a flicker of hope in her breast. The pair were surely not constables or thieftakers, who were carting her off to Newgate Gaol to be tried and hanged. She'd concluded they must be kidnappers, instead. Ruthless rogues who believed she was Arabella, the Duke of Cumberland's mistress. Desperate men who would demand a ransom for her safe return. Or rather, Arabella's safe return. Her very life could hinge upon their believing she really was Arabella. As Rose Trelawney, tavern wench and thwarted thief, she was not worth a farthing.

"I demand to know where you are taking me." She drew herself up on the rowboat's crosspiece, trying to look like a proper duke's mistress. "Rest assured, His Grace shall hear of this outrage," she threatened with as much conviction as she could muster. "Answer me, pray, sir!"

"Ye'll find out soon enough," the taller man growled softly. "And why."

Having spoken, his sculpted mouth clamped shut in a thin, cruel line. To her disappointment, he said nothing more.

A nighthawk flew over the foggy river on silent wings. It uttered a piercing shriek as it hunted its prey along the grassy banks.

Huddled in the bows, the freckled one's knees pressed painfully against hers; the dark-and-brooding one rowed like a man possessed, and Rose fancied she knew how that prey felt.

Small, powerless—and very much afraid.

Drummond rowed, throwing his back into the task. He ignored muscles that screamed for rest, a mind that sought peace, a wound badly in need of tending.

In the three weeks since they'd become fugitives, he'd slept little. The few hours he'd snatched in cairn, ditch or brier had been poor and plagued with dreams; nightmares in which he saw the moors stained red with blood, and the sky turned dark with the sooty wings of the corbies.

That he was not among the dead that day, he owed to a common horseshoe nail, which had saved his life, he believed. He wore it now, looped about his throat on a leather cord. It served as a reminder; a symbol of his shame, his guilt, his failure.

If he hadn't stepped upon it in the bracken that morning, when the Bonnie Prince's army stopped at the burn to drink, his foot would not have swelled with poison.

If the poison hadn't driven him half mad with fever, Cameron would not have ordered him left behind at Kilravock Castle, in the care of Andy and Laird Rose's servant, Granny McRee.

For it was while he languished there, cosseted like an invalid, that the others marched on to their deaths.

Aye, if not for that bluidy horseshoe nail, he'd be in Heaven now, with the rest of them, and his heartache over.

If! 'Twas the sorriest word in the whole damned language!

After leaving the Clava Cairns, the ancient sanctuary where they'd gone to ground in the aftermath of the battle, he and Andy found all highways to the coast patrolled by Redcoats.

The English were searching for the Stuart Prince and for Jacobite fugitives, like themselves.

They'd worked their way home to Castle Dunmor, but discovered only tragedy awaiting them there. A wanted man now, with a price of five hundred guineas on his head, he and Andy fled south to avoid the English, who swarmed like blowflies over Scotland's corpse.

Slogging along on foot, they'd followed the little-known reivers' tracks to avoid English check-points, shunning the highways.

Little by little, their destination had become London, the very heart of enemy England. Their purpose was twofold: Revenge and escape!

They crossed the border at Coldstream on the first moonless, starless night after the battle. Using the darkness as their cover, they dodged the Redcoat sentries who patrolled the river crossing, on the lookout for fugitives like themselves.

When they were but halfway across, a sentry's voice rang out in challenge. When they gave no password in return, he fired his musket at their retreating backs and roused his fellows to hunt them down.

Wet, half starved, bone-weary and still weak from their wounds, he and Andy fled the mounted dragoons like hunted hares.

In the coming days, they hid out in thickets of thorn and bracken, swearing they'd rather be shot or drowned than hanged by the cursed British. Or worse, burned to death in their own homes—a common fate for those captured after the battle.

Drummond tightened his jaw. He did not fear death now. In truth, nothing scared the man he'd become; the carefree fellow he had been before no longer existed.

Like his older brother, Laird Cameron McLeod, sixth laird of Dunmor, he'd been left behind on Culloden's windswept moors. . . .

Remembering, his eyes burned and his throat ached, but he would not weep. He was a man, by God. And though his heart ached for those he had lost, and for the land he called home, he had sworn an oath upon the bodies of Cameron and their fallen kinsmen. He would not fail them now.

"I will seek out whatever is nearest and dearest to Cumberland's foul heart," he had vowed. *"And when I find it, I shall destroy it utterly! Someday, Cumberland will drink from the cup of grief, and learn 'tis a bitter draught to swallow!"*

As he rowed toward the Pool, his eyes fell on the English lass who was nearest and dearest to Cumberland's foul heart.

He saw how the starlight caught the sheen in her eyes—and prayed he could keep his vow to destroy her.

Chapter Three

The Pool of London was a forest of tall masts and gently bobbing vessels drawn from all four corners of the world, Drummond discovered after they abandoned the rowboat.

He jostled the lassie along the torchlit wharves, which were lined with chandlers' emporiums and grog shops, while Andy brought up the rear.

As Drummond and his cousin traveled deeper into enemy England after crossing over the Borders, they had met up with other fugitives of the battle, like themselves. One of them had given Drummond the name of a Scottish vessel, the *Salutation*, which was scheduled to be docked in the Pool of London on this date.

Her master, Captain Hamish McKinnon, the other man had promised, was a loyal Jacobite. McKinnon had spread word up and down the coast that he planned to delay his departure from the Pool to the New World until high tide this evening, and would grant free passage to those Highlanders who sought escape to New France.

For Drummond and Andy, McKinnon's vessel offered the fastest, most direct escape from enemy London. Yet how in the world was he to find the vessel he sought before the tide turned, and she set sail without them? There were literally thousands of vessels anchored here. How could they hope to find her in time?

No sooner had the thought filled his head than he came to an abrupt halt. His eyes widened in disbelief. His flagging spirits lifted, while a broad grin curved his lips.

For once, Lady Luck had smiled upon him!

The gilt script that curled across the bows of the vessel before him read *"Salutation."* He snorted in disbelief. The vessel he sought was right there, in front of his eyes! A bonnie merchantman that rocked gently at her moorings, her black-and-white paintwork and her rigging just as trim and neat as a pin.

Her figurehead raised a wooden goblet over the lapping dark water, a reminder of the secret salute loyal Jacobites made to their "King over the water," as the exiled prince was known. It was a fitting name for the vessel that would carry fugitive Highlanders to safety in New France.

By now, the Bonnie Prince was in hiding once again, a bounty of thirty thousand pounds on his head. And in the Highlands, women wept for the sons, sweethearts and husbands they'd never hold again.

Drummond hardened his jaw. Once they were at sea, he would avenge them all. The next time, there would be no weakening on his part.

"Andrew?" Emotion cracked his voice.

"Aye, Drum?"

"Stay here with her while I speak wi' the captain."

"Not bluidy likely," Andy protested, eyeing the girl. "I'll go."

Drummond drew himself up to his full height. "Do ye forget, mon? I'm the McLeod now."

"Aye. I ken." With that, Andy trotted up the gangplank, asking the captain's permission to come aboard as he went.

"Why me?" Drummond muttered under his breath.

"Because *you* wanted to kidnap me."

He shot her a scowl that was as black as Old Nick's. "Hold your tongue, ye wee besom. I didna ask your opinion."

"I didn't ask t' be kidnapped, either," she countered, her chin lifting. "But that didn't stop you, did it?"

He had the insane urge to laugh at her bravado. But the urge evaporated when he looked down at her.

Rain had washed away her paint and powder. In the flickering torchlight, she looked younger, more vulnerable than he had expected. Aye, and not half sae brave as she made out.

Can ye do it, laddie? taunted the small, niggling voice of his conscience. *You've balked once tonight. When the time comes, can ye drown her like a wee kitten?*

He found himself staring into her wide, frightened eyes, fringed with curly dark lashes. In the torchlight, they were the pale amethyst of heather. Highland heather.

He squared his jaw. What irony, for an English whore to have such bonnie eyes, and lashes like sable brushes. Yet, what had she done with her God-given beauty? Squandered it. Sullied it. Used it to snare the murdering "Butcher," that's what.

Disgust choked him. Grief clenched a fist about his heart and choked all pity from it.

"You were taken for a reason," he rasped.

"Was I, indeed? Well, I can think of no good reason for abducting an innocent lady so cruelly—"

"Innocent! There were no innocents at Riverside House. Nor," he added, spitting on the ground, "any ladies."

"—though I warrant I can guess yours," she continued as if he had not spoken. Her hand strayed to her throat "You mean to ravish me, once we are out to sea. I know it."

"Oy. Oy. What's this? Wants ter ravish ye, does he, the evil sod! Make sure 'Big Ben' pays ye first, all right, ducks?" a passing doxy warned over her shoulder.

Ample hips swinging, she sashayed to the corner, winking at him—Big Ben?—as she went by.

"Be off with ye, ye frowsy drabs," he growled.

"Big Ben? He-he. That's a good 'un, Kitty." The second woman brayed with laughter. She puckered her lips at him, too. "Oooh, I wouldn't half like to ring your chimes, lover. Give us a kiss!"

Arabella shifted against him. He could feel her muscles bunching, tensing. She was ready to run. "Dinna try it, lass," he warned.

"Help! Somebody, heeeelp! You, Kitty! He kidnapped me—heeelpp!" With an ear-splitting yelp, she suddenly shoved him in the chest.

Knocked off his feet, he went down in the mud. He made a grab for her skirts, but his hand closed on air as she flew off like a Fury.

She pelted down the cobblestoned wharf after the doxies, risking a turned ankle as she ran.

The bully-boys of a press-gang broke ranks like skittles to let her through, whistling raucously as she fled on, showing a trim pair of ankles.

With a curse, Drum heaved himself to standing and charged after her.

* * *

She must get rid of him, she told herself, pressing her side, where a painful stitch pricked like a needle. She'd escape, then get word to Jim.

She caught up with the doxies outside a grog shop. The pair were soliciting a trio of sailors.

"Please, I need your help," she panted.

"Our help, ducks?" the one named Kitty snorted as she turned to look at her, then spat in the dirt. " 'Strewth, with a clock like yours, you don't need our help. Fact is, you're bad for business, so scarper, or Lil will scratch yer eyes out. Right, Lil?"

"Right," Lil agreed with a lurid grin.

"I need your help." Rose's heart hammered as her abductor careened around the corner like a runaway cannon. "Oh, God. Here he comes again."

"Arabella!" he roared. "Hold!"

"The devil I will." Hastily lifting her skirts, she drew from her petticoats a slim gold chain, which she pressed into Kitty's hands. "Here. Take this for your trouble. Go to the Golden Swan on Tavern Street. Ask for Jim Trelawney. Got it?"

"Cornish Jim? The duke's man?"

Rose nodded. "Was, aye. Tell him the goods are safe, but I'm to be taken aboard the *Salutation*. She sails with the next tide. Tell him Rose needs him, quick as may be. Now, go. *Gooo!*"

"Got ye, ye slippery chit," the dark brute

roared. He grabbed her wrist as Kitty ducked under his arm and sped away.

"Not so bleeding fast, matey. Them doxies be ours," a sailor protested, just before his fingers hooked over her shoulder. "Find your own."

The Scot had to let her go to defend himself.

"Ah, shit," she heard him growl as she twisted away, and her spirits soared.

She'd escape him yet. She had to. Jim needed her.

"Inform the McLeod that we sail with the next tide, Andrew," Captain Hamish McKinnon told Andy after he'd given the password.

Such caution was necessary, he knew. The English would consider the capture of a Scottish vessel, its hold filled with Jacobite fugitives, a rare prize, he thought grimly.

The captain's stare was piercing as he looked at him. "The McLeod or no, I willna wait, mon. I've forty fugitives below these hatches, and every head wi' a price on it. I'll not jeopardize those forty for anyone, laird or no. Understand?"

"Aye, sir. If we're not aboard within the hour, Godspeed ye to New France without us."

McKinnon's bushy gray brows rose. "Us? How many are ye?"

"Three, Captain."

"Very well, then. One hour. No longer."

There was no sign of either Drum or the girl where Andy had left them.

He paced the wet cobbles in the drizzling rain, his dread mounting. Whist, where the devil was Drum? Time was running out. Twice he ducked into the shadows between the warehouses, to avoid being challenged by the night watch or the Redcoats patrolling the wharves. Thank God, they moved on without spotting him.

Just when he'd given up, his cousin spilled from the mouth of a dark alley. He looked angrier than Andy had ever seen him—and much the worse for wear. The wench plastered against him looked no better. Andy had to look away, for the desperate plea he saw in her eyes filled him with such guilt, he could not stare her down.

"We're to go aboard straightway. Ye had a wee bit o' trouble, aye?" he observed.

"I did," Drum agreed. He raised his left wrist. It was tied to the girl's by a length of dirty rag. "But I managed. She'll no' run from me again, by God. Will ye, lass?"

His soft-spoken words were laden with menace. His tone alone would have cowed most men. They had no effect whatsoever on the lassie.

"The duke will stretch your neck for this, you rogue," she promised.

Drum clamped his hand over her mouth, yelping as she sank her teeth into his palm.

"Damn ye, ye wee cat, I'm bleeding. Have done, I say."

"We'd best go aboard, Drum," Andy urged. "She sails with the tide, with or without us."

"Lead on, then," his cousin urged, shaking his throbbing hand.

"Shall I take her for ye?" he offered.

"Nay. You've a powerful soft heart when it comes to the lassies. I don't. Do I, Mistress Slater?"

"I doubt you even have a heart, you bastard!" she hissed.

Drum chuckled. "Run from me again and you'd best keep running, for if I catch ye, I'll wallop your arse till it blisters. And rest assured, I will catch ye."

"You're no better than a—a beast."

Andy winced.

A fierce light ignited in Drummond's gray eyes. "Nay, Arabella. I'm a Highlander—and bluidy proud of it," he ground out. "Now, walk."

Andy followed them up the wooden gangplank. The lassie, still linked to his cousin at the wrist, was forced to scurry to keep up with Drum's long strides.

Pity filled him. The girl's defiant words had not deceived him. Beneath that false bravado, she was terrified. He shook his head. Drum was wiser than he knew. Had she been in his charge, he'd have let her go at the first hint of tears.

The rain had eased up, he saw now. The oily dark waves that slopped against the piers were rimmed with moonlight. The tide had turned. Within the hour, they'd be setting sail, leaving all he held dear forever.

Chapter Four

"Welcome aboard, my laird, your ladyship," Captain McKinnon greeted them. Doffing his tricorn, the stout little captain swept her a gallant bow.

"My thanks, Captain, but I am not his lady," she announced, crisply and clearly, before McLeod could silence her. She glared at him, daring him to contradict her.

"—yet," the rogue added instead. Catching her about the waist, he drew her close.

She pulled herself free. "Captain, you strike me as a reasonable man. I beg you, listen to me. This—rogue—abducted me. Until tonight, I had never set eyes on him."

"Abducted, madam?" McKinnon frowned. His

shaggy gray brows wrinkled as he looked from the Scot to her. "How so, my lady?"

McLeod had the gall to chuckle, then squeezed her in what, to the casual eye, surely appeared just another embrace. In reality, the force of the brute's bear-hug nearly cracked her ribs and drove the air from her lungs in a loud, unladylike, "Oooff!"

"Pay her no mind, Captain. My bonnie . . . er . . . bluebell was forced to leave her pretties behind when we fled the Highlands." McLeod actually winked at McKinnon. "For that, she holds me to account. Do ye not, my wee bannock?"

He chucked her beneath the chin, chuckling when she went for his fingers like a terrier after a rat.

"I'm not your wee anything, you rogue," she snarled. "What I am, sir, is your prisoner. Your captive. Captain, he's lying. Before today, I'd never set eyes on him. I swear it."

Drummond chuckled even harder. He nudged her and rolled his eyes. "Now who's the wee liar? How would I ken that mole upon your left breast? Or the tiny birthmark ye sport upon your bonnie wee ar—?"

"My laird! Enough, sir!" McKinnon protested.

McLeod's eyes were murderous as he looked down at her. They promised hell to pay if she didn't pipe down.

Turning back to McKinnon, he explained, "My betrothed is unwell, Captain. Once she is rested, she'll be herself again. But for now, if you would show us to our berths . . . ?"

"Your berths. Of course." Lips pursed, McKinnon glared at Andy. "My laird, your serving man didna explain that your betrothed was with ye. The Lady . . . Arabella, is it? . . . shall use my quarters for the duration of the voyage." The captain gave her a pitying smile.

"We are touched by your generosity, Captain," McLeod said with a gallant half-bow. "I'm sure we'll be verra comfortable there, shall we not, my dove?"

Before she could comment, the captain cut in, "*We*, sir? Ye canna mean to share the cabin? Not without benefit o' matrimony?" He was aghast.

"Come, come, Captain. These are unusual times. Besides, we wouldna dream of being parted, would we, poppet?" Drummond ground out, jabbing her sharply in the ribs with his elbow.

He bared his teeth in a wolfish grin. One that became a grimace of agony as she stabbed her heel into his shin—an act her full skirts hid from the captain.

"On the contrary, you lecherous, lying brute, I'd sooner kiss the Devil's arse," she purred, batting her lashes at him, "than go anywhere with you."

McLeod fell prey to a loud fit of coughing—or pretended to. "Ye see, Captain? Mad as a hatter. Addled as a rotten egg."

McKinnon's smile faded. His expression became stern. "You have my sympathies, sir. However, it remains my Christian duty to uphold the morals of all those aboard this vessel. I will not knowingly condone adultery. You, sir, shall make your berth below, in steerage, with the others." He coughed. "Unless . . . may I make a suggestion?"

"By all means," her captor ground out.

"I have seen how the lady clings to you, my lord."

He chuckled like an indulgent uncle. But then, he could not see the rag that bound their wrists together.

"If you are of a mind to be wed, I would be honored t' perform the service," he added.

"Wed!" McLeod almost choked on the word. "You jest, Captain?"

"At least we agree on that point, *dearest*," she cooed, flashing her kidnapper a sugary smile. "Captain, if you'd show me to my quarters, I would be most grateful. I confess, I am sorely fatigued." She pretended to yawn, delicately covering her mouth with her hand.

McKinnon inclined his head. "But of course, dear lady," he murmured. "This way."

"You heard him, McLeod," she hissed, jerking her wrist. "Untie me."

"When hell freezes over, my wee haggis," McLeod ground out. "McKinnon! Fetch your prayer book, mon. I've changed my mind. We'll be wed straightway."

"What?" she exploded.

Her last hope died when she turned to look at him. Despite all the merry excuses he'd made to the captain, this had been no game for him. No sparring match with words. He was in deadly earnest. She could tell by his eyes. They were gleaming with triumph—and cold as ice.

"You heard me, chick. Come, marry us, Captain. And, Captain? Make haste." He shot her a look that made her skin crawl, adding in a lecherous purr, "I've a powerful urge t' consummate!"

"All right, Jim, lad. Where is she?" Tom Wainwright snarled. He twisted his meaty fist in the collar of Trelawney's shabby shirt. Then, crushing it against his windpipe, he slammed the crippled groom against the stable door. "An' don't tell me ye don't know, old son, or I'll break both your bleeding legs, so help me God."

"Where's who? What the devil are you talking about?" Jim protested, fighting for breath.

"Rosie, that's who. As if you didn't know, you double crossing, thieving bastard!"

"Isn't she with you?" Jim shot back, wrenching free of his hold. He shoved himself away from the stable door, rubbing his bruised neck and the lump on the back of his head. "She left here with you. You promised to take care of her."

"I did," he allowed, "but she took off, didn't she?"

"What?" Jim's head came around as if jerked by a string. "What do ye mean, took off? Took off where?"

"That's what I'd like t' know. She scarpered with a coupla strange coves in a rowboat before I could stop her. Took the goods with her an' all. That makes me unhappy, Jim, lad. Very unhappy, indeed."

Jim frowned. "You know Rose, Tommy. She's a good girl. We're close, me and her. She wouldn't just run off with someone like that. Not without telling me. She'll be back before you know it. Who's she? And who were the men in the boat?"

Trelawney nodded at Arabella, who was hanging on Tom's arm. Dark-red ringlets spilled over her shoulder. Her shining eyes were as green as the Eyes of the Tiger in the fading light. Tom chuckled. Chances were, poor old Jim was wishing she was his woman—along with every other man in London.

Her looks and her skills in the bedchamber had won her the heart of the duke. Gifts of jewels had followed, as they'd planned from the first. It was the pick of those jewels that had vanished now. Twin emeralds, both the size of robins' eggs, each worth a sultan's ransom. But he'd get 'em back, an' no mistake. Never mind who he had to destroy to do it.

"Never mind who she is." He dismissed Jim's question, giving 'Bella a possessive squeeze. "It's the goods I'm after."

"Devil take the bloody goods! What about my sister?" Jim insisted. "If she's really gone, I have to find her. Get out of my way, Tom."

Tom drew back his fist and clipped Jim solidly under the jaw. The stupid git flew backward, slammed into the stone wall behind him, then slithered to the ground, out cold. Tom smiled. So much for Cornish Jim and his famed right hook.

"Time t'get going, love," he said, flexing bleeding knuckles.

Taking 'Bella's arm, he steered her back through the crowded tavern.

"Where are we going?" she demanded as they wove their way between the sweaty bodies jostling in the taproom, which smelled of ale, horses, smoke and meat pies.

"Back to the river. The ferrymen will have seen the gel and her fancy man. Sooner or later, we'll find out where the bastards have gone."

"I want t' go back to Riverside now," Arabella suggested in a petulant tone. "Before my maid misses me. Perhaps Billy has sent me a bauble from the north. He promised he would." She pouted.

"The devil you'll go back there," he rasped, his fingers closing about the little bitch's wrist. "That wasn't the plan, remember? Once we had the emeralds, you said you'd never see His Grace again. That's what you wanted, right?"

"I suppose so," Arabella agreed sulkily.

He grabbed her wrist. Squeezed. Thrust his face into hers. "I said, is that right?"

"Ouch! Yes, yes, it is! Ohh, don't, Tom. You're hurting me—"

"Just so you understand," he said softly.

"Wh—what are you going to do? When you find her, I mean?"

"What do you think I'm going to do?"

"Take back the emeralds?"

"Clever girl. And then?"

She swallowed. "K-kill her?"

Tom smiled.

A watery moon was rising over the back streets of London when the pair left the Golden Swan. A hackney cab waited outside the tavern, the driver dozing on his perch. Tom tossed the cabby a ha'penny.

As he handed Arabella aboard the shabby vehicle, a pair of doxies rushed up to it.

"Seen Cornish Jim, have yer?" the pretty one asked him breathlessly. Hands on her hips, she looked Tom over with a calculating eye.

"What you want him for, ducks?" he quipped, giving her a wink. "Won't I do, then?"

"Hey. You promised, Tom," 'Bella reminded him. "None of that."

He quelled her with a look and turned back to

the doxy. "Like I said, what do ye want with ole Jimmy, ducks?" he asked her.

"I've a message for him. From his sister. Urgent, it is," Kitty insisted. "A matter of life an' death, ye might say. Concerning some 'goods,' if ye take my meaning."

Tom and Arabella exchanged long looks.

"Is it, now?" he said. "Well, you've found him, so spit it out, love." He spread his arms wide and made a bow. "Cornish Jim, at your service."

"You? You ain't Jim," Kitty said, eyeing him doubtfully. She'd heard 'Bella call him Tom. "Are you?"

He chucked her beneath the chin, drawing a dangerous look from Arabella. "What do you think, luv? 'Course I am. Jim Trelawney, prizefighter. Cornish Jim, they called me, when I was the duke's man. What mischief has my bloomin' sister been up to now, eh, Gawd bless her?"

With a shrug, Kitty told him.

Rose was still reeling from the speed with which McKinnon had married them when she felt the ship get under way.

A grinding shudder ran through the vessel like a huge animal groaning in its death throes. Then the looming dark wharf with its choppy silhouette of warehouses and granaries began to slip away into the night—or rather, the ship did.

Forgetting that she and McLeod were still joined at the wrist, she panicked and tried to rush past the Scot to the railing in a last bid for freedom. Instead, she ran headlong into his outstretched arms.

"Whoa, now. Where are you off to? Or are ye just eager for me, my bonnie?" he taunted in a husky tone, thrusting his handsome, hateful face into hers.

They were so close she could see each dark whisker of stubble that rose from his rugged jaw. Could feel his breath, warm on her cheek. See the flecks of pewter and gold in his gray eyes, which were still cold in the light of the lanterns that swung from the yardarms. Still empty.

She averted her face and refused to look at him. She could not find a voice to answer him as, taking her by the wrist, he hauled her across the decks and down a narrow, dark gangway.

Opening a door, he ushered her into a lamplit cabin.

"After you, Lady McLeod," he mocked.

Nudging her ahead of him, he followed her inside, locked the door behind them, and pocketed the key.

Quite alone with him, and far removed from the civilizing influences of cousin and captain, she felt desperately afraid.

Did this . . . madman mean to consummate their mockery of a marriage, as he'd threatened? She shivered. If he did, she had little hope of stopping him. He was tall and lean, yet power-

44

fully built, while she was small and light. Made for flight, not combat.

Besides, even had she been able to outwit him and escape, there was no one and nowhere to run to, not here and not now, she thought miserably. Her only way out would be to dive overboard, into the oily black Thames. And although she could swim very well, there were corpses bobbing about in the river, both human and animal, along with all manner of other nasty flotsam and jetsam.

She flinched as McLeod suddenly ducked his dark head. She sucked in a frightened gasp, expecting him to grasp her by the chin and force his mouth on hers—or worse.

Instead, he drew a dagger from his boot. Its steely blade winked in the lantern light. A pitiless smile curved his lips when, her eyes wild with terror, she shrank away from the shining blade.

"Nay, little Sassenach. Not yet," he menaced in a liquid purr. "And never sae easy as this . . ."

As he bowed his head to sever their bonds, a lock of his inky hair flopped over his sweaty brow. It tickled her cheek.

"I wanted ye tonight. Did you know that?" he asked softly, tracing the curve of her face with his knuckle. His skin felt very hot against hers. "Back at Riverside House, when I held ye in my arms? Ye felt sae soft and warm, and your poor wee heart was beating sae very fast! I thought . . . just for a moment. . . . that if I had ye, I could

45

feel again. That *you* could make me feel. . . . But I was wrong. You canna. No one can."

Her breathing quickened as his arms went around her.

She held her breath, closed her eyes, but the kiss she feared never materialized.

"Shoo, my flighty wren. Dinna fear. Your virtue's safe with me," he whispered in a lilting burr that turned her blood to ice.

Releasing her, he strode across the cabin, removed his torn black frockcoat and deposited it on the sea chest at the foot of the bed.

The lantern above him swung slowly to and fro with the motion of the ship. In its light, his hair—black as sin—fell to his broad shoulders in inky waves, in striking contrast to the grubby linen of his full-sleeved shirt. His gray eyes were fringed with long black lashes, beneath brows as savage as quill strokes on vellum. They were eyes that were empty of everything but ghosts.

Even drunk, as he surely must be at this moment, and clad in such worn, rustic garments, he had the devil-take-ye good looks that women sighed after.

All women but her, that was.

She gnawed at her lower lip. A man like McLeod had no need to force a woman into his bed. Many with far greater claims to beauty than she had surely flocked to it, striking brute that he was. Besides, he had said her virtue was safe.

What had he meant by that? That her virtue

was safe, but something else was not? And if so, what something had he meant?

Her life!

Oh, God. That was it. It must be. He meant to kill Arabella Slater—and she had done her utmost to prove she was Arabella!

Somehow, she had to convince him otherwise.

"I know who you think I am," she began hesitantly, her voice husky with apprehension. "But you are mistaken, sir. I am not Arabella Slater. Nor was I ever an actress on Drury Lane, or the Duke of Cumberland's mistress. My name is Rosamund Trelawney. I served ale in the taproom of the Golden Swan, on Tavern Street, before I broke into Riverside House this afternoon. If you demand ransom of His Grace for my safe return, he will not pay. Truly, he does not know me from Adam, sir."

"Ransom?" McLeod chuckled unpleasantly as he drew his shirt over his head. A rusty nail, looped on a leather cord, nestled in the dark hair that lay like a shadow across his broad chest. "Is that what you thought? Nay, Arabella. I'm afraid it isna ransom that I'm after."

His admission drove the last shred of hope from her.

"Then—then what do you want of me?" she asked.

"Your life," came his answer, confirming her fears.

And with that, he collapsed face down, on the bed.

"Hold fast! Hold fast!"

His tartan breachan streaming behind him on the wind, he raised his claymore to the dour gray sky and charged into the hell that was Culloden.

He remembered nothing after that first reckless moment until he came to, to find his horse gone, and death—not glory—awaiting him.

Scottish dead and Scottish dying lay all around him.

Painfully turning his head, he saw a handful of English dragoons. They were going from body to body, finishing off the wounded, the stunned, the fallen.

One trooper strode toward an injured High-lander, close to where he lay. He heard the harsh bark of laughter as the Redcoat raised his musket aloft.

He tried to warn the Scot, to draw the trooper's attention, but . . . he could not speak.

"Quarter!" the Scot groaned. "For the love of God, give quarter, Sassenach!"

"Your Grace?" The trooper looked at the cor-pulent young officer astride a white horse for his answer. "Do I grant 'im quarter, sir?"

Cumberland shook his white-wigged head. "I think not, Sergeant Higginbottom. By my orders, there'll be no mercy shown today. We shall teach this Highland rabble a lesson they'll never forget, ja?" He smiled.

"Very good, sir."

As if in some macabre ballet, Drum saw the trooper's bayonet fall once, twice, with a bright, hard wink of steel. A fountain of crimson spurted over the sod.

He would never forget that flash of sun on blade. The crimson gout that fountained over the turf.

"Nooo!" he roared, finding his tongue at last. But his cry was snatched away, lost on the wind as other Redcoats poured over the hill in a scarlet tide.

As he shoved himself up onto his elbows, the arm of the corpse he cradled slid limply to the turf. The broad hand with the long fingers—so like his own!—was stiffening. As the auburn head lolled to one side, he saw dark-blue eyes, wide-open, staring blindly at the sky above.

It was Cameron! Ah, God, ah, God, not him!

Never again would his older brother see the sun rise on a new day, nor watch the eagle fly. Never again would he smell the wild thyme or taste the heather on the wind, as they hunted the red stag together. Never more would he hear the pipes skirling, or feel the cool mist of the glen on his cheek.

Never more. . . .

Kneeling, he kissed Cameron's waxy lips. "Farewell, my brother. Go with God," he whispered.

Then, drawing the ragged tartan over his brother's face, he crawled from the battlefield—

*   *   *

"Aaagh!"

He sat bolt upright, shaking all over, his cry echoing in the silence. His heart was thundering in his chest. His face and shirt were clammy with sweat.

He flicked his head to clear it. It was the same dream. The nightmare he'd had every night since the battle. Only this time, the ending had changed. This time, Cameron's corpse had not whispered in his ear.

Swinging his legs over the side of the bed, he stood, wincing with pain as his swollen foot protested his weight. His gaze fell on the heap of rags across the cabin. He frowned.

No. Not rags. A woman. Arabella.

She was curled in one corner, her dark-green skirts pulled up, around her shoulders, for warmth, her petticoats drawn modestly around her legs.

In the lamplight, with her eyes closed and her exquisite face pillowed on a mass of golden-brown curls, she looked as innocent as an angel.

Too innocent to kill.

Pushing the unwelcome thought away, he drew on his wrinkled coat and limped to the door.

From now until the time came to take her life, he would keep his distance. It would be easier that way.

For both of them.

Chapter Five

When Rose awoke the next morning, the Mc-
Leod was gone and Andy, the sandy-haired one,
was there instead.

There was pity in his eyes as he took her
numb, icy hands in his own and helped her to
stand.

"Lay doon on the bed, my lady," he urged
softly. "Get some proper sleep."

He was so gentle, so caring for her comfort,
she burst into tears, much to his dismay.

She continued to weep off and on for the next
two days. By the third, she had no tears left to
shed. Her voice was hoarse. Her eyes were
rimmed in red.

That same morning, she dried her face, blew

her nose and swore she would never shed another tear. What was done was done, and she could not go back, nor change it. Consequently, she must go on as best she could.

Her chances of ever seeing Jim or England again were nil, she decided, weighing her options. To all intents and purposes, she was on her own from here on, bound for New France with a madman for a husband. And a madman, moreover, whose dearest wish was to see her dead, and himself a widower!

Well, she wasn't dead yet. And chances were, it was the strong spirits he'd imbibed that had been talking when he'd said, oh-so-chillingly, that he wanted her life. Sober and cool-headed, there was an excellent chance he intended no such thing. Perhaps he'd even apologize for frightening her . . . ?

So, whether she flourished or failed was up to her, from here on. And since—through no fault of her own—she had lost everything she owned not once, but twice before this, she was determined not to sink further into the mire a third time.

Perhaps being kidnapped wasn't so much a disaster as an opportunity in disguise, she told herself. Not an ending at all, but a chance for a fine new beginning. The opportunity to rise from the ashes of ruin, like the phoenix, and soar to even greater heights.

In the taproom at the Golden Swan, she had

heard that in the New World there was fertile land for the asking. Forests with acre upon acre of virgin timber. Lakes and rivers, and land, land everywhere!

Like her mother, Bettina, before her, God rest her soul, she dreamed of owning land of her own. When she was a little girl, Mam always said that land was wealth, and that wealth was power. She had not meant power over others' lives, but over one's own.

Poor Mam. She had died soon after giving birth to Sir Roger Trelawney's third by-blow, a second son the priest had baptized Roger in Papa's honor, only minutes after her mother's death. Alas, the poor little babe lived only an hour himself.

A few years later, their Papa had likewise passed on following a stroke, and then there had only been Granny to care for her and Jim. Papa's widow, the haughty Lady Philippa, had ordered them—Sir Roger's illegitimate children, but his only surviving issue nevertheless—evicted from the farmhouse Sir Roger had deeded over to their mother, along with their ailing grandmother. They had been driven off their own land by laborers brandishing pitchforks.

Eleven then, but already proud, Rose had felt her cheeks burning with shame. She'd promised herself that some day, somehow, she would own land of her own that could never be taken away from her. She'd have a sprawling farm and a fine snug house—all of it. It would be a wonderful place that the wealthy widows and spiteful dukes of the world could never, ever take from her.

A husband and several children had once been a part of her dreams, too, but McLeod had destroyed all that. Or . . . had he? She frowned. Would the Pope recognize their marriage as lawful, when she had taken wedding vows in another woman's name? She shivered. She hoped not. To be bound to that silver-eyed devil forever would be a living nightmare.

She sighed. What on earth had that wretched Arabella done, anyway, that McLeod would risk hanging to steal her away?

There was only one thing for it. She had to find out.

The merchantman plowed through the gold-rimmed waves, her prow rising and falling like a bird riding the wind. Her full sails were the color of buttermilk in the light of the setting sun.

Drummond faced into the breeze, blind to the beauty of the sunset, deaf to the wild song of the wind through the sails. His face stern, his powerful hands curled over the taffrail like the talons of a hawk, he stared straight ahead—and into the past.

Ship, ocean and sunset fell away. He imagined himself a lad again, standing on the hills of Lochalsh, below the cattle pass.

Shading his eyes against the dazzling sunlight,

he could see the Isle of Skye, where father's cousin, Alexander McLeod, served the MacDonald, Lord of the Isles.

The wee island rose from the shimmering gray water and sea-spray like the misty isle of a dream, crowned by the jagged crags of the Cuillins.

Colonies of seabirds nested amongst the isle's black rocks, their keening cries melancholy, even from this distance. Seals basked in the sunshine, the bulls barking and roaring as they fought over the females, the cows protectively rounding up their mournful-eyed pups.

Before Father's death, he and Cameron had been sent to Skye from Glen Dunmor every year, to spend the summers with their cousins. Cam and his cousin Duncan had taught him how to fish and swim. Alec had taught him how to row and fight. And from Elspeth. . . . from cousin Elspeth, he had learned how to kiss.

"Halloo, the shore!"

Cameron's cry echoed down the cavern of the years. Time rolled away.

Drum saw the prow of a small craft part the gauzy mist like a blade, piercing a veil.

Cameron sat on the dory's crosspiece, his hand raised in salute. His long, dark-red hair shone like a nimbus about his head in the light.

"Come on, Drum," he called. "Come aboard. I've been waiting for ye."

His brother wasna dead. It had all been some terrible dream!

With a shout of joy, he started forward to join Cameron in the boat. But as he drew closer, boat and island began to fade away.

"Wait! Come back!" he begged. "Dinna leave me here! Ye canna go without me."

"My laird? Laird Drummond! Are you unwell, sir?"

The stern voice, that firm hand on his shoulder, jolted Drum back to his senses and the present.

"What?" He whirled to face the speaker, saw the captain standing there, pipe in hand, and frowned.

"Forgive me, sir. I was thinking. I—I didna hear ye."

McKinnon nodded, yet eyed him curiously. "That's quite all right, my laird. I don't believe I saw you at services this morning, sir?"

"I was—"

"Unwell, perhaps?" McKinnon supplied, his shaggy brows arched as he puffed on his clay pipe again.

"Aye." It was as good an excuse as any.

"When you are feeling up to it, I recommend that ye try them. Morning services, that is." McKinnon puffed out his chest, tugging on the lapels of his frockcoat. "The bracing air, the spindrift, the glorious sunshine! 'Tis a most uplifting experience to stand on deck and thank

God for our safe deliverance from the British. Uplifting—and cleansing, too, ye ken?"

"I'm sure it is, Captain," Drum agreed sourly. "But for myself . . . Well, let's just say my faith is no' as strong as it was."

To Drum's surprise, McKinnon nodded sympathetically. "Grief, great tragedy, does that to some of us, my laird. It makes doubters of us. But while we may desert Him on occasion, He never deserts us. When you are ready, He will be there."

"Aye. But maybe I won't," Drum growled.

"Your lovely bride is English, is she not, sir?"

The gray eyes narrowed. "What has that to do with anything?"

"A mere observance, sir. Her accent?" He shrugged. "I couldna help but notice. Is she from London?"

"Aye."

"Ah. A city sparrow. My own wee Maddy hails from Cornwall. I call her my seabird. I was reflecting earlier that this voyage must be particularly difficult for Lady Arabella. Without exception, everyone aboard this vessel has lost loved ones to her countrymen. It canna be a pleasant thing to think aboot."

"You may save your pity, Captain. My wife can take care of herself."

"Forgive me if I sounded pitying. I assure ye, it was not pity I intended to offer, sir. Merely an observation that it is unfortunate there are so few ladies aboard. If my wife was here, she would take your lady under her wing. Kind, she is, my Madeline. Verra kind-hearted. She would show the rest of them the true meaning of Christian compassion and charity." A shaggy gray brow lifted.

"What are you trying to say, McKinnon?"

"Just that women—some women—remind me of birds, my laird. They make a pretty flock, preening their feathers, twittering and warbling sweetly. But set in their midst a strange bird, one with feathers of a different color mayhap, or a different note to its song, and they change. Left unchecked, they will fall upon that strange bird and pluck out its eyes. Destroy it utterly, regardless of its innocence. Dinna let them destroy your wee city sparrow, my laird."

After McKinnon wandered off to attend to the smooth sailing of his vessel, Drummond continued to stand by the rail. He stared out at the darkening sea, over which phosphorescence began to shimmer as daylight faded.

His fellow passengers came above decks for the evening prayers, singing the old hymns with a sweet melancholy that would have wrung tears from stone.

He did not join them. He felt he was not fit for their company, sick as he'd grown. Nor was he worthy of it, he decided. They, at least, had fought the English. They had not languished abed, sipping gruel like a child, as he had done.

He shifted his weight to his right foot. His left was agony in his boot. The lightest pressure made him want to swoon like a babe, or else be sick. The rest of him burned with a hot, dry fever, or shivered with chills. From time to time, his mind wandered, too. Thoughts came and went, insubstantial as thistledown.

Sometimes he believed himself again at Culloden Moor. Cameron's body lay slack in his arms, his eyes turned up to Heaven. With his dying breath, Cam fought to tell him something, over and over again. But, though Drum strained to catch his words, he could not make them out over the gunfire and the shouts.

What his brother had said had gone with him to the grave, but Drummond's lust for revenge on "Butcher" Cumberland had not abated one whit. It lay now like a cold, dark fire, banked in his belly.

Cumberland had shown no mercy that morning. Had granted no man quarter, as was customary in battle. Instead, he had ordered wounded men bayonneted or shot, and ruthlessly slaughtered those thirsty fellows who had crawled to drink from the moor's only well.

It was just a matter of time now. He could feel it. When the black rage grew too strong to contain, he would kill the duke's mistress, as he'd sworn to do.

Surely then, Cam would stop whispering in his ear?

Chapter Six

"I'm telling ye, he's up on deck and willna be doon. Have a bite. Nibble on a biscuit, at least."

"I'd sooner nibble on his black heart," she murmured, "if he has one, which I doubt."

"Oh, he has one, all right, lassie. And more conscience than is good for a mon. That's his trouble, aye? Here. Eat!"

"Oh, all right." With a sigh, Rose accepted the hard ship's biscuit from Andy and took a small bite.

She had no appetite, but she chewed it anyway, reluctant to hurt Andy's feelings. He had been kind to her since McLeod dragged her down here after their mockery of a wedding. Indeed, any hatred she'd felt for the sandy-haired

Scot had been replaced by gratitude long before her seasickness passed.

Without his care, she would never have survived.

The first two days, the rolling motion of the ship had made her sick to her stomach. Yet day or night, Andy had been there, holding the bucket steady, wiping her mouth, crooning nonsense to her in the odd language he called "the Gaelic" whenever she wailed that she was dying.

Four days came and went before she was able to leave her bed and totter about to take stock of her surroundings. When she did, she discovered that the cabin was quite spacious, and that the box bed on which she slept was bolted to both wall and deck.

A bow window bellied outward at the farthest end. Watery daylight shone through its bottle-glass panes, giving the impression that the cabin was underwater. Beneath the window squatted a large black sea chest with brass trim. A heavy leather-topped desk was bolted to another wall. Over it hung a whale-oil lantern with a brass shade. On its leather surface lay quills, a porcelain inkstand, a jar of pounce, a box of parchment and a leatherbound Bible.

It was a fine cabin, neat as a pin, and reminiscent of Hamish McKinnon, its owner. But it was proving a prison of sorts just the same, exactly as she'd feared.

This morning—the one and only morning

she'd ventured forth to morning prayers up on deck with the other passengers—the Scots' hostile glances had confined her to a small, inconspicuous corner of the deck. Only the captain had smiled and bidden her a good day.

She was leafing aimlessly through the Bible on the evening of the fifth day, feeling decidedly sorry for herself, when McLeod began pounding on the cabin door. She had locked it when Andy left.

"Open up!" he roared.

Only a fool would comply with an order like that.

"Never."

"I said, open up, damn ye, woman!"

She shrieked and ran backwards as a booted foot suddenly slammed into the cabin door, loosening the iron hinges from the jamb. All thoughts of finding a weapon vanished as a second kick followed the first in rapid succession. The rusty hinges surrendered. The door lurched sideways.

McLeod exploded through the opening like an avenging angel, dominating the close confines of the cabin with his crackling presence. He was at once so virile, so threatening, so very large and intimidating, Rose's courage fled her.

In that moment, she wanted nothing so dearly as to crawl into her bed, cower beneath the woolen blanket there, and pray for a quick and merciful death to take her.

Instead, she snatched the feather bolster from the bed and hurled it at him.

He caught it and flung it aside. A handful of downy feathers billowed from a wound in its casing. They drifted down to the planking like flakes of snow.

McLeod seemed to grow taller and taller, dwarfing the roomy cabin as, with a pitiless smile, he vaulted over the desk, like Jack leaping over the candlestick, landing not two feet from where she stood.

Trapped, with nowhere to run, Rose did as Jim had instructed she should do if ever attacked by a man. She waited until he took a step toward her, then brought up her knee and slammed it into his groin with all the strength she could summon.

Despite the padding of her skirts, the momentum of the blow all but rocked her off her feet.

His gray eyes widened, as if he could not believe what she had done to him; then darkened to pewter with pain. When he doubled over, groaning and guarding his middle, she backed away. Gritting his teeth, he took a giant pace forward. Rose took a dozen steps back.

Now, once again, the desk lay between them— her only bastion against the murderous rage in his eyes.

Her bosom heaving, a sick feeling of doom in the pit of her belly, she stood there, waiting, trembling, waiting . . . her mouth dry as sawdust, her palms slick with sweat. Would he again spring nimbly over the table, like Jack over the candlestick?

Nay. Not this time! With the speed and grace of a panther, McLeod suddenly darted around it and caught her to him by a lock of her tumbling hair.

"Now," he murmured, breathing low and hard. His eyes were hot as cinders as they bored into hers, just inches from her face. "Now ye shall come with me, ye wee hellion."

He grasped her by the wrists and dragged her toward the door.

Digging in her heels, she pulled back. "I won't go. Not until I know where you're taking me."

"You'll find out, soon enough."

"Andy! Andy!" Her courage failed her when she looked up at him. There was no pity in his eyes. No compassion. Nothing.

A chill skittered down her spine. *He is mad,* she thought. *He has lost his mind!*

"Let me go. Andy, help me!"

"Aye, lassie. That's the way. Go ahead and scream," the McLeod urged. "Beg for quarter as those poor laddies begged. Not a soul aboard this vessel will help ye. They lost too many at your true love's hands."

"What true love?" she panted, struggling to twist free of his grip. Her wrists burned from the friction of his punishing fingers.

"Cumberland—as if you didn't know. William

Augustus, Duke of Cumberland. I swore I'd take from the Butcher what he loves best. And what he loves best is you!"

She recoiled as if he'd struck her, his words like a fist to her belly. Oh, God. He still believed she was Arabella, the pampered mistress of "Butcher" Cumberland. The English duke's armies had slaughtered over a thousand Highlanders on a moor named Culloden.

She swallowed. If only she'd been able to convince him of her real identity.

"Well? Do ye deny it?" he rasped, his eyes flaying her alive.

"I most certainly do!" she shot back, still trying to wrench her hands free of his grip. "I was never his woman, I swear it. I told you the night you kidnapped me. *I am not Arabella.*"

"Nay? Then why did ye let me think it? Why did ye let me call ye by her name, time after time?" he demanded, thrusting his face into hers.

His eyes glittered, too bright by far for sanity. He was breathing heavily as she struggled against him, yet the sweat on his brow and upper lip was cold and clammy—surely not from his exertions?

"Because I was afraid, that's why," she yelled, jabbing her elbows into his middle. "I thought my life depended on being Arabella. That's why I said nothing. But I'm not her. I never was. Never could be."

"More lies," he growled. "Silence. Enough!"

"No! I hate the bloody duke as much as you do. He ruined our lives. He had my b-brother beaten. You must believe me. You have to!" A desperate sob broke from her. *"I'm not Arabella."*

"You will say whatever you think I want to hear," he said softly, half carrying, half dragging her to the gangway steps.

She hung back, digging in her heels, hanging on to the polished wood moldings, the railings, clawing at anything she could hook her fingers over. "As God is my witness, my name is Rosamund Trelawney, sir. I—I served ale in the taproom of the Golden Swan on Tavern Street . . ."

She tried to sound calm and convincing as she spoke. Oh, God, how could she reach his heart, or stir his pity, with such wildness, such emptiness in his eyes?

". . . I was born near Penzance in C-Cornwall. Jim and I came to London with our Granny to find work when I was eleven. Soon after, she died, and we were left all a-alone."

There was ruddy color in his gaunt cheeks despite the glacial glitter of frost in his eyes. His fingers were dry and hot, manacles of fiery steel about her wrists.

"A tavern wench? But of course," he mocked. "Who else would I find primping in milady's chamber, pray?" His eyes blazed as he dragged her across the starlit decks.

"I went there to rob her. Arabella, I mean. Tom

set it up. I—I was supposed to steal the emeralds the duke had given her for Christmas," she babbled as he hauled her after him to the taffrail. "We planned to sell them, split the money and live in luxury. But at the last minute, I—I changed my mind. I'm not a thief, don't you see? I was p-putting the emeralds back when you surprised me. I—I could show you?" she offered. "Just—just let go of me. For a moment. That's all I ask, sir."

An evil smile curved his lips. "Bravo! You're a better actress than the critics gave ye credit for, lassie," he panted. "And—were I a trusting mon—I'd believe ye."

Clamping his hands around her waist, he lifted her up onto the narrow taffrail. His hands still on her hips, he whispered in a silky purr, "Almost."

The hairs on the back of her neck stood up as she risked a glance over her shoulder—and wished to God she had not.

Beyond and far below her precarious perch on the rail, the ocean winked where it caught the moon's light. Tonight, it was smoke-black crystal, like his eyes. Beautiful. Bottomless. Deadly.

One hard shove. That was all it would take. A sudden push and she would pitch backward into the drink, and it would all be over. The *Salutation* would sail on, and she would be left behind to feed the fishes. Or at best, to tread water until exhaustion claimed her and the sharks started circling.

She couldn't let that happen. She had too many dreams to die now. What of her precious land? Of the farm she wanted . . . ?

Shivering uncontrollably, she locked her fingers over his upper arms in a vise grip, clawed at the flapping folds of his full-sleeved shirt, wound her fist in the slim leather cord about his throat, and hung on for dear life.

"Please, sir. It's no act. I swear it, on my brother's life—upon my own. I beg you. Don't do this to me, my lord," she implored. Too frightened to be brave now, she babbled huskily, "For pity's sake, listen to me. I don't want to die!"

"Dinna beg me, lassie. Beg God! Ask His forgiveness for your sins!"

McLeod loomed over her, dark hair flying about his head like writhing serpents, silvery eyes blazing. A dark, avenging angel, come to exact retribution.

Grasping her by the shoulders, he pushed her. With a shriek, she tipped backward.

But by some miracle, he did not let her go.

Way above the decks, the wind shifted. New gusts hit the shrouds. As the canvas filled, it flapped and snapped, the sounds loud as pistol shots.

The sharp reports distracted McLeod. His dark head jerked around. His blazing eyes narrowed.

"Cameron!" he roared. "Behind ye, mon! Dragoons!"

In that instant, Rose threw herself forward, toppling to the deck and taking him down with her.

McLeod's knees buckled. "Damn their black hearts! I'm shot, Cam," he whispered. "Hellfire, I'm shot."

With a curse, he crumpled to the decks.

Pushing herself up onto her knees, too terrified to move, she stared down at his lifeless body.

He was dead. Somehow, she'd killed him.

"She killed the McLeod!" The shout went up, echoing her fears.

An angry buzzing spun her around.

Over her shoulder she saw that a circle of sailors and angry Scots had gathered.

Those ghouls must have heard her cries and come to watch the Sassenach meet her end. Yet none of them had lifted a finger to save her.

"I heard shots, Captain McKinnon. The Sassenach shot him!" a young black-haired woman cried.

" 'Tis a lie! I did nothing but defend myself," Rose protested, slowly rising.

Had she escaped murder at the McLeod's hands only to fall prey to a Sassenach-hating lynch mob?

"He—he tried to throw me overboard. What should I have done? Let him? All I did was push him away, to save myself. And then he . . . he fell."

"Lewis. Attend your laird and his lady," Captain McKinnon snapped.

The crowd of onlookers parted to let the captain through.

"You, Robbie, give Master Lewis a hand, lad. The rest of you, disperse straightway."

A wave of relief washed over Rose as Andy thrust his way through the wall of bodies. He stood protectively before her, his expression warning the others to keep their distance.

"Stand back, laddies. You, too, Mistress Margaret. We must take my laird below."

With a grunt, he and a sailor named Robbie lifted Drummond—a much larger, longer-limbed man than either of them—and carried him across the deck.

A huge bull of a man planted himself solidly in their path to the hatchway.

"Stand back, all of ye," Andy repeated. "Make way for the McLeod and his lady. You heard the captain. Come on, now, move your carcass!"

"We know who and what she was, Andrew Lewis. And why the McLeod brought her aboard. I'll no' step aside for a Sassenach whore," the enormous, bearded fellow snarled. He spat on the decks. "No more will my daughter."

The strapping black-haired young woman beside him tossed her head. She shot a spiteful glare at Rose.

"The lady is the McLeod's bride. Insult her and ye insult our clan, ye loud-mouthed clod," Andy rasped.

His face, only inches from the other man's, was as fierce as any terrier's now. His blue eyes were unwavering.

"A warning, Angus. Guard your tongue."

"And another for you, Lewis. Watch your back." The man lumbered aside to let them pass, his massive arms still folded over his barrel chest.

Drummond's head dangled as they carried him across the deck and down the steps of the hatchway.

Rose followed, dragging her heels. "Is he dead?" she asked, trying not to sound too hopeful.

"Not yet."

"Oh, dear."

She sounded so disappointed, Andy snorted with laughter. Could he blame her for wanting to be rid of Drum, after what he'd put her through? Probably not.

"I think he's swooned. To be honest, I've been expecting it," he panted as they maneuvered him around a tight corner. "The hard-headed clod wouldna heed me, ye ken?"

"About what?"

"About what ails him."

"Which is . . . ?" She hung back, obviously fearing contagion. "Cholera? The pox? Strong liquor?"

"Nay. 'Tis the bluidy nail again, like as not. Left man, left! Aye. Now, right, Robbie. Hard right!"

She frowned as he and the sailor worked their way around a narrow angle, with Drum carried like a rolled-up Turkey carpet, sagging between them.

"The nail? Never heard of it."

"A horseshoe nail. Drum stepped on one last month. Almost lost his foot from the poisoning. He swore the wound was healed, but I'll wager he lied to me. We'll see soon enough, aye?" He was breathing hard. "The door, lassie. Quickly, now."

She lifted the sagging door aside, and they lugged their burden into the captain's cabin.

They dropped Drum in an ungainly heap upon the bed, and then the sailor left.

After he'd caught his wind, Andy bade Rose close the door as best she could, and then drew a dirk from his boot. He handed it to her. "Here, take this while I hold him down. Use it t' cut off his boot."

"Why would he need holding? He's unconscious. It's not as if he's going anywhere," she reasoned.

He gave a grim laugh. "Because if I'm right, his foot's full of poison. He'll thrash like a wounded bear t' keep ye from touching it. And he willna care where his fists might fly."

She was hugging herself about the arms, chilly and trembling in reaction to her near brush with death, but she gamely murmured, "Oh, all right, then. Which foot?"

"The left. If the boot willna slide off, then cut it. Wait, now. Ye'll need the lamp t' see by."

As he feared, the boot was stuck. And each small tug the lass gave on it wrenched a groan of agony from his cousin. The sheen of sweat glistened on his brow like amber oil in the lantern's light.

"You were right. I need to cut it."

At his curt nod, she deftly sawed through the coarse leather and pulled the ruined boot free.

"Oh, my Lord," she whispered, covering her nose with her hand. "Look at it."

The sickly sweet stench of poison that rose from the limb was one she remembered all too well.

"His foot's full of poison. It's very bad. I've seen it before."

"Ye have?"

She nodded. "Last year. My brother's arm turned this way after Cumberland's thugs beat him."

His brows rose. "Beat him, ye say?"

She nodded, but did not elaborate.

From the ball to the arch, Drum's foot was hugely swollen. Inflammation mottled the flesh a fiery red-and-white, while a large area around the gaping puncture had a moist look to it. A greenish-yellow hue showed beneath the skin. Fully half the foot must be riddled with pus, Andy guessed, sick to his gullet.

"How he's managed to walk on that foot is nothing short of a miracle," the girl murmured.

To his surprise, she sounded almost sorry for his cousin. Under the circumstances, he could not help admiring her cool head.

"He's too hard-headed for his own good. Must it come off, do ye think?" he asked thickly.

"Take the foot off a man like that? Huh. He'd sooner die."

"Ye're right there, lassie. So, you'll try to save the foot, then?" he nudged slyly. "I've a packet of herbs ye can use. I dinna ken what's inside it, but Granny McCree claimed 'twas a sovereign remedy for poison."

"Who's Granny McCree?"

"The old woman who had the care of him at Kilravock. I'll be back shortly," he added, heading for the door.

"Wait, I—"

"Ye must make the poultices verra hot, ye ken?"

She stared at him, her eyes round with dismay in the golden gloom. "You're not jesting, are you? You really expect *me* to have the nursing of this wretch, after he tried to kill me? Why should

I care if he dies of poisoning? I'd be safe from him then."

"For now, perhaps. But ye'll need his protection by and by," he said grimly. "I promise ye that. And in order t' protect ye, he must be alive, aye?"

Her fair brow creased in a frown. "Why would I need his protection?"

"Because the McLeod is all that stands between you and the others. Angus Stevenson and his daughter, Margaret, in particular. Ye had the good fortune to meet her father on your way down here, aye?"

She wrinkled up her nose. "That great oaf was Angus?"

"Aye. And his lass was the one shrieking that ye killed the McLeod." He nodded at Drum, shaken by how pale and still he looked, but doing his best to hide his concern. "Neither father nor daughter has any love for Sassenachs—the English. The daughter, in particular, would like nothing better than t'see you tossed overboard in a sack, and nurse him herself."

He could see the conflicting emotions chase each other across her expressive face as she weighed her choices—and came to the same conclusion he had reached.

"Where's the water?" she snarled. "And we'll need sea salt, too. Lots of it. And clean cloths. And spirits."

He grinned. "I'll fetch them for ye straightway, my lady."

"Sweet Jesu!"

Drummond heard his own voice echoing down a long, hollow cavern.

"Aye, my son?" Andy quipped. "What can I do for ye?"

He cast his cousin a look like thunder. "Ye daft fool. Give me a hand, instead of gawping."

Balanced on one foot, Drum pulled the rusty horseshoe nail from the ball of his muddy, bloody foot, then tossed it into the bracken with a snort of disgust. "I trod on a blasted nail."

Andy rolled his eyes. "Is that all, mon? Are ye a lad or a lass, to be squealin' over a pin prick?"

"Pipe down or ye'll find out," he threatened as he dropped to his knees.

Ignoring his belly's growls of hunger, he leaned over, cupping his hands to drink from the swift-flowing burn.

The burbling water was brown and gleaming in the light of the setting sun. He remembered the taste of it now, like clover on his tongue.

Flinging his breachan over one broad shoulder, he straightened up, towering over Andy. "If ye still doubt my manhood after I wallop your scrawny arse, Andrew Lewis, ye can ask Moira. I was man enough for your sister, God bless her." He grinned and adjusted his belt.

"Why, ye clarty dog." Bristling like a collie,

Andy brought up his knotted fists and threatened, "I'll teach you t'sully my sister's name, by God! Come on. Put up your paws, McLeod—if ye're man enough!"

"Fight me, would ye, ye snappy wee cur? Come on, then—but first, ye have t' catch me!"

So saying, he lunged past Andy, tipped his cousin's feathered bonnet over his eyes, and then leap-frogged onto the horse's broad rump.

He landed astride, planted solidly in the saddle. "Haaa! Get up there, ye scrawny nag!"

The ugly stallion—he'd named it George after the hated English king—shot forward like a ball from a cannon. With a shrill scream, it galloped away.

Grinning, Andy followed him.

Drum began to burn with fever three nights later. The same night, God help them, Lord Murray's spies returned to camp. They brought with them the news that Cumberland's armies had left Aberdeen. Even now, they were marching on Inverness!

At first, Drum had blamed his feverishness on a touch of the spring ague. But within hours, his foot had grown so swollen, his boot so tight, each step was agony—and the cause of his fever was plain.

Before long, he was begging Andy to cut the leather from his foot, whimpering at even the lightest touch. Fever and headache throbbed like drums behind his eyeballs.

The nightfall of the fourteenth of April, the Jacobite army had begun marching in earnest, pushing on through a fine yet soaking rain in their eagerness to engage the English armies. A year before, the Stuart had led them to victory at Prestonpans, forcing the English to run for their very lives. Morale was now sky-high. The Bonnie Prince himself believed them invincible!

By then, Drummond's condition had deteriorated. He could no longer stay in the saddle unaided and was desperate to hide his condition from Cameron. His brother—who was also the McLeod, and laird of their clan—would not let him fight if he knew how sick he was.

Despite Andy's efforts to tie him into the saddle, Drum was found out when he slithered silently from his mount to the sucking mire, his teeth chattering, cold sweat dripping from his brow.

On Cameron's orders, he'd been loaded onto a supply wagon like a sack of oats. They'd carted him to the nearby castle of Lord Rose of Kilravock, where the Bonnie Prince and his right-hand men were quartered for the night.

The Rose family, though not Jacobites themselves, had offered the Stuart the hospitality of their keep, as any Highlander was honor-bound to offer a passing traveler. The prince had not refused their kindness. Neither had Cameron, Drummond remembered, drifting on through the blackness again. . . .

Chapter Seven

While Andy went to fetch the things she needed, Rose busied herself in undressing the Scot. She had to do something to keep from trembling uncontrollably—a delayed reaction, she fancied, to almost being killed.

Hefting his solid body to the left, then right, she lifted his unwieldy limbs and, with much huffing and puffing, stripped his sorry, threadbare garments from him.

Once he was naked, she stood back and inspected her patient, fists on her hips.

A little over a year ago, her brother had been beaten by a gang of Cumberland's thugs. Their hobnailed boots had mangled his poor arm beyond repair, and he had suffered several other minor but painful small wounds, too. It was these smaller wounds she sought now.

Pursing her lips, she observed that the Scot was far taller and larger than Jim. He was probably older than Jim had been, too. Twenty-seven or twenty-eight to Jim's twenty-three. He looked very dark and masculine against the grayed white of the bed linens. A sharp contrast to Jim's slighter, shorter build and fairer coloring.

A cursory glance told her that, apart from the minor scars all men acquired as lads, which were now faded to white lines and small crescents, and a few yellowing bruises she fancied she might have inflicted, McLeod's broad-shouldered, lean-hipped torso was unblemished. She would even go so far as to say—albeit reluctantly—that it was beautiful, in an athletic, masculine sort of way.

His was the body of a rugged outdoorsman; a man who strode the moors and rode horses with the same gusto with which he hunted, fished, fought or wielded a sword against his enemies. Hours of exercise and a lifetime spent in the unforgiving climate of the Highlands had strung powerful, ropy muscle beneath the smooth flesh, and weathered the parts of him exposed to sun and wind.

His arms and thighs were also powerfully made, hard curves of sinew and muscle stretched taut over long bones. The hands were large and long-fingered, too, with calluses roughening his palms and fingers. Silky hair sprinkled the forearms. His chest was divided by a T of more silky dark hair that thinned out across his abdomen and hard, flat belly, before reasserting itself in a great dark pelt at his groin.

Here her perusal came to an abrupt halt.

Heat filled her face, for *there* all association with her brother's naked body abruptly ended.

Dear Lord, what could she have been thinking? She could not nurse this—this male brute back to health. There was a world of difference in tending to the intimate needs of a hurt brother whom she loved dearly, and in performing the same services for an overtly masculine stranger who had tried to kill her.

How would she bring herself to bathe his body? Or to help him to make water when he was too weak to aid himself?

Cheeks burning, she tugged a corner of the bed linen over his upper thighs, hiding the offending and decidedly large organ that, quiescent now, draped to one side. Telling herself that out of sight was synonymous with out of mind, she smartly lifted her gaze to the much safer territory of his chest.

There, glinting dully between whorls of springy black hair, lay a rusty nail on a leather cord. A strange keepsake, unless—? It must be the nail he'd stepped on. The horseshoe nail that had laid him low. Why on earth had he kept it? she wondered absently.

She tried to come up with some plausible answer to her question, but in all honesty, her mind was not on the wretched nail at all. Not remotely. It persisted in wandering to parts south, and lingering thoughtfully on the triangle of linen and what lay beneath it.

Those parts of him had, to her shame, stirred an undeniable quiver of curiosity within her. They had also triggered an answering pulse, a flame of something fierce and unknown, deep in her belly.

Exerting an iron will, she forced herself to look away. To look anywhere but there.

To her relief, the way the lantern-light spilled over his striking face caught her attention. It revealed a reddish sheen in his coal-black hair. Accented the jut of a prominent cheekbone under taut flesh.

He looked quite different in repose. Striking. Rugged. Not an avenging angel at all, but a dark angel who had fallen from grace and been barred from Heaven's gates.

In sleep, his broad brow was unlined. A thick lock of crisp hair fell carelessly across it. She reached out to brush that lock aside, but caught herself and quickly withdrew her hand. Nay. Tempting as it was, she would content herself with looks alone. Who knew where a touch might lead, when she was feeling as jittery and peculiar as she did?

His eyes were closed below the thick, straight

black brows. His lashes were thick and dark, too. His nose was long, but not too long, and slim. It balanced perfectly the determined jut of his chin and rugged jaw. The latter was set off by a well-defined, dark-rose mouth.

She stared at his lips, fascinated. It was such a beautiful, sensual mouth. One that filled her mind with deliciously carnal images . . .

She shuddered. Whatever was wrong with her?

Shrugging off her wanton thoughts, she forced herself to examine his wound.

It did not look good, and a feeling of hopelessness washed over her. The suppurating puncture in the ball of the Scot's foot appeared to be his only injury, thank God, but it was a foul one that might easily cost him the limb, if not his life.

"Ask the captain for some rum," she instructed when Andy returned to the cabin. "Or whiskey. Whatever he has."

"To drink?" The Scot blinked in owlish surprise. He glanced from his practically naked cousin, then back to her, and she could read his thoughts as clearly as any book: was the English lassie a wanton and a drunkard to boot?

"I shall need it to cleanse the wound, Andrew," she snapped, saying each word crisply and hoping her cheeks were not still that telltale guilty pink color.

"Och, aye. Right away, my lady."

When Andy left again, she tested the dirk's blade on the ball of her thumb. With only a gentle prick, a drop of blood welled. She sucked it clean. The dagger was as sharp as Jim's razor had been. *Perfect.*

Firmly anchoring McLeod's leg under her arm, she held it there with the weight of her upper body, grasped his heel, and drew a deep breath. Uttering a hasty prayer, she made a small, deep nick in the center of the wound, where the flesh was most swollen and puffy-white.

Immediately, pus pumped out, flowing as steadily as blood onto the rag she quickly held under it.

When the flow stopped, she took up a clean cloth, wetted it in the steaming salt water Andy had brought, then swabbed and pressed and coaxed the foul-smelling muck to drain from the wound.

The heat of the poultices drew the poison to the surface, then out through the opening she had made. But she had to repeat the distasteful process several times, scraping away dead skin, blood and matter, before she was satisfied the wound was thoroughly free of poison.

It took ages, but eventually only blood seeped from the raw red wound. Loose flesh sagged now over the area where the poison had collected, but no ominous traces of white remained under the skin.

She took the tin cup of whiskey Andy handed her, swigged a fortifying mouthful herself, and then poured the remaining liquor into and around the raw, gaping wound.

While she gasped and beat on her chest as the whiskey burned a fiery path down to her belly, McLeod groaned and thrashed as the alcohol bit into the wound. He snagged a handful of her skirts in the process, but although he twisted his fist in the cloth, he did not waken.

"More rags. And more water—cold will do, this time. And get rid of this lot. Better yet, burn it," she instructed hoarsely, handing Andy the basin with the fouled cloths.

"Sweet Mary! Will ye look at that. Who'd have thought a wee prick wi' a nail could do such damage? Will he lose the foot?"

Andy's face was stark with worry. His eyes glistened. With tears, she suspected.

"Not if *I* have to take it off, he won't," she said vehemently. There were limits to what she would attempt as a "physician." Amputation was one of them. If the leg turned gangrenous, someone else would have to tend to him. "Now we must bandage the wound, and work to break the fever."

"And then?"

"And then we start all over again. We drain, we sponge, we wait—and we pray." Her violet eyes met his bright blue ones as she repeated, "Especially pray."

*   *   *

McLeod slept for several hours with scarcely a sound. Indeed, his breathing was so shallow that at times she held a cold metal blade up to his lips, to see if he breathed at all.

She passed the rest of the day and most of that night perched uncomfortably on the edge of the box bed beside him, reading from McKinnon's ancient Bible—not because she was of an overly religious turn, but because the cabin offered nothing else by way of reading material. She suspected McKinnon might have taken whatever books he owned with him to his temporary quarters. He seemed of a scholarly nature.

Several times, she set aside her reading to sponge her patient with cool water, or to spoon a few drops of broth between his lips.

His skin felt dry and very hot to her touch, or by turns chilled and clammy. When he shivered, she heaped over him the coarse woolen blankets Andy had brought. But his teeth still chattered.

". . . winter sae blessed cold as this, Auntie?" he babbled in his sleep. "Was it still snowing when ye came up the glen, then, Cameron? Whist, brother, step closer t' the fire and warm yersel'. Ye'll take a wee dram, aye?"

As the fever rose, his mind rambled constantly. He conversed with the friends and family who peopled his dreams, a woman he called Auntie Flora, Duncan, the "gillie," whatever a gillie might be. And a girl he called Elspeth. He said

86

the latter's name with such affection she suspected the two of them were once sweethearts—and felt a tiny, irrational twinge of jealousy.

By the wee hours of the next day, she knew the sponging was not working. His skin was burning and dry to the touch. His eyes glittered. Two bright spots of ruddy color rode high in his cheeks, and his lips were cracked and blistered. She had to make him take more liquids, somehow. To cool him from the inside, as well as out.

Propping his head on one of the bolsters, she again perched on the side of the bed, armed with a bowl of clear broth. Taking up spoon and basin, she scooped up some broth and then pressed the side of the horn spoon against his closed lips. She hoped the pressure would nudge him into opening his mouth and drinking.

It worked. Or rather, it worked at first. But after only a few spoonfuls, he suddenly gave a tremendous heave, as if he meant to rise from the bed.

"Come on then, ye bluidy murderer! Take me if ye can! I'm not some puir old woman who canna fight back!" he roared hoarsely.

A weighty arm that ended in a huge clenched fist suddenly flew out. It slammed the basin from her hands, spraying broth in every direction, and flinging her clear across the cabin.

"No!" she cried, lunging for his arm. "You must be still," she panted, wrestling that powerful arm down to the feather pallet. "Stay abed, you wretched man."

But no sooner had she pinned one arm down than he flailed about with the other.

"Let me up, damn ye!" he roared. "Get off me, ye old witch!"

His strength seemed superhuman. Flinging herself over the bed, Rose pulled herself up onto her knees. She then leaned across his chest, using her weight to hold him down.

Being sprawled across him was akin to riding an earthquake. His powerful body bucked and rippled, heaved and rolled, as if some massive, otherworldly force was fighting to get out from under her.

But, despite his nakedness and the proximity of their bodies, she had little time for embarrassment. Indeed, all her energies were devoted to keeping the brute abed, where he would not harm himself, and where his wound could knit and heal.

When he was finally still, and his breathing deep and even again, she rolled off him and lay at his side, exhausted.

She was acutely aware of every throbbing bruise, every battered bone in her body as she arched, stretching like a cat. Hmm. How gloriously soft the feather bed felt beneath her aching back. And how good it was to lie on goosedown, rather than on the bare deck, as she would have to do again tonight. If she closed her eyes for just a minute, surely no one would be any the wiser. . . .

She was roused from a deep, exhausted sleep much later by the feel of something wet on her cheek, and the taste of salt on her lips.

Tears, she decided drowsily—but not her own. Her own eyes were dry; the last of her tears had been shed days ago.

They must belong to the laird beside her. The man on whose brawny shoulder her head was resting.

She must have been exhausted, to have taken such liberties, but was it any wonder, tired as she was? She pushed herself up onto her elbows.

It was no dream. In her exhaustion, she really had fallen asleep—had trustingly rested her head upon the shoulder of the Scot who, a day ago, had tried to drown her. The man who, six days ago, had held a pistol beneath her breast and sworn to shoot her. And now her cheek rested on his shoulder. One of her legs was thrown carelessly across his thighs. How the world could change in the blink of an eye!

He was still asleep, she discovered, yet silent tears slipped down his hot, stubbled cheeks like rain. His eyes moved beneath the closed lids. That, and the little murmuring sounds he made, the occasional restless twitches of his body, suggested he was dreaming.

The sight of a strong man weeping was one she had always found deeply moving. Indeed, she had never forgotten the sight of her Papa, weeping over Mam's body, then just an hour later over that of the infant son she had borne him.

But the sight of those silent tears streaming down the cheeks of a man like McLeod—the hard, ruthless brute who had tried to kidnap, then kill her—had a profound and unexpected effect on her.

"I canna hear ye, Cam. Ye must tell me again," he babbled. "Tell me how t' help ye. . . . ah, God, Cam, no! *Nooo!*"

Moved to tenderness, she took him in her arms.

Cradling his body against her own, she stroked the damp black hair away from his burning brow. Her cool fingers caressed his back and shoulders as she crooned to him. "Hush, now, hush. It will be all right. You'll see." She gently rocked him back and forth. "Sleep, now. I'll be here."

They were simple words. Words a mother might say to soothe a child with a nightmare. But he opened gray eyes brilliant with fever and stared up at her. The broad brow creased in a frown, as if he could not place her.

"Ye willna leave me?" he croaked through cracked lips.

She shook her head. "Never," she murmured, saying what she thought he'd want to hear.

"Never." A faint smile caught up the edges of

his mouth. His fingers tightened around her hand. "Never."

The solitary word faded to a slurred sigh as he fell back to sleep, his fiery cheek pillowed by the soft curve of her breast.

Chapter Eight

Rosamund scowled at Andy and crossed her arms over her chest. "I thought you were kind. I was wrong. You're a slave-driver—no better than him."

She jerked her chin at McLeod. He lay quietly now, his breathing deep and even. It was a healing sleep, very different from the first few days she'd nursed him, when he'd thrashed about, calling on Andy and others and fighting her gentlest touch. Two weeks had passed now. And, while he was well on the road to recovery, she was exhausted.

Andy shrugged. "We do what we must, aye?" He grinned. "Fate, lassie. Destiny. We're all slaves to it in some way, like it or no'."

"My name's not lassie, nor milady. I told you. It's Rosamund."

"Aye. I ken it verra well. 'Tis Rosamund Trelawney," Andy supplied cheekily. "Ye served ale at the Golden Swan until Jim—"

"Who's Jim?" she tested him.

"Your brother, James Trelawney. Until he and his friend Tom Wainwright decided to rob Riverside House. But you took Jim's place—"

She pursed her lips. "All right. That's enough. Mayhap I did tell my story more than once. But I didn't show you the jewels they were after, did I?"

Reaching down the neck of her hunter-green bodice, she withdrew two large green jewels that winked in the meager light. "The Eyes of the Tiger," she murmured. Her own eyes were almost dreamy as she stared at the huge twin jewels. "You haven't heard of them?"

Andy shrugged and shook his head. "Never."

"They were a gift from the duke to his mistress, Arabella, last Christmas. They say they're the same emerald-green as her eyes. I don't know about that. All I know is, they are worth a sultan's ransom. I'm going to sell them to buy land, once we reach the New World."

Andy snorted. "Land? You'll be lucky t' buy flour with those two useless chunks of glass. They won't be worth a farthing in New France. You'd be better off with a brace o' hogs or a horse and some chickens than those, lassie."

93

"But why?" she exclaimed, crushed.

"Because gold and coin have no value in the wilderness. Tools . . . livestock . . . seed . . . useful things, they're what count. But never mind that for now. We'll no' reach Quebec or Fort Charles for weeks yet. Tell me about the duke. You've no fondness for the mon yourself, I'm thinking." It was a statement rather than a question.

"I loathe him," she said vehemently. "Him and everything about him. Jim used to be his man, you see?"

"His valet, you mean?"

She laughed and shook her head. "Not likely! My brother Jim was a prizefighter. A champion," she explained proudly, dropping the jewels back down her bodice with a provocative wiggle that made Andy's throat instantly dry. "Cornish Jim, the crowds called him. We'd come from Cornwall just a few years before, you see? His Grace was his patron."

He stared hard at the two small bumps the jewels made in her bodice, before catching himself, turning red and looking away.

"For a while, we were quite comfortably off. We lived in a lovely little house in Sadler's Wells with servants, good food, fine clothes, everything. Jim said"—her voice broke—"Jim insisted that I attend Miss Pennington's Academy, so that I could become a proper young lady, as Father would have wished, and marry someone of substance, as Mama would have wanted. We were so happy, you cannot imagine."

Andy nodded. "That explains it."

"Explains what?"

"Why ye dinna talk like a London tavern wench. Ye sound well-bred, educated, most of the time."

Pleased, Rose primly ran her hands down over her threadbare gown. Although well-worn now, the hunter-green fabric had once been of excellent quality. She held her head a little higher. "The house we lived in was almost as nice as the farmhouse where I was born."

"And then what happened?"

She scowled. "Cumberland happened. Like I said, he was Jim's patron. But when my brother refused to 'throw' a fight, His Grace and his cronies lost heavily on their wagers, and the duke set out to ruin him. That same night, he publicly withdrew his patronage. First thing the following morning, his creditors called in their notes." She bit her lip. "We had no money to pay our debts, and so we lost everything. Our house, our furniture—all of it—in one fell swoop. We were cast into the London streets like beggars, left without a farthing in our pockets, and only the clothes upon our backs. But that wasn't the worst of it."

"What could be worse?"

"The following night, Cumberland sent his thugs to teach my brother a lesson." Her eyes

95

darkened with pain at the memory. "They taught him, all right. With their hobnailed boots.

"When they were done, Jim's right arm was so badly mangled it would not heal. In a single night, his livelihood as a fighter was lost, and mine along with it. We were half starved, and Jim's arm was badly infected when we met Tom Wainwright. He found us a place to stay. We couldn't afford a physician for Jim's arm, so Tom brought a midwife. She was a gin-sot, but she told me what to do for him. Tom hated Cumberland, too."

"Why?"

"I never asked. It was thanks to him we found work and lodging at the Golden Swan when Jim recovered. I slept in the garret there, while he slept in the stables with the other grooms. It wasn't much, but it was better than life in the streets, or the workhouse."

"A fine friend, your Tom, to have a lassie steal for him," Andy observed. His mouth was pursed in disapproval.

Rose shrugged. "That was my fault. I begged him to let me take Jim's place that day. My brother's crippled arm makes him clumsy, you see. I was so afraid he'd be taken up by the night watch." She frowned. "Andy, when the McLeod lifted me into the rowboat that day, you told him you'd seen a tall, dark man by the bushes. Remember?"

He scowled. "Aye. But if that was your Tom,

ye needn't pine for him, my lass," he cautioned, hearing the wistful note in her voice. " 'Twas your braw Tommy that raised the hue and cry. He betrayed ye, he did, lass. Wanted ye caught."

"You believe me now, then? That I'm not Arabella?"

"I do." He grinned. "A part o' me suspected from the first, when I saw the loot ye'd hidden under your skirts, aye? Came rainin' down like manna from Heaven, it did. Gold chains, silver combs, all manner of whatnots!"

She laughed. "So it did. Before I left the tavern, I sewed pockets into my petticoats, to carry the loot. You'll help me to convince him, if he recovers?" she asked, nodding at Drum's prone body.

"*When* he recovers, aye," he promised. "And if I canna convince him, I give ye my word, I willna let him hurt ye."

It was more than she'd dared to hope for. Leaning over, she kissed Andy's cheek. "You're a dear man, Andrew. Thank you."

He blushed.

"Where's Cameron?" Drum asked, surfacing momentarily from the deep, dark pool in which he drifted.

"Who's Cameron?" he heard a woman's voice inquire.

"His brother," he heard Andy answer. "The McLeod."

"The McLeod?"

"Aye. That's the laird, or chieftain, of our clan. Drummond's the McLeod now. . . ."

Drum thought his voice sounded like an echo in the endless blackness in which he floated.

"Come on, lad. Bid our kinsmen Godspeed and farewell. They march within the hour, ye ken?"

His cousin looked pale and anxious as he looked down at him. Why, Drum wondered? What had gone wrong?

"I shall go with them," he heard himself mutter. "Prince Charlie needs my strong right arm. Get away, old woman. I will get up, whether ye like it or nay. Andy. Andy!"

"Aye, laddie, aye. I'm here. Pipe down, now."

"Bring me my claymore. Cameron, wait! I'm coming with ye."

He flailed about, throwing off the grubby linens, thrashing from side to side.

Andy stepped back as Cameron leaned low to kiss him farewell.

"Are ye away, sir?" Drummond heard Andy ask.

"Aye, cousin. We march within the hour. Will ye stay back wi' him?" Cameron's chiseled features had softened. "He's a pain in the arse, but he's all the family I have. I'm of a mind t' keep him."

"I'll stay with him, sir," he heard Andy promise.

Silently he begged Cameron to wait for him, but could not find the strength to say the words aloud.

"I'll be off now, little brother," Cameron murmured. "Nay, nay, dinna fret. Bide here until you're well again. If I should perish in battle, tell Fiona I love her, will ye, Drum?"

He could not find the strength to answer.

"Drum!"

"I'll tell him for ye, milord. When he's well," Andy offered.

Cameron clamped his hand over Andy's shoulder. "Take care of each other, aye, laddies?"

"We will, my laird. May God be wi' you all, and wi' our prince."

Soon after, the Mcleod and his clansmen left the chamber.

Still locked in his stupor, Drummond heard their claymores scraping against the stone walls, heard the shuffle of feet and Highland voices raised in farewell. Then all fell silent.

"Wait!" he cried. "Cameron! Dinna go!"

"Be still, laddie. Be still." Someone spooned a potion down his throat. "Have done wi' your ravings, do! You're too weak to fight the fever, let alone the cursed English. At Kilravock ye'll bide, for the while, else I'm not Granny McCree."

"Let me up, damn ye! Let me up, I say. Sweet Mary, I must. . . ."

*   *   *

"Must what?" Rose asked as her patient opened his eyes.

Now that the sickness was leaving him, the fever waning, they were a beautiful clear gray, no longer frighteningly cold, or glittering with hatred. Still, she regarded him with wary curiosity as he shoved himself up onto the bolster. Memories of their last confrontation still loomed large, and she was uncertain how much of that time he'd recall.

"That I must . . . bid ye a good day, lass," he said in answer to her question.

"For a start, I'm not a lass," she said pertly.

"Nay?" He looked her up and down, making her wish she'd done more than braid her brown hair in a fat rope that hung down over one shoulder. "Whist! Dinna tell me you're a lad?"

"No. Of course not—"

"Nor Granny McCree?"

"Hardly." She frowned. "Nay. I have the great misfortune to be your wife, my laird Drummond. The Lady Rosamund McLeod." She bobbed a sarcastic curtsey. "At your service, sir."

"My *wife?*"

He managed a wan yet wicked grin that would have been engaging in such a handsome, gaunt face, were he any other man.

"Ha! Then I'm the man in the moon, aye? Come here, milady—wife—if that's really who you are. Offer your laird a wee bit o' wifely service."

He lifted a limp hand and, to her amazement, squeezed her derriere.

She yelped and swatted at his head. "You must be getting better, to be doing such wicked things."

"Sweeting, if ye were truly my wife, ye'd ken I'm *always* doing such wicked things." He lifted the rumpled linens and winked invitingly. "Won't ye join me, my bonnie? I've a mind to refresh my memory of our wedding night."

She felt her face flame. "I will not." She skittered away like a nervous filly.

His teasing laughter and wicked invitation unsettled her. They stirred the same feathery pulses she felt whenever she looked at his naked body. They made her feel breathless and silly, for no reason at all.

"Lie back while I fetch you some broth from the galley. You'll be hungry, I expect."

"Starved, aye." He jiggled his dark brows. "But it isna food I'm wanting now. Come here, woman!"

His laughter followed her as she bolted from McKinnon's cabin, headed for the galley.

In the narrow gangway en route to the ship's kitchen, she encountered the mate, Mr. Sinclair, coming in the other direction.

She looked away as he pressed himself back to let her pass. The mate had a sly, knowing way about him she did not care for.

"Lady McLeod. A very good day to ye, ma'am."

"And to you, sir," she murmured, meaning to brush past him.

But to her distaste, instead of stepping aside, Sinclair stepped toward her, blocking her path. He was now so close she could see the countless pox scars that blemished his olive skin.

"Let me pass, sir."

"All in good time, milady. Or should I say *Arabella*?"

"My name, sir, is Mistress McLeod. Rosamund McLeod."

"Don't lie t'me, lass. I know the truth," he rasped, thrusting his face into hers. His spittle sprayed her cheek when he spoke. "I know your name and I know what you were. Cumberland's whore! If you want me t' keep my mouth shut, meet me tonight after ma watch. Down in the ship's stores." His black eyes glittered with lust. "If not, everyone aboard will know your clarty secrets."

"I'd not meet with you in broad daylight on London Bridge, sir. Not if I had a thousand secrets to keep," Rose snapped.

As he reached for her breast, she squirmed aside and went on about her errand.

"Go on wi' ye then. Ye'll not be sae high and mighty when I'm done wi' ye, bitch," Sinclair muttered under his breath as she hurried away.

Chapter Nine

When she returned to the cabin, it was obvious McLeod had remembered everything

He was sitting up. His arms were crossed over his bare chest and he was wearing a scowl as black as sin.

Asleep, he'd looked like a dark angel, fallen to earth. Awake and unshaven, his gray eyes heavy-lidded, he looked like the Devil himself, but so handsome the breath caught in her throat.

What on earth was happening to her? Had she so short a memory, so little pride, that what he had done counted for naught?

She sighed. Apparently so, for at some time during the past fortnight, McLeod had ceased to be the black-hearted beast who'd tried to throw her overboard. His horns and tail had miraculously vanished and, although he hadn't exactly exchanged them for wings and a halo overnight, he *had* become a man, rather than a demon. A sick, vengeful, grieving man, true, but one she had held and comforted in the long, lonely nights when he called for those he'd lost.

At times when she stroked the crisp raw silk of his black hair or sponged his broad, hairy chest, she'd found her thoughts drifting. She'd wondered what it would be like to be loved by this man, as deeply and loyally as he had once loved those he mourned. What would it be like to be his wife in every way, instead of in name alone? If they shared one life, one future, one bed?

She hugged herself about the arms. The thought of sharing McLeod's bed, of his touching her, kissing her, stirred her in ways she did not comprehend. It excited and scared her at one and the same time—not unlike the wretched man himself. Of one thing she was certain. He would love the woman who shared his life with the same fierce intensity that he hated his enemies.

The thought of being loved like that made her shiver.

"Here. Drink this," she urged gruffly, handing him a steaming basin and a horn spoon. "You must be starved."

He eyed the thin, greasy soup with suspicion. "How do I ken it isna poisoned?"

"That's the fun of it, aye, milord? You don't." She shot him a grin that was calculated to gnaw at his innards. He must have remembered bits and pieces of what had happened after he took her from Riverside House and in the days before he passed out. He was probably expecting some sort of retaliation on her part. Well, let him fret over it. The uncertainty would do him good. Perhaps it would help to sharpen the wits that sickness had dulled.

As she expected, he waved the basin away, although she could hear his belly rumbling from where she stood. He'd had only pap and gruel for she didn't know how many days. He must be starved for something more filling by now. His refusal of the soup suggested he was afraid of what she might do to him. She hid a smile. The shoe was on the other foot, now.

"Here, take it," she urged. "I can't stand here all day."

"I'm no' hungry," he snarled, casting her a foul look.

"What a shame. My appetite's increased. The result, I believe, of a clear conscience."

Without further ado, she perched on the corner of the box bed, took up spoon and bowl and polished off the soup. It was a greasy concoction that featured beans, salt pork, turnips and onions as the only identifiable ingredients. "Hmm. 'Tis quite tasty, for once," she lied.

"You? A clear conscience?" He snorted, carefully staring anywhere but at the bowl she was holding. "That's a strange thing for a thief to be having, Arabella—"

She sighed. "My name, sir, is Rosamund," she cut in crisply. "Must we go over that again?"

"Aye, aye, whatever ye call yourself—"

"Trelawney. Rosamund Trelawney. And I am not a thief." That wasn't entirely true, she thought with a twinge of conscience. Thanks to his untimely arrival at Riverside House, she had never returned Arabella's jewelry to its casket. So, strictly speaking, she *was* a thief. However, she had not intended to steal anything, after her change of heart.

"All right, Rosamund, or whatever your bluidy name is. I'm in no mood t' discuss conscience or the lack of it. And as to ye being a thief"—he smiled nastily—"if ye didna want me to mention the stolen emeralds, ye should have taken them from your bodice."

He chuckled, relishing her shocked expression, the hand that flew to her breast, betraying the jewels' hiding place. "That's right, lassie. Every time ye leaned over me, I've been treated to a fine display of your bonnie wee treasures. And the emeralds, too, aye?" he added with a roguish wink.

Heat burned its way up her cheeks. "Is that

how you thank me for my care? By making lewd sport of me?" She sniffed. "Ha! Ingratitude is surely a Scottish trait."

"As murder is an English one?" he shot back. His sensual lips thinned. "Ye've a sharp tongue to ye, woman."

"If I am less than gently disposed toward you, sir, 'tis your doing. You brought me here."

He frowned. "Ye were in the wrong place at the wrong time."

She rounded on him in disbelief. "Is that your idea of an apology?"

"I'll no' apologize, ye wee besom," he growled, tossing the bed linens aside and springing to his feet.

He stood there, swaying unsteadily, his left foot—still heavily bandaged—placed gingerly on the boards. Yet he was flinty-eyed and thin-lipped as he glowered down at her.

She eyed him critically. Although he appeared much improved, the lout was still weak, far from recovered. He trembled with the effort it had taken to stand.

"Why not?" she demanded, fists on hips.

"Because of you, I lost the means to avenge my brother's death."

"Oh? And exactly how was that my doing?" she demanded, bristling. Her thick brown plait flew out as she whirled to face him. The end almost put out his eye. "Explain yourself."

"If ye hadna been robbing Arabella's chamber,

she'd be here now, and ye'd be"—he grinned nastily—"wherever it was ye came from."

He managed to make it sound as if she'd crawled out from under a rock, or a cesspit, or some other verminous hole. "Of all the cockeyed, twisted reasoning. So you will admit no mistake on your part, sir?"

"My only error, madam," he ground out, "was in taking ye with us."

He abruptly sat down again. Even from across the cabin, she could see his legs quivering.

"Your plan was a mistake to begin with, McLeod. But you'll never admit it, will you? Arabella Slater was a kept woman. No more, no less. She had no say in her master's doings. None at all."

"Maybe not. But she *was* verra dear to the duke, aye?" His upper lip curled in contempt and remembered loathing. "The Butcher would have tasted Scotland's sorrow had I killed her."

She rolled her eyes in disgust. "Him, sorrow over the likes of her? Not for a minute. After a week, he'd have found himself another bedmate. While you—! It would have been too late for you, McLeod. By then, you would have taken an innocent woman's life—risked your own immortal soul—and for what? For nothing. You, sir, should thank me." She tossed her head.

"How so?"

She threw up her hands in exasperation. "Because if you'd killed her, you would be no better than the man you despise! It was Cumberland who ordered your kinsmen slain. Cumberland whose life should be forfeit. Not Arabella. Nor me either, come to that. Our deaths cannot bring Cameron back, nor ease your—" She fell abruptly silent.

"Dinna stop now, lassie," he said through thinned lips. "Say it."

"Very well. Your . . . guilt."

"Guilt!" he exploded. "About what?"

"That you lay at Kilravock while your kinsmen marched on to their deaths." In a lower, gentler voice, she added, "The sad truth, McLeod, is that there's nothing you could have done, except add your number to the fallen. You have naught to reproach yourself for. Only . . . you cannot accept it."

His eyes had darkened as she spoke. Now, like banked coals, they were almost black and glittered with fury. "Ye mentioned my brother, Cameron. What do ye know of him? And when did ye become such an authority on *me*, madam? Someone's been telling tales. Was it Lewis?"

She gave a little smile and shook her head. "Poor Andy. Nay. It was you. You told me yourself."

"The devil I did."

"In your sleep."

His dark brows lifted. "Did I, now?"

"Aye." There was a weighty pause as she moved around, straightening up the cabin. "You talked about your Auntie, too. Flora, I think her name was. And a woman named Elspeth."

A muscle pulsed at his temple. "And it was ye who tended me? The whole time?"

She nodded mutely.

He seemed about to say something, then the anger suddenly fizzled out of him like a damp squib. His shoulders slumped, and in a world-weary, grudging tone, he began, "I suppose ye're right, then. I owe ye my thanks. For saving me from myself, I suppose. And for seeing to my foot."

"Oh, I'd say you owe me more than that," she retorted with a weary smile. "You're indebted to me that it's still there. Your foot, I mean. Andy was all for taking it off."

"Was he now? But you disagreed?" He sounded surprised.

She nodded. "Yes. I said I thought we should wait." She smiled. Her thick lashes fluttered.

"Aye? Then I'm deeper in your debt than I knew, madam," he said through clenched teeth, unsettled by her honeyed expression, so at odds with the gleam in her amethyst eyes.

"Oh, don't thank me. I certainly didn't do it for you."

"Who, then?"

"For myself. If anything was coming off, I thought it should be your blasted *head*."

*   *   *

There were dark thunderheads huddled on the horizon like prodigal sheep three evenings later as Rose, Andy and the other passengers stumbled stiffly above decks from the hatchways for the evening prayers. A fierce wind was ripping the gray waves into a choppy froth.

The Scots eyed her askance, as usual, and muttered behind their hands. But after a moment or two, the imminent storm drew all their attention, and she was forgotten.

"We're in for a rough night of it," Andy observed, his expression serious. "If the storm hits during the service, dinna wait for me, lassie. Get doon to the cabin. Stay with my cousin. He's still weak, aye?"

She nodded. "Feverish, too. Where will you be?"

He turned as pink as a girl. "In steerage with the others. There's a lassie. Mistress Kirsty McLachlann's her name. She's an orphan." He coughed. "She—ah—she has only her uncle t' see to her welfare."

"Oh? And what's wrong with her uncle?"

"He's Angus Stevenson," Andy said, scowling. "That's what's wrong with him. He already has his hands full wi' that daughter of his."

She smiled knowingly. "Then, of course, you must see to Mistress Kirsty's safety."

He nodded. "But will ye be all right? Alone with himself, I mean?"

"The McLeod? Of course. Haven't I been all right so far?"

Andy pursed his lips. "Aye. I've been hoping . . . since the two o' ye are already wed . . . that perhaps if ye were left alone for a wee bit, ye could maybe . . . ?" His voice trailed away. He shrugged and sighed. "Ye ken what I'm trying to say, aye? After all, ye're marrit. And the Catholic kirk doesna countenance divorce."

"No, it doesn't, does it?" she agreed glumly. Tawny eyebrows rose. "An annulment, perhaps?"

"That would take forever, lass. Ye'd have to send to Rome for it. His Holiness himsel' has t' grant his approval, ye ken? Could ye not—could ye not see your way to—making the best of it?"

She shot him a look that spoke volumes. There was more chance of a cow jumping over the moon than of she and the laird of Dunmor ever growing close, as Andy so obviously wanted. Still, it was her opinion that a little hope never hurt anyone. "We shall see."

Although the storm was yet some distance away, she could hear the thunder's ominous rumble now. It sounded louder, closer that it had moments before. Lightning flickered on the livid horizon. The jagged bolts were like eerie white sprites, caught up in a jerky pagan ritual.

While the passengers hastily muttered their prayers under the captain's leadership, the crew scuttled back and forth like crabs to prepare for the weather's assault, battening down the hatches, lashing the cannons into the gun ports, shinning up the ratlines to follow the mate's roared commands.

The *Salutation*'s crew was still lashing down the cannons when, halfway through the second hymn, the swollen black clouds overhead burst. Rain poured from the dark sky, roaring as it fell, drumming on the decks and soaking the kneeling worshipers.

Before they could sing their Amens and take cover below, the decks were awash. The sails snapped and cracked, whipped in all directions by the screaming wind as the wet, terrified Scots fled for the hatches, stumbling over each other in their haste to get down to the holds.

Caught in the teeth of the violent wind, *The Salutation* bucked like a terrified stallion, then bolted.

Rain streaming down her uplifted face, Rose crossed herself. She stared skyward in amazement, Andy's instructions forgotten.

High above her, the lanterns that hung from the yardarms were swinging violently, drawing crazy arcs of light against the charcoal sky. The shrouds whipped furiously about, while sizzling green light leaped from mast to mast, then spread over the pitching decks in an eerie green fog.

"It's St. Elmo's fire. Come below!" Andy yelled, appearing from nowhere to take her hand.

Sandy hair streaming, he tugged her after him across the decks.

The last thing she heard before they went below and the hatches were battened down was Captain McKinnon roaring orders to his crew over the wind and the rain.

"It's going t' be a long night, laddies!" the Scot bellowed. His blue eyes blazed. "You, Duncan, jump to it! Stow those lines aft. Robbie, look lively, lad! Secure the starboard guns. . . ."

A hot surge of lust jolted through Drummond as Rosamund spilled through the cabin door. His mouth went dry.

In the murky gray light, she looked like a mermaid, a sea-siren who lured sailors to their watery deaths with her beauty and her song.

Drops of water spiked her dark lashes. More dewed her lovely, glowing face. Her golden-brown hair was plastered to her head and flapped in wet dark strands down her back. Her soaked bodice clung to the curves of her breasts, while the taut nipples stood at attention beneath the wet green cloth.

He stared at them, wanting to do far, far more than look. He wetted his lips, wondering how she would taste, how she would feel in his arms.

"You're awake," she exclaimed, pulling up short on the threshold.

"Aye."

"The fever is gone?"

He cleared his throat and nodded curtly. "For now, aye." To be replaced by a fever of another kind entirely. "I wanted to come aloft, but I couldna find my boots . . ."

"There's only the right one. I had to cut off the other one when you were ill. I'm sorry. We had no choice."

"Never mind that. What's happening aloft? I heard the guns rolled out." He forced himself to look at her face, praying she would not look down. "Did the lookout spy a sail?" Pirate ships were all too common in these waters. No vessel, however innocent, would risk sailing without cannons in the gun ports.

Before she could answer him, the ship heeled, pitching her across the cabin toward him.

Everything that hadn't been bolted down came with her.

On reflex, his hands shot out, anchoring around her upper arms. Once she'd recovered her footing, his grip softened. It was the only thing that did. His treacherous body was hard and fully aroused, crushed against her damp, feminine curves.

As he was about to release her, the ship gave another violent heel in the opposite direction.

They lurched across the cabin a second time, and he wrapped his arms around her, twisting at the last moment to absorb the brunt of the fall himself.

He landed against the bulkhead with a thump that drove the breath from his belly.

He lay on his back with Rosamund sprawled, face down, across him. Her breasts were flattened against his chest, her belly and thighs were riding the hard ridge in his breeches. Her skirts were rucked up, exposing shapely stockinged legs and an expanse of slender ivory thigh.

He clenched his teeth, muffling a groan, for her frantic efforts to right herself were adding to his aroused state. The urge to sweep her beneath him, toss up her skirts and take her, right there on the canting deck, was nigh overpowering.

"Sweet Lord," he muttered fervently, wondering if the minx knew the effect she was having on him.

"Sir?" She quickly scrambled off him, and his eyes narrowed. Her speedy change of position, the way she refused to look him in the eye, confirmed that she knew all right. Oh, yes, she knew.

He sensed her frowning in the shadows. "My lord? Are you injured?"

"Nay, nay, 'tis naught," he rasped through clenched jaws. "Why has McKinnon run out the guns?"

"He hasn't. What you heard was thunder. There's a bad storm overhead," she explained breathlessly. "It took everyone unawares, even the captain."

"What about Andy? Is he all right?"

"He's down in steerage. There is a girl—Kirsty,

116

I think her name is. He was concerned for her safety."

His brows rose. "Was he now? And what about yours?" He caught her chin between his thumb and finger and tipped her enchanting, heart-shaped face up to his.

Her lashes lay like silky moths upon her cheeks. Her mouth was a crushed flower—a budding red rose, with petals soft as velvet—that he ached to taste.

In a husky voice, he asked, "Who's worrying about your safety?"

She quickly looked away, color rising up her cheeks. "I chose to stay here, milord. With you."

He rolled his eyes heavenward. "Thank God for foul weather!"

A frown knit her smooth white brow. "What do you mean by that, sir?"

"Nothing. Nothing at all. Look at ye, lassie. Ye're soaked. Grab that blanket and crawl over here, whilst I douse the lantern. We must get ye warmed, or ye'll take the ague."

"Must you douse the lantern?" she asked in a small voice. The prospect of being alone in the dark with him was not one she found appealing.

"Aye. It could start a fire, with the ship lurching about, ye ken?"

"Oh, yes, of course. I didn't think of that. Go ahead, sir."

A moment later, they were plunged into darkness, broken only by murky flashes of lightning through the bow windows.

"Are ye afraid of the dark?" If she wasn't now, perhaps she should be, he thought ruefully. The thoughts he was having about her—the things he would like to do both to and with her—would surely seem monstrous to a lass like her.

He groaned silently as she sat down beside him, shivering. Her thigh brushed against his as she wriggled about to get comfortable, and the scent of cold rain and warm woman filled his nostrils, teasing his senses.

"Come closer," he urged, pulling the blanket up and over them both. "It will be warmer that way."

"I've never been very fond of storms," she admitted, staying right where she was. She shuddered. "I'm not afraid of them, exactly. They just . . . unsettle me." Her voice shook ever so slightly.

"Och, aye. My mother was the same way. I remember when I was just a little lad there was such a storm one summer it roused us all from our beds. Even auld Duncan, father's gillie, was . . ."

When he'd finished recounting his anecdote, she was much more relaxed. As he talked, she had edged closer to him—was now actually leaning against him. Her head was resting on his shoulder, and he could feel her breath fanning his cheek. The rise and fall of her breasts was deep and even in sleep.

He gritted his teeth. With her head lolling on his shoulder, her soft breasts crushed against his side, and her tantalizing fragrance filling his nostrils, the night ahead promised to be torture.

In more ways than one.

The vessel pitched and rolled all night long, shaken in the jaws of the violent squall. The ship's rough motions woke her.

To her horror, she discovered that her head was cradled on McLeod's chest. His chin was resting cozily in her hair and his arm was draped over her shoulder. Her cheeks flamed when she realized that his long fingers were curled lightly over her breast.

She lifted his hand away, startled by the dry heat she could feel raging just beneath his skin.

Despite his returning health, he was still far from recovered. Every afternoon and evening brought on a recurrence of the fever he'd experienced at the height of the sickness. When it rose, a ruddy flush stained his hollowed cheeks. A feverish glitter made his eyes unnaturally bright. And when he slept, although it was a very long, deep sleep, he awoke sweaty and unrefreshed.

She frowned. Granny McCree's herbs were long gone. All she could do was sponge him with cool water and pray the fever would break.

She fumbled around on hands and knees, defying the ship's violent lurching and the dark to find the pitcher and cloth she'd used to sponge him.

With everything turned upside down, it took ages to find the metal pitcher. Not surprisingly, all of the water had been lost when the ship heeled, but the cloth she found nearby was soaked.

It was better than nothing.

Kneeling beside him, she swabbed the wet rag over his face and neck several times. He muttered in his sleep and tried to push her hand away, but he did not waken.

Twice more that hellish night, she forced herself to wake up and repeat the process. Both times, she heard the storm shrieking about the ship like a wild banshee, and the groaning of the timbers as winds and waves battered them about.

She awoke shortly before dawn to a loud hammering noise, certain she was hearing the knell of doom.

Through bleary eyes, she looked down. McLeod's dark head was cradled in her lap, and his long fingers were linked through hers. How had that come about?

Throwing off the tatters of a fitful sleep, she slipped her hands free and squirmed out from under McLeod's weight to answer the knocking.

It was Andy, come to rouse them.

"The storm's blown itself out. Captain Mc-Kinnon has ordered all passengers and hands to assemble on the upper deck."

"All right. Let me set the cabin to rights, and then I'll come above."

She was bending over the bed, smoothing the rumpled linens over the pallet, when she felt a pair of hands slide around her waist from behind.

As McLeod drew her back against him, she flung around in surprise. She was brought up short by the bulk of him, her palms pressed flat against his broad chest.

"What are you doing!" she protested.

His eyes were heavy-lidded, smoky now. "I'm yielding, lassie. Succumbing t' my baser instincts. As, I pray, will you—"

Before she could do or say anything to stop him, he ducked his head and kissed her, full on the mouth.

His hands skimmed lightly down her throat, noting the pulse that fluttered in the hollow at its base, before reaching behind to draw her closer.

She stiffened. She couldn't breathe, couldn't move as his large hand cupped the back of her neck. The other cradled her cheek.

"Don't!" she whispered as he ducked his dark head, denying the strange ache, the heat in the pit of her belly that his touch kindled.

"Shoo, lassie. There's nothing t' be scared of,"

he murmured as if he were gentling a frightened wild animal. "Nothing at all . . ." His tongue traced the outer margins of her closed lips, skillfully teasing them apart. " 'Tis just a kiss, aye?"

"Just a kiss," indeed. It was not "just" anything!

When she opened her mouth, he touched her tongue with his own and stole her breath away. The teasing kisses she'd known before paled by comparison to McLeod's searing blasts of sensation, his hot, demanding kisses.

When their mouths met, it was as if she'd been struck by lightning. Her world narrowed, centering on his hungry lips. On the way they tasted, the dangerous way they made her feel. On the frightening, exciting things that happened inside her when he ground his hard, muscular body against hers.

Her heart pounded like a triphammer, racing out of control. She felt dazed and confused, while her knees were boneless with a surrender she could not control.

"Our first kiss," he murmured when he broke away. Pulling back, he looked down at her, smoothing the ball of his thumb over her full, pink lower lip.

"And most assuredly our last, sir," she said shakily, jerking her head away.

He chuckled. There had been no sting to her words. How could there be, when her body quivered uncontrollably under his touch, and grew languorous with desire? Or when she looked as rosy and flushed as she did now, and seemed not to know what to do with her hands.

He could have told the lovely witch what to do with them, he thought, but . . . blast it! She settled for crossing them over her sweet breasts in a maidenly show of modesty.

"Och, Rosamund, dinna fash yersel'. 'Twas but an innocent wee kiss from a mon to his bride. Admit it! Ye've been wondering, too. And ye wanted it as much as I did." He swayed a little as he drew his shirt over his head and then tucked the fullness into his breeches. He could not even dress himself without feeling weak.

"The devil I wanted it, sir," she retorted. Cheeks pink, she pushed past him, her hair a fragrant, silky floss against his cheek as she went by. Pausing on the threshold, she turned to face him. "And as for it being innocent—! It was no more innocent than *you*, milord."

He chuckled to himself, thoughtfully touching his lips where the taste of her still lingered. She didn't want his kisses—but she hadn't said she disliked them, any more than she'd lifted his hand off her breast in the night.

"Sassenach?" he called after her.

She paused in the doorway, glaring daggers at him. "What now?"

He ran the tip of his tongue over his lips and winked. "I like the taste of ye. I like it verra much."

She blushed. "Devil take you, McLeod!"

He was smiling as he followed her through the door.

Rose and a limping McLeod followed Andy up the gangway and onto the decks.

They emerged into the lemon-colored light of early morning to find the sea the color of beaten silver in the dawn, its surface as calm as a millpond.

The *Salutation* had fared less well. Two of her crew had been washed overboard at the height of the storm. Three others had suffered injury. The ship was also severely damaged. Much of her canvas was ripped, and one of her masts had shattered, among other things. The passengers were heavy-eyed and stiff, battered and bruised from the long, rough night.

"Praise God, we have weathered the storm, good people," McKinnon's voice rang out. "Unfortunately, we have not done so unscathed. My ship's carpenter and the sailmaker have badly needed repairs to make, if we are to continue on to the New World." He looked down at the sea of concerned white faces from his vantage point on the quarterdeck.

"As some of you know, the ship's stores were awash at the height of the storm. Sacks of flour, cornmeal and other dried goods were contaminated by saltwater, or completely waterlogged. Several hogsheads of fresh water were ruptured—and we are still a month from our first landfall in the Indies.

"With that in mind, I have reached a difficult decision. One that I expect each of ye to abide by." He paused for effect and looked around. "Until such time as we can replenish our stores, all victuals are t' be rationed, as is the fresh water. The lion's share shall go to the crew, who will need their strength t' sail this vessel. The remainder will be divided evenly among you."

There was a moment of absolute silence as his words sank in; then an angry mutter arose.

"What about you, McKinnon? Are your victuals t' be rationed too?" one man yelled.

"Four bluidy weeks? We'll starve t' death, ye fool!" yelled another.

"All victuals are to be rationed, aye," the captain repeated, his stern yet calm tone quelling the hecklers. "Mine as well as yours. If we conduct ourselves in a Christian fashion, I am confident we shall survive this difficult time in good shape."

A murmur of unrest ran through the crowd. Despite his assurances, McKinnon's words held an ominous ring.

"Mr. Sinclair!" the captain barked.

"Sir?" Sinclair arrived at a run.

"You, sir, will ensure that the distribution of provisions is equably handled. Each daily ration is to be divided into two portions, to begin with. These are to be handed out following the morning and evening prayers. The ship's biscuits, dried apples and whatever foodstuffs remain undamaged shall be evenly apportioned amongst us all. Fresh water, likewise. Set those men not on watch to casting lines over the side. Fish will be a welcome addition to our meager diet, as time goes by."

"Very good, sir."

His blue eyes stern, McKinnon looked from troubled face to face. "I know these are difficult times for you, my friends. But remember, ye've already endured far greater hardships in our homeland, and survived. I beseech each of ye to remember that Mr. Sinclair is only carrying out my orders, and to obey him. He will report to me all who refuse t' comply with the rationing. They will be dealt with accordingly."

He paused, giving time for his words to sink in. "Likewise, any mon caught stealing food will receive twenty stripes o' the cat, to be delivered before this gathering. 'Tis a harsh sentence, but I'll thank all of ye to keep in mind that any theft from our stores, however small, is food taken from the mouths of every soul aboard this vessel.

"Now, if there are no further questions, we shall begin our morning prayers, and give thanks to Almighty God for delivering us from the storm."

It was a subdued little group that attended morning prayers that day, despite the calm seas and the glorious, sunny weather.

The passengers grumbled about the terrifying night they'd spent, tossed out of hammocks or bunks, thrown this way and that about the dark, airless, leaky hold, convinced they would all be drowned.

Rose was relieved when most of the Scots went below to restore order to their quarters, leaving her alone at the taffrail with McLeod, who professed himself eager for some fresh air, after so many days spent in the cabin's close confines.

Rose curled her hands over the polished teak rail and closed her eyes, enjoying the sun's warmth on her face—and the memory of McLeod's kiss, which had set her senses whirling like leaves in autumn.

If she closed her eyes, she could still feel the pressure of his lips on hers, the sensual play of his tongue, which sent heat lapping through her.

There was all the time in the world to go below. For now, she would stay where she was and bask in his sunshine.

Drummond squinted against the brilliant light, watching as Margaret Stevenson and her cousin promenaded about the decks.

The lengths of fringed tartan they'd thrown about their shoulders twisted and flapped like sails in the lively wind. From time to time, black-haired Maggie would cast a saucy eye in his direction, favoring him with a bold smile no proper lass would cast a married man—or a bachelor, either, come to that.

But to his surprise, he felt no response to the lassie's silent come-hither. The invitation in her eyes left him cold.

Turning back to his bride, sloe-eyed Maggie forgotten, his only thought was that Angus Stevenson must surely have his hands full, with such a daughter. He could almost pity the great lout.

"What beautiful shawls Scottish women have. And no two alike, that I've seen," Rosamund observed, watching the young women. She was not alone. The men of the *Salutation*'s crew were eyeing them covertly, too, though for far different reasons. "Do your Highland women weave the cloth themselves?"

He nodded. "Aye. They learn the sett of their clan's tartan at their mam's knee, so that they may pass it down to their daughters. Usually, the wool is spun from the crofters' own sheep."

"A sett?"

" 'Tis the tartan's pattern. Each one is different."

"I see. Then your clan has its own tartan, too?"

He nodded, his gray eyes bleak. "Aye. And bonnie it is, too."

His face was thinner since the sickness, his profile as spare and chiseled as a hawk's, she thought. His flesh was pale against the wild black mane that fell about his shoulders. He'd donned his full-sleeved linen shirt, much darned, and wore it now without coat or stock, baring a vee of smooth throat.

"Will you show me?" she asked.

"I canna, lassie. My plaid is long gone."

"All of it?"

"Aye, every inch, more's the pity. Me and Andy, we threw our breachans down a well before we fled the Highlands."

"But why?"

"Because the wearing of the tartan betrayed us t' the Redcoats as Highlanders, ye ken?" A grim smile played about his lips. "There were things we had to do. We didna have time to die just then. So we abandoned our tartans and bonnets."

"Then everyone who knew the sett of the McLeod tartan is gone?"

"Nay. There are a few aunties left on the isle of Skye. And my cousin Elspeth would know it."

She smiled. So. Elspeth was his cousin. She was glad to hear it. "You will return to Scotland, Drummond. Someday, when these troubles are over, you will go back, I'm sure of it," she said gently. "And when you return to stay, your womenfolk will weave the McLeod tartan again. People—even nations—forget, do they not? And like their subjects, kings also die. Your—exile—cannot last forever."

"Mine shall," he murmured, "for in the Highlands, I'm a wanted mon. One wi' a price on my head for murder. Five hundred English guineas, that's what I'm worth t' the English. Dead or alive." His gray eyes gleamed.

He hadn't intended to tell her. Had never intended to tell another soul. Nor had she asked him to explain. But the quiet way she listened, with her golden-brown head cocked to one side, her lovely eyes grave and non-judgmental, made him want to unburden himself to her, somehow. Perhaps . . . perhaps if she knew all of it, she would understand why he had done what he did—and forgive him for abducting her.

The words spilled from him. And once started, he could not seem to stem the flood.

"We went back home, after we fled the battle at Culloden, Andy and I," he began. "Home to Glen Dunmor. Did I speak of it in my sleep?"

She solemnly shook her head.

He tried to smile but could not quite manage it. The lump in his throat made swallowing painful.

In his mind's eye, he saw himself as he'd been then, with his ragged green-and-blue plaid wrapped about his lean waist, the free end thrown over his shoulder to furl in the wind. The tartan had been held in place by his silver clan badge, a red stag, leaping. He'd carried a dirk strapped to one hairy, sinewy thigh by a strip of leather, while a *claidheamh mor*—his traditional Highland sword with a basket hilt—jutted from the scabbard at his lean waist. Its damascened blade showed yet another stag, leaping through thickets of rowan.

"As we slipped up the glen, we saw the bluidy Union Jack flying from our battlements. The English had beaten us to our home. There were Redcoats in the keep, bastard Redcoats everywhere. They were searching the crofts and horse sheds, hunting down those who'd escaped from Culloden Moor. Loyal Jacobites, like mysel'. A thousand dead was no' enough for them." His nostrils flared. His upper lip curled. His hands were white-knuckled where they gripped the taffrail.

"They'd billeted their dragoons where Dunmor McLeods had lived for seven centuries. Almost thirty generations of our clan," he said with pride, "from the time of the Viking, Olaf the Black, King of Man and the Isles, down to Cameron, and then mysel'."

A muscle flexed as his jaw hardened.

"Their nags were stabled in my Great Hall. Horse droppings steamed on the stone floors where our kings and lairds once feasted. The communion chalice my mother gave the Catholic chapel was serving as their piss-pot, may God damn their black souls."

She made no comment, but he saw that her eyes were brimming with tears. She reached out and placed her hand over his on the rail. Her grip was surprisingly strong and comforting, and he made no move to shrug it off.

"My Auntie Flora had the raising of us, after Mam died, ye ken? Cameron had left her in charge of his household when we marched off t' fight the English. She armed the servants with pitchforks and scythes and ordered them t' drive out the bluidy Redcoats."

"A brave woman."

"Aye, and an old one. But her age didna spare her, not from the cursed English. An officer—Captain Harry Williams, his name was—bashed in her head wi' the stock of his musket. He said 'twas her proper punishment for daring t' resist his men. Auntie was gravely wounded. A crofter took her and her maid in. They did their best, but she was near death when we found her."

"And did she recover?" Rosamund asked in a whisper.

He sighed heavily. "I dinna ken, lassie. But I ken verra well what happened to Captain Williams. The English officer." A wolfish grin split his lips, yet his eyes remained glacial. "Before we fled the Highlands, I killed the bastard." A shadow crossed his face. "Now, I am the last McLeod of Dunmor."

"And the first of the New World," she reminded him softly.

He glanced at her face, surprised. "Aye, I suppose I shall be," he agreed, and offered her his arm. "Will ye walk with me a wee bit, Lady McLeod?" he asked. "I've a mind t' find my sea legs."

She shyly linked her arm through his elbow. "If you will call me Rosamund, sir, I would be honored to help you look for them."

He chuckled. "Rosamund it is, then. And you. Will you call me Drum or Drummond?"

"Nay, McLeod, I will not."

Laughing, they set off, arm in arm.

In the three weeks since McKinnon had ordered the rationing, both passengers and crew alike had given the ship's stores a wide berth.

But on their way back down to the hold from the bilges, where he and Jamie Gordon had gone to relieve themselves, Andy froze in mid-stride.

He could hear a man's deep voice and breathy female giggles rising up through the hatchway that covered the entrance to the gloomy storeroom.

On closer inspection, he saw that the hatch had been lifted aside, then crookedly replaced from below.

". . . . ye're a hard man, Calum. But, och, all right. There! And what must I do for an extra biscuit. My *what*? And how about a wee cup of water? Och, ye wicked devil!"

Jamie elbowed Andy in the ribs and snickered, making a lewd hand gesture.

There was a pause, a shocked squeal, followed by the low murmur of a man's voice.

"Whist, I canna, sir. If my Da' finds out, he'll kill both of us."

There was a pause, then a long-drawn-out female sigh. "Ooooh, Calum, ye're awful bad, ye are."

Whoever the woman was—and Andy thought he knew her identity—she'd obviously chosen to risk her father's ire and accommodate her companion's demands. The moonlight that fell through the grilled hatch onto the food stores gleamed on bulky sacks and huge wooden hogsheads—and on a pair of plump white thighs, half hidden beneath a welter of petticoats, snowy bright in the ashy light.

As they watched, a dark male shape crouched down between them.

Jamie Gordon jabbed Andy in the ribs again. "Lookit! Lookit!"

"Have done, will ye," Andy hissed.

"They're after havin' a poke." Jamie chortled.

"I'm no wean. I ken what they're aboot, laddie," he whispered scathingly, disgusted with the lad.

James's teeth flashed white in the shadows as he grinned.

There was a settling male grunt, another female gasp. Then the shadows began bucking violently. Moments later, the woman's low, impassioned cries rose up from the bowels of the ship, bringing heat to Andy's ears.

"Ah, weeell. He spent himsel' too soon. The poor lassie should have asked me. I'd have lasted a wee bit longer, aye?" Jamie boasted, giving Andy another nudge.

"Get along with ye, ye blasted windbag," he growled.

Without further ado, the pair stumbled back to their hammocks in the hold.

"It was with true regret that I ordered ye to assemble here this morning, my friends. But there is no help for it," McKinnon began, his expression stern indeed as he looked out over the company of crew members and passengers. Every face was turned to him. "As your captain, I am bound to enforce the strictest. . . ."

Rose tried to concentrate on what he was saying, but it was very difficult.

Why had the captain seen fit to call an assembly today of all days? she grumbled. She had so many other distractions this morning.

McLeod's fever had risen very high for the past two nights, and she'd had little sleep. He had remained abed this morn, rather than accompany her above decks, as he had been doing. The light was so bright today, reflected off the shimmering ocean and dazzling canvas, it hurt her eyes. She had to squint gritty eyes against it. Squinting and lack of sleep had caused a throbbing pain in her temple.

The worst distraction by far, however, was her hungry belly. She sighed. All she could think about was how hollow she felt. She simply could not wait for Captain McKinnon to finish his long-winded speech, so that the morning rations could be distributed! As it was, her innards seemed to be gobbling themselves.

". . . nevertheless," the captain was saying, "we canna allow the thief to go unpunished. Are there any among you who can confirm or refute the names Mr. Sinclair has given me? Anyone else who has witnessed someone pilfering from the stores?"

Catching the tail end of what he was saying, Rosamund frowned and straightened up, all ears now, her attention riveted to what the captain was saying. There had been pilfering! Indignation filled her. There was precious little food to go around, as it was. What gave anyone the right to a larger share than the rest of them?

"I have!" rang out a woman's voice. It was so loud, Rose flinched. "I saw someone!"

Every head turned to watch as Margaret Stevenson left her trio of female friends and slowly crossed the deck. With a great show of reluctance, she lifted her skirts to climb the few stairs up onto the quarterdeck where McKinnon waited. Her bear of a father lumbered after her, his expression that of a pious man compelled to do his duty, no matter the cost to himself. That old hypocrite. He was relishing his moment in the sun.

"Mistress Stevenson. A good morning to you."

"And to you, Captain," Margaret murmured,

bobbing McKinnon a curtsey. She would not meet his eyes, but looked demurely at the planking.

"Come, come, now, my dear. There's nae need to be afraid. You're among friends here, lassie," Captain McKinnon said in a kindly, encouraging fashion. "Who was it? Speak out, loud and clear. Tell us who it was and what ye saw, and we shall deal with him as he deserves."

Margaret Stevenson's head had been bowed. But now her chin came up as she stood on tiptoe to see over the Scots' heads. Her eyes flashed with spite.

"Who do you think it is?" Rose whispered to Andy at her side.

Before he could answer her, Maggie tossed her thick, glossy black hair over her shoulders and looked boldly out over the gathering.

The tension built unbearably for a few moments as she appeared to be searching the upturned faces, looking for one face in particular.

Malice and triumph glittered in her bright blue eyes as she pointed an accusing finger over the heads of both Scots and crew, to where Rose and Andy stood apart from the rest.

On reflex, Rose turned around, to see whom Maggie could be pointing at behind her.

There was no one there.

"It was her—the Sassenach whore," Maggie's voice rang out. "I saw her climbing out of the ship's stores wi' a handful o' neeps and biscuits! She's your thief!"

Chapter Ten

" 'Tis a lie!" Rose protested as the crowd stirred, buzzing like an upturned hive. "I did nothing!"

She felt the color drain from her face in shock as the angry Scots turned as one to look at her. "I've not gone near the ship's stores. Not since the rationing began."

"I believe you, madam. Truly, I do," McKinnon said. He seemed deeply troubled, at a loss to contain the situation. "However, two independent witnesses have come forward to accuse you. One is a member of my crew, and the other is Mistress Stevenson here. They both tell quite another tale, madam."

"Wh-what they tell is lies, Captain," Rose stammered. "It wasn't me, I swear it. You must believe me. If they say so, then they are mistaken."

"Forgive me, my lady, but I may show no partiality in this matter. You have been accused. And there are witnesses."

"Will! Alistair!" barked Sinclair's voice.

"Milady . . . ?"

Rose looked up to find two crew members in jerseys and canvas breeches standing before her.

"What is it?"

Alistair looked sheepish. "Mr. Sinclair's orders, mum."

"I don't understand . . . ?" It was only when they reached for her arms that she realized why they were there, what it was they wanted. Her.

She had been accused by two independent witnesses: Sinclair and the Stevenson wench, who had both openly expressed their dislike of her. And in one fell swoop, their lies had condemned her. She had been accused, tried and found guilty, on their say-so alone! And now they would carry out the sentence McKinnon had prescribed. What had it been? A frisson of pure terror sliced through her like a knife to the belly. *Twenty stripes with the cat.*

Dear God, they meant to flog her!

"Andy!" From the corner of her eye she saw him dive for the gangway, bolting below like a frightened rabbit, diving nose first into its burrow. Her friend, her only friend, and he had abandoned her.

Her knees buckled. But before she could run or fight—do anything—the sailors grabbed her by the wrists. The Scots parted like the Red Sea to let them through as they jostled her across the deck.

"Andy, heeelp! Let go of me, you bastards! Let me go!"

Despite her furious struggles, they managed to wrestle her to the masthead, where the mate, Mr. Sinclair, waited with a length of coarse line. A gloating smile played about his fleshy lips. Anticipation glittered in his black eyes as he quickly lashed her wrists together and then bound them to the mast, high above her head.

"Not sae hoity toity now, are ye, milady?" he whispered thickly in her ear before he stepped away.

It had all happened so quickly, she was in shock. One moment she'd been standing off to one side, only half listening to the captain; the next she was here, bound to the mast, the coarse rope chafing her slender wrists. The way Sinclair tied her left her dangling. She was forced to stand on tiptoe, breasts thrust up and forward, arms and back painfully stretched, muscles screaming, feet barely touching the ground. It was painful now. How much worse would it be when they began?

She pressed her cheek to the rough wooden mast, frantically searching the gathering for a kind face, a sympathetic expression—for Andy's pug-nosed, freckled face. Her lower lip trembled. She was perilously close to tears, despite her promise to herself, for she found only closed, hostile faces. Faces that were eager with anticipation. Or faces grown stony with bitterness and hatred for what she was, instead of who she was.

Directly ahead of her, the crew had been assembled to witness the thief's punishment. This was McKinnon's unsubtle reminder that aboard ship, his word was law, and that discipline would be strictly enforced. There was no sign of Andy anywhere. She swallowed. Had he truly abandoned her now, when she needed him most?

"Arabella McLeod, you have been found guilty of the theft of victuals from the ship's stores," Captain McKinnon's voice rang out. "The punishment for that theft is flogging. Twenty lashes, to be laid on by the mate, Mr. Sinclair. Is there any reason this sentence should not be carried out?"

"Aye, Captain. I am innocent," she protested hotly, eyes blazing.

"Say again, madam?"

"I said, sir, that I am innocent!" she cried in a louder voice. A low moan escaped her as Sinclair strutted past. As he drew level, he slapped the knotted leather tails of the cat across his palm, smiling in spiteful anticipation when the sounds made her flinch.

"Soon, bitch. Soon," he rasped, running his tongue over his fleshy lower lip.

"I am deeply sorry, milady, but there are witnesses who swear otherwise," McKinnon continued. "Mistress Stevenson and Mr. Sinclair have nothing to gain by lying. There is no chance, perhaps, however slight, that you are with child?"

The captain's tone was hopeful. It drew angry looks from his fellow Scots. A woman who was with child could legitimately "plead her belly" and request a postponement of her punishment. McKinnon was trying to let the Sassenach off!

"How can she be breedin'? She doesna share her husband's bed!" Angus roared.

"Milady? Please. Answer the question," McKinnon urged, ignoring the man's outburst. "Are you with child?"

"No, Captain." She spoke so softly, only those nearby could hear her. "I am not with child. But I swear to you, before God, that I am innocent of these charges, sir. Does my word count for naught?"

"I am deeply sorry, milady. The witnesses say otherwise. There is nothing more I can do for you." From his position on the quarterdeck, McKinnon's shoulders slumped a little, as if in defeat.

In a louder voice, he announced, "If no one will speak out in this woman's defense, Mr. Sinclair will administer the punishment forthwith. Twenty stripes, Mr. Sinclair. You—uh—you may begin when ready." His voice was thick with emotion.

"Very good, sir."

Sinclair approached the mainmast, strutting jauntily like a bantam cock. A faint, unpleasant smirk curled his lips as he clamped his meaty paw over the neck of her gown. With one violent wrenching movement, he jerked down the garment and the shift beneath it. His actions bared her shoulders and half her back.

She felt the wind feathering gossamer strands of golden-brown hair across her bare skin in a gentle caress, and thought she might faint. *Wanted* to.

The mate raised the whip aloft.

Chapter Eleven

"Enough, Sinclair. Lay a finger on my woman and I'll make ye eat that bluidy whip, inch by inch, so help me God."

McLeod's tone purred with menace as he strode slowly across the deck.

The wind plastered the full-sleeved shirt to his powerful shoulders and rippled the threadbare cloth about a torso lean as a blade. Wild, black hair streamed back from the chiseled profile, revealing smoky eyes that smoldered like brimstone. His was a ruthless mouth, made hard with anger.

"Ye're no' the captain of this vessel, McLeod," Sinclair snarled, brandishing the cat. "I follow McKinnon's orders. Not yours. The captain's ordered the sentence carried out—and it will be."

"No, Sinclair. It will not."

McLeod took a stride forward. Straightway, Sinclair lunged at him, wildly swinging at him with the cat. The nine knotted leather tails flailed across his cheek, leaving reddened welts in their wake. McLeod grabbed for the flying tails, wound them about his fist, and jerked the whip toward him so suddenly, Sinclair had no chance to let go.

He lurched forward, slammed jaw first into McLeod's right fist. The punch rocked him backward, onto the deck. He scrambled to his feet. Strings of blood and saliva unraveled from his badly split lip.

"That's it. You're in for it now. I'll gut ye from stem t'stern now, ye bluidy bastard! See if I don't!" Sinclair roared, reaching for the dirk in his belt.

"Come on, then, mon. I'm no' bound, and I'm no' a helpless woman," McLeod reminded him softly. He brought up his fists. "If ye have the stones t' fight me, ye'd best kill me, for I'll finish ye when I'm done."

Sinclair swallowed. His hand froze on the hilt of his dirk. His dark eyes slid questioningly to the quarterdeck. "Captain?"

"One moment, Sinclair. My lord Drummond, you are undermining my authority on this vessel."

"And you, sir, are making a grave mistake."

"On the contrary, your wife was found guilty of stealing victuals from the ship's stores. There were witnesses—"

"So I have been told. Your mate, Sinclair, who made improper advances to my wife—and a young woman who, for reasons of her own, dislikes my bride. But I have witnesses who say otherwise."

McKinnon's face brightened. "You do?"

"Aye, Captain. With your permission, I would like to free my wife before I tell ye who they are."

"By all means. Please, do."

Drawing a dirk from his own belt, he slashed the ropes that held her, catching Rose in his arms before she could topple.

"Chin up, my brave wee lass. Dinna let them cow ye now," he murmured, supporting her against his chest.

Gratitude swelled inside her. In another moment, Sinclair would have cut her back to ribbons with the cat.

Trembling, she accepted his arm, yet carried her head high as he led her across the deck to where Andy waited at the head of the gangway leading below.

There, he covered her hand with his own and squeezed it. "Go below with Andy, lass. Ye'll be safe there."

"But, what about you? What if they—"

"Hold!" a voice rang out.

She froze. Instead of doing as he'd bidden, she

drew a shaky breath. Fingers digging into his arm, she held onto him as if he were a lifeline.

"When the Sassenach stole from the ship's stores, she stole from us all. This is Hamish McKinnon's vessel. McLeod has no say here," challenged an onlooker. "Will we let his wife go unpunished? Would ye let *my* wife off sae free and easy, Captain? Is there one law for the wife of a laird, and another for us common folk aboard this vessel?"

Ugly murmurs of assent followed the question.

The McLeod stilled. Slowly he turned to face her accuser. His eyes, Rose saw, had paled to a dangerous silver. "Hear me, McNab. All of you, hear me well, for I will say it but once. My wife is innocent. She stole nothing," he said in a voice of deadly calm. "And therefore, she is undeserving of punishment."

"With all due respect, sir, how can ye be sure of that?" Her challenger sneered insolently.

"I can be sure, Mr. McNab, because these thefts took place at night, when the lady was where she belonged. In my bed." He drew her against him and added, "With me." He looked out over the gathering, daring them to gainsay him.

"Was she now, sir?" McNab jeered. "And would that be every night, or just one or two?"

McLeod smiled, his eyes heavy-lidded, half-closed. He appeared deceptively calm. But Rose could feel the tension coiled within him. The anger straining to break free.

"Look at her, mon. Quickly, now, laddie, before Mistress McNab catches ye! She's bonnie, my bride, aye?"

"Verra bonnie indeed, sir," the man shot back so quickly he drew everyone's laughter but his spouse's.

"Then ye've answered your own question, mon. *Every night*."

A titter of laughter ran through the crowd. McNab was red-faced and embarrassed, his long-nosed, scrawny wife livid.

"I say again," McLeod continued when they fell silent, "my wife wasna running aboot, pilfering biscuits and neeps. Nor was she lifting her skirts for one o' the crew, as was the *real* thief."

" 'Tis your word against the mate's and Angus's daughter, McLeod," challenged someone. "And what mon would point the finger at his own wife?"

"That's where you're wrong, Innes. 'Tis not my word alone. Andy!"

"Here, Drum."

"Tell the captain what you saw."

"Him!" Innes jeered. "He's your bluidy cousin! He'll say whatever ye ask him to, McLeod!"

"Enough, Master Innes. Let Master Lewis speak for himself," Captain McKinnon commanded. "Go on, Master Lewis. Tell us what you saw."

"Very guid, sir. Well, James Gordon and my-self were on our way back from the bilges one evening," Andy began. "It was the next day that the first theft was discovered, aye? We—er—we had gone aloft to—er—to relieve ourselves, sir. We were coming back when we overheard a woman and a man down in the stores. The woman was"—he coughed—"she was giving herself to the man, in exchange for extra rations." His face was red.

"James Gordon? Step forward, lad. What have you to say?" McKinnon asked. "Is what Master Lewis has told us the truth?"

"Aye, Captain," James chirped up. "It's true all right. Just as Andrew said."

"I see. And who were these people you and Master Lewis are accusing. Can you name them?"

"I can, sir," Andy put in.

"So can I," Jamie agreed. "The man was the mate, Calum Sinclair, captain. And the woman with him was . . . Mistress Stevenson. Maggie Stevenson."

A muttering began and swelled as the Scots reacted to the names.

"That's a clarty lie, James Gordon!" shrieked Maggie Stevenson. "Calum! For God's sake, tell them it isna so."

"Aye, Sinclair. Tell us, laddie," McLeod purred. His piercing silvery gaze fell on Sinclair, who was cradling his bruised jaw, then shifted to Margaret Stevenson, who was trying to break free of her father's punishing grip on her wrist.

The mate scowled, refusing to meet Drummond's steely gaze. He tried to slip away, past his fellow crew members, who were openly hostile to him now. He had been an unpopular mate who had been free with his fists and cruel to them all. They were happy to see him brought low now.

"Not so fast, laddie," McKinnon barked. "You, Ranald, administer the punishment, sir. Mr. Culross, Mr. MacPherson, stand by to escort Mr. Sinclair down t' the brig when sentence has been carried out," the captain ordered. He turned back to Sinclair. "Ye've made your last voyage on any vessel of mine," he told him. "I only hope and pray the Lady Arabella can find it in her heart t' forgive us all."

Angus Stevenson stepped forward, holding Maggie by the scruff of her neck. "By your leave, Captain, I'd like your permission t' chastise my daughter mysel'."

"As ye will, mon," the captain agreed.

"If you have nothing further to say, Captain, I'd like to escort my wife down to our cabin," McLeod observed.

"Of course, my laird. Lady McLeod, may I extend my deepest apologies to you, madam?"

"Apology accepted. I do understand, truly, Captain," Rose assured him. It was no more than the truth. The captain had publicly committed himself to punishing any thief with twenty lashes. Two separate witnesses had claimed she was that thief. Had McKinnon backed down, he would have lost the respect of both his crew and the passengers.

She felt the captain's eyes on their backs as McLeod led her away. As he handed her down the gangway, she heard McKinnon bellow, "All of ye scurvy deck-rats, back to work, now! Look lively, you swabs, if ye know what's good for ye!"

Once they were safely inside the cabin, Rose's shoulders slumped. After a few moments, some of the strain left her face and a little of her color returned.

"That was a close call, milord," she murmured with feeling. "I don't think I've ever been so happy to see someone as I was to see you." She hugged herself about the arms. Her lower lip trembled as she came to stand before him. She blinked back the tears that tipped her lashes. "Truly, I cannot thank you enough for your timely intervention."

She went up on tiptoe, intending to kiss his cheek in gratitude, as she'd so often kissed Andy or her brother. But the McLeod was not Andy, nor Jim.

When she cradled his handsome face between her hands, she could feel the roughness of his beard on her palms, the rugged shape of his jaw. Her heart beat a little faster as she closed her eyes, drew a deep breath and touched her lips to his.

A shiver ran through him as their mouths met. She felt it through the pads of her fingers, clear down to her toes—and in certain other places she never dreamed a kiss *could* be felt. A low, throaty moan escaped her.

"Tsk, tsk, Rosamund," McLeod chided, his voice a husky rasp that was almost a purr. His gray eyes were slumberous, heavy-lidded. "That wasna a proper kiss," he said. " 'Twas but a wee hen's peck."

Her face turned pink with embarrassment. She stared at his mouth. Oh, God, his mouth . . .

"What do you mean, it wasn't a proper kiss?" she blurted out.

He shrugged. "What I said. Perhaps that wee, feeble peck would pass for a kiss in England, but in Scotland? Never! There, kisses are a wee bit—"

"What? A wee bit what?" she demanded, straining eagerly toward him. She was filled with a sweet, desperate hunger. A longing she could not bear another moment.

Gray eyes dancing, he drew her toward him. "Come here, and I'll show ye."

Chapter Twelve

For a moment he simply held her, cradled her to a chest as hard and unyielding as the bulkhead at his back. And then, cupping her face, he captured her mouth beneath his and kissed her with the same tender fury he had used the first time. Kisses that were explosions of sensation and pleasure, that left her trembling and breathless.

With the first touch of his lips, she made another soft sound, deeper, throatier than the first, and melted against him. Whether it was a moan or a sigh, a sound of pleasure or surprise, he could not have said.

Teasing her lips apart with his tongue, he took her mouth, holding her closer, letting her feel his hardness, his need. He showed her with his kisses, with the skillful play of his tongue and lips, how very much he wanted to be a part of her. How he ached to take her body as he was taking her mouth, to fill her with himself.

As he deepened the kiss, he gently curled his hand over her breast. The small, soft mound swelled to fill his palm. Lust sizzled through him, primitive and raw, as the small nipple hardened in response to his touch.

God, how he wanted her.

Ever since the storm three weeks ago, he'd wanted her so fiercely, desire had become a roaring, physical ache in his gut. He wanted to strip off her clothes. To free her golden-brown hair from that plait and comb her long fairy curls with his fingers. To lay her down and taste her . . . touch her . . . everywhere. And then, when he'd learned the taste and scent of her, he would explore her softness. Rekindle—through the sweet surrender of her body—all that had been taken from him.

The ability to feel. To give. To trust. To care.

To love . . .

With a shiver, she opened her mouth, gasping as his tongue surged inside it, to war with hers.

The nipple under his thumb hardened, making the ache in his groin unbearable. He rubbed the nubbin again, and a shivery moan escaped her lips, caressing his cheek like a warm, sweet breeze.

"I want more than kisses from ye, Rosamund,"

he whispered thickly in her hair when their kiss was ended. "I will have all of ye, lassie, or nothing at all. If ye dinna want the same from me, then ye must say so now, before 'tis too late. Shall I stop?"

In answer, she took his hand and placed it over her breast. She was trembling when she looked up at him, yet her answer was there, too, shining in her eyes like stars. His shaft bucked.

She wanted him, too.

"I willna hurt ye, my wee wren," he promised liltingly, pulling his shirt over his head. "Ye shall have your pleasure, too, my lassie. More pleasure than ye've dreamed of."

Cupping her chin, he tilted her face and kissed her tenderly, pressing her back against the bulkhead as he did so.

As they kissed, his hand dipped beneath her hems and traveled up her silky legs, thrusting up skirts and petticoats to caress her dainty ankles, calves and knees.

Kneeling at her feet, he untied her garter ribbons with his teeth, then rolled down her stockings, one by one, before venturing higher, to caress her thighs.

Moments later, he wetted his finger in his mouth and eased it between the velvety petals of her sex, hidden by a nest of curls.

His groin tightened. She was wet and ready for him. *Och, so blessed ready*.

With a shudder, he eased his finger deeper, until it was lodged fully inside her. He groaned with pleasure against her sweet mouth as the tender flesh sheathed his finger. She was so tight. Surely she was innocent?

Taking her hand, he placed it on his shaft.

Her caress was light as butterfly wings. Hesitant. Exquisite. The blood thundered through his veins, scattering conscious thought. Sweat began a trickling, sensual journey down his face.

"Careful, dearling. Easy, now. He wants ye verra badly," he warned thickly.

He took his time to undress her.

Lingering on each hook and lace, he slowly drew aside ribbons and ruffles to bare each new delight. The grace of her ivory throat. The tiny dip of her navel. The lush curve of a rounded, womanly hip.

Kissing and gently nibbling the rosy flesh he bared, he savored the taste, the intoxicating scent and changing textures of her body. Inhaled the faint yet tantalizing fragrance that was hers. How many nights had her scent haunted his dreams?

"My sweet Rosamund," he whispered as she stepped from her petticoat. Her beautiful body was cloaked in golden-brown ringlets that spiraled over creamy flesh to her waist. "Do ye ken how lovely ye are, ma *sonsie bean*?"

Plunging his fingers deep into her hair, he tipped her head back, wanting to kiss her again. His mouth was hungry, his kiss wild and deep.

He tasted her again and again, until she moaned against his lips.

The sounds she uttered made his belly contract and his stones ache.

Twisting restlessly in his arms, she pressed against him. "Please, McLeod. Oh, please—!" she whispered urgently.

"Aye, lassie, aye," he breathed. "Let me take off my breeks."

Violet eyes widening, she watched as he slowly shoved his breeches down over his lean flanks, over the pelt of springy black curls. His manhood sprang free of confinement with a will of its own as he kicked off his clothes.

Noticing her startled expression, he grinned. "Dinna fash yerself, lassie. He's not half sae big as he looks. Besides, it's no' as if ye hadna seen him before, aye?"

His gray eyes danced as she blushed a luscious pink. The color of guilt.

He lifted her against his hardness, grinding his knee against her mound in his need.

"Say it, lassie," he rasped hoarsely. "Say ye want it. Tell me ye want *me*."

"I want . . . oh! Yes. *You*. Oh, *please!*"

Her skin was flushed and rosy. Everywhere he touched her, tasted her, she was hot silk and warmed honey. His hungry mouth drew another wild, impassioned cry from her as, cupping her breasts, he kneaded them, tugging each carnation-pink bud between his teeth in turn, until they stood up, red as rubies.

Her plump breasts rubbed against his chest, and the heated slip and slide of her bare body against his was more than he could bear.

He swept her up and placed her on the edge of the bed, then knelt between her thighs, putting his mouth to her soft cleft. His tongue danced over the hidden jewel between her legs, and a sizzling fire took hold.

With a hoarse cry, she knotted her fingers in his hair, crying out as the blaze consumed her with overwhelming sensation. Tears streamed down her cheeks as she pulled him up and over her.

He stepped between her legs, lifted them high and thrust forward. With a groan, he drove deep, deep into her sweet flesh, taking her maidenhead in one clean thrust and sheathing himself to the hilt.

She twined her legs about his waist to hold him inside her. The fierce embrace of her thighs proved almost too much. His face an intense, dark mask, he slowed the tempo of his thrusts, riding her slowly, deeply, postponing his own release.

He meant to be inside her when the dam broke a second time. To watch her face, her lovely, expressive eyes as her body contracted along his length, rippling, shimmying like tiny, seductive fingers. Only then would he seek the savage pleasure of his own release. Only then would he spill himself inside her.

And when he did, when he was lost in the pleasures of her sweet, female flesh, he prayed he would forget—for that moment in time—the sorrow and guilt that had become his constant companions. . . .

The delicious, stretching sensations, the surging fullness went on and on. Drummond withdrew and thrust, and each powerful stroke deepened his possession, increased the erotic sensations exploding through her.

Insatiable, she arched upward to meet his thrusts, unable to get enough of him.

"Dinna move, lassie. Dinna move," he commanded thickly. "Och, lassie, ye're sae tight." A lock of black hair flopped over his forehead as, braced on his palms, he planted a tender kiss full on her swollen mouth, then nipped each ruby nipple with his teeth. "Tighter than a miser's purse, by God."

"Forgive me," she whispered, wondering why he sounded so pleased if she was too tight.

"Forgive ye?" He almost shouted the question, his expression incredulous. He kissed her again, quick and hard this time. "Ye teasing wee vixen. Ye sheath my cock like a glove, then beg my pardon for the pleasure ye give me?"

For the first time since they'd met, laughter danced in his gray eyes. A deep, rich chuckle welled from his throat. His sensual mouth curved in a genuine smile that utterly transformed his rugged, stern face. It gave her a glimpse of the man he'd been before sorrow embittered him.

His smile was like the sun coming out. Shining down on a small forgotten plant that had lived too long in the shade, and grown half-starved for warmth and light.

The forgotten flower of her heart.

When Mcleod smiled, her heart bloomed inside her. A shining new emotion emerged, like a beautiful new butterfly emerging from its chrysalis and spreading its tissue wings. Or a pink rosebud, tightly furled, opening its petals one by one to the light and warmth of the sun.

The emotion was fragile, vulnerable, *real*. One she had never expected to find here, with him. Her captor. Her would-be assassin. *Her husband.*

She was so stunned, she could not bring herself to give the emotion a name, not even in her secret heart.

She ran her hands down over his hard, lean body. He was so beautiful, so hard, so strong. So different from her own warm, downy softness, she thought.

She stroked his broad back, all muscle and sinew, then the wide chest, bisected by a shadow of dark hair that led down, past his flat belly, to the ridge of hard, jutting flesh that gave her so much pleasure.

Fingers biting into his shoulders, she clung to

him, caught up in a delight too exquisite for words.

A throaty moan escaped her as a second, almost unbearable explosion ricocheted through her; her lips were pressed to the silky, salty maleness of his skin.

As her body pulsed around his shaft, he grew very still, poised above her with his dark head thrown back, his smoky eyes closed. And then he gripped her hips, shouting her name as he drove into her one last glorious time. He shuddered and fell forward across her.

She lay there unmoving, scarcely breathing, waiting for the tides to recede. For the rippling pulses inside her to wane. In the stillness, she felt his seed spurt into her and wondered, with a feeling of wonder and joy, if he had started a babe in her belly.

When he made to roll off her, insisting that he was too heavy, she held him fast. She didn't want to let him go. Not now. Not ever. She wanted to lie there, joined to him, and savor the way she was feeling forever.

Their legs entwined, their fingers linked, the McLeod fell asleep while she lay wakeful, marveling that this man—her kidnapper, her unwanted husband, her dark and bitter enemy lord—should be the one her heart had chosen . . .

. . . to love.

Chapter Thirteen

"I believe you are hard on the road to a complete recovery, my lord," Rose observed soon after the night they became lovers.

"If I am hard, lassie, 'tis you I have to thank," McLeod insisted, his eyes twinkling. "And for my recovery, too."

"Don't thank me. I did only what any woman would have done—if she valued her life," Rose retorted with a saucy grin of her own. She pretended she had not noticed his ribald jest. "I knew even *you* could not kill the woman who'd nursed you back to health, wretch that you are."

"Nursing? Who's talking about your nursing, lassie?" McLeod asked with a wolfish grin. "I was talking about your. . . . wee arse," he declared, grabbing her. "Will ye feel this bonnie backside! It could hae brought Lazarus back from the dead—and with a smile on his face, by God!"

With a growl, he nipped at her ears, her neck, until she shrieked and begged him to stop, laughing until the tears rolled down her cheeks.

Like most of their conversations, she mused much later, that one had ended with the two of them falling onto the bed, tossing their garments to the planks and making love. Again.

Although she was reluctant to admit it, Rose secretly credited much of Drummond's rapid recovery to their very passionate, very frequent lovemaking. She could not explain why the two were connected, but she knew in her heart that they were, nonetheless.

Now that Drummond's health was improving by leaps and bounds, his appetite increased accordingly. He was always hungry, but could not fully satisfy his hunger on account of the continued rationing. When his attention was drawn elsewhere, she sometimes slipped some of her own meager rations onto his platter.

To be honest, sharing was no real hardship for her, since her own appetite—never very robust— had become even poorer since the storm.

The mere sight of a moldy ship's biscuit, the thin broth of greasy salted pork or a mildewed turnip made her feel queasy. Rather than spiking her appetite, a single whiff would send her running to the bilges to empty her stomach.

As the days passed, the McLeod's fevers had tapered off, much to her relief. To all appearances, his sleep was now deep and healing, for the most part. And, although she suspected he was still plagued by occasional nightmares about Culloden, haunted by the guilt he felt for his kinsmen's deaths, he never shared his torment with her.

In an effort to rebuild the strength he had lost during his sickness, he had taken to diving over the side to swim in the warm waters of the sparkling, deep-blue ocean whenever the *Salutation* lay at anchor. While he swam, she hung over the rail to watch him, keeping a sharp eye out for the dark fin of a shark cutting through the turquoise glass.

At other times, he worked alongside McKinnon's crew, shinning up rope ladders, hanging in the shrouds like a spider in a web, or climbing the ratlines to the crow's nest with the agility of a monkey. He swabbed the decks and manned the capstan, too, his deep tenor swelling the crew's sometimes bawdy, always rollicking sea chanties.

As the vast ocean fell away behind them, the muscles that had grown weak and lax during his sickness grew strong and flexible again. The sun that beat down on the merchantman's scrubbed decks bronzed his corded limbs and sinewy torso a rich, dark gold. The deepened color of his skin was now in striking contrast to the midnight hue of his hair and the sensual smoky gray of his eyes.

She watched him from beneath her lashes whenever he was above decks, unable to take her eyes off her vital, virile, handsome lover. Lover? Aye, she always thought of him as such, for she could not think of him as her husband, herself as his wife.

For him, their marriage had simply been a means to an end. His means, her end—or so he'd thought. Their shipboard wedding had been just another distasteful yet necessary step to accomplish her abduction.

The original reason for their marriage no longer existed. And, although they made love frequently, McLeod had never said that he loved her, nor that he was *in* love with her. If he had, perhaps she would have felt like a wife rather than a mistress.

Much to her annoyance, she discovered she was not the only woman on board who enjoyed watching her husband. Along with half of the married matrons, who sighed after him when their husbands were not looking, Maggie Stevenson, that little sneak-thief, watched him, too. She shot Rose a smirk of triumph whenever softhearted McLeod tossed her a kind word. Maggie latched onto his smallest comment like a hungry dog tossed a bone, and milked what sympathy she could from her fading bruises.

"The Stevenson wench is enamored of you,"

Rose observed one day as they promenaded the decks, an exercise that had become a thrice-daily ritual.

"Enamored? Dinna be so daft, love! I did but toss her a kind word or two. You saw the black eyes and the bruises her Da' gave her. The wench could hardly move for a fortnight. I'm thinking Mistress Maggie has paid for her theft and whatever dalliance she had with Sinclair. The lassie seems starved for a gentle word, aye?"

"Then let her find it elsewhere, sir," Rose said with a sniff. "If Andy had not come to get you, I would have been flogged for her thievery. Forgive me if I feel less than charitable toward her."

She was about to flounce away from him when, gray eyes dancing, he caught her about the waist.

"Jealous, my wee Rosamund?" he asked, his voice a velvety purr that left a catch in her throat.

"Dinna be sae daft, mon," she came back, parroting his Highland burr as she pushed him away.

The passengers seemed equally inclined to let Maggie Stevenson's theft go unpunished, except for the beating her father had given her. Rose pursed her lips. They had been far less indulgent when they believed she was the guilty party. Then again, perhaps they had all suffered so dearly at the hands of the English, they wanted no further violence.

Some of the Scots actually gave her a curt nod

or a mumbled word of greeting whenever they met on deck, but to most of them she remained the hated Sassenach wench, the English pariah. Perhaps she always would.

When they reached New France, she planned to spend as little time as possible at the Scottish settlement of Fort Charles. The farther she could put herself from the hostile Highlanders, the better, as far as she was concerned. While they thought of nothing beyond beginning their lives anew far from the hated English, her own dreams were all of the wilderness. Of the land she would someday own in New France, if she could sell the emeralds in Quebec. God willing, Andy's scathing comment that seed and hogs would be of more value in the New World than the Eyes of the Tiger would prove incorrect.

As the end of the voyage grew closer, her curiosity about New France increased.

If she timed their daily promenades to coincide with those times when the captain came above decks to smoke his pipe, she discovered she had a captive source to quiz for information. McKinnon's vivid descriptions augmented what little she was able to pry from McLeod each night in those lazy, golden moments after they made love.

They were bound, she discovered, for Fort Charles, which was a Scottish settlement some twenty miles from the St. Lawrence, a river that McKinnon claimed was wide enough to accommodate ocean-going vessels for several miles of its length.

" 'Tis a wild country, madam. But one sae blessed beautiful it takes your breath away," he declared with a dreamy look in his eyes. "Green valleys and plains dotted with wildflowers and countless butterflies. Vast forests. Roaring waterfalls. Aye, and every acre teeming with wildlife and vegetation! I once saw a dozen black bears fishing from an icy river."

"Fishing! How so?"

"They scooped up the salmon with their paws while their cubs waited on shore to eat."

Her eyes shone at his vivid descriptions.

"And the settlers. What are they like?" she asked eagerly. "Shall I be accepted by them?"

"The citizens of Quebec are French, madam. They have little liking for Englishmen. However, they are verra fond of beautiful women such as yourself, whatever their origins."

"Thank you, Captain. You are indeed a gallant man."

"You are most welcome, my dear. Now. Where was I? Ah, yes. The people of Fort Charles are much like these good souls." He gestured vaguely at the passengers. "Fugitives from Scotland, who blame the English for all their woes. Or immigrants, weary of trying to eke out a living on Scottish soil. In time, they will come to accept you, my lady, never fear, just as they've accepted my Maddy."

"As Drummond McLeod's wife or for myself?"

He would not meet her eyes. "That I canna say, madam."

"You don't have to, sir. How many people live at Fort Charles?"

"There were over four hundred souls when I set sail for Scotland last, my dear."

"All within the settlement's walls?"

"Nay, not all, though many do live within the settlement. Others farm their own cleared lands some distance from it."

"But surely it is dangerous, with bears and such creatures roaming freely about?"

"It is, aye. But then, every new frontier has its hazards," McKinnon admitted. "New France is no different. Attacks by renegade Indians account for a few deaths every year, unfortunately. Bears and mountain lions and the winter take their own tolls. But for the most part, the natives are peaceful people, content to trade their pelts with goods from French or Scottish traders."

"How difficult is it for a man to make his mark in the fur trade, Captain?" McLeod cut in.

Rose looked up, surprised to see that her husband was still standing there, listening. In her eagerness to quiz the captain, she had quite forgotten him.

"Not difficult at all, sir. A young, strong fellow such as yourself could amass a considerable fortune in just a few good seasons." He cast a pointed look in McLeod's direction, adding, "Especially if he had a stable backer t' finance his ventures."

"Ah. And would ye know of such a stable man of means, sir?" McLeod asked, a small smile playing about his lips.

The captain pursed his own. "Indeed I would. In fact, I might be persuaded t' back ye myself, my laird."

McLeod grinned. "Would you, now? 'McLeod and McKinnon, Fur Traders,' mayhap?"

"Make it 'McKinnon and McLeod, Fur Traders' and the answer is aye, milord." The captain winked. His bright blue eyes were very merry.

To Rose's dismay, McLeod's casual question led to a lengthy discussion between the pair over a "wee dram o' whisky." A discussion from which she, little by little, was politely yet firmly excluded, despite her most determined efforts.

By the time McKinnon had finished expounding on what was obviously a subject dear to his heart, the morning had flown and Rose was disgruntled to discover that the prospect of becoming a fur trapper and trader had taken firm root in McLeod's ambitions.

By sunset of that same day, her husband and McKinnon had shaken hands and given each other their word, as men of honor, to be partners in the venture.

As soon as they reached their destination, McLeod would embark on his first foray into the wilderness as a fur-trapper and trader, delaying only long enough to equip himself and acquire several pack animals.

The captain was apparently a man of some substance in New France. He had offered his financial backing for Drummond's first trapping expedition, and would furnish Drummond with everything he needed by way of pack mules, beaver traps, something called snowshoes, weapons, trade goods and provisions. In return, McKinnon would receive a share of the profit from the sale of the furs when her husband returned in the spring.

They would remain partners until such time as McLeod was able to fully support himself and her, so Drummond said. He would be gone until the spring, he added, his gray eyes dancing with anticipation.

"Oh? And what am I to do all winter while you are gone?" she demanded irritably that night, after he'd excitedly explained his plans to her.

He would not look her in the eye, but seemed uncomfortable and averted his gaze. "I have arranged comfortable lodgings for you, never fear. Ye are t' stay with Mistress Maddy McKinnon. When Hamish puts out to sea and I am gone, the two o' ye shall prove company for each other, I fancy," he added, as if this were her heart's desire.

"You fancy, sir? But what of me? Am I to have no say in this?" she exploded, springing off the box bed. "Have you once again taken my life into

171

your hands, without so much as a by-your-leave?"

He scowled at the stress she placed on the word *again*. His jaw hardened. "Aye, I have. And shall continue to do so, for as long as you are my wife."

"That I am your wife, sir, was all *your* doing," she reminded him waspishly. "Or had you forgotten? I wanted no part of it—or you."

His scowl became a look of deep displeasure that darkened his eyes to pewter. "If our marriage so displeases ye, madam, perhaps we should live apart when the trapping season is over."

Her lips tightened. "As you will. But must I stay with this woman who will loathe me because I am English?"

"Aye. You must. And she will not hate ye. Madeline McKinnon is English, too. Did Hamish not tell ye? There is an excellent chance ye will find yerselves with much in common." There was a hopeful note to his voice now, as if he thought this tidbit might win her over.

"I don't care if this McKinnon woman is sister to the bloody king, sir," she snapped. "I would prefer to find my own lodging."

Turning on her heel, her hair and skirts flying, she stalked toward the cabin door.

He got there before her and blocked her way, immovable as a wall.

"You will have your land, Rosamund. And

your independence, too, if that is what you wish. But not now," he told her softly.

"No? Then when?"

"That I canna say." A bleak look came into his eyes. He sighed. "Too much has happened, lassie. I need . . . space and time in which to come t' terms with mysel', aye? The courage to accept what I canna change. God willing, I shall find what I need in the wilderness. And when I come back to ye, we will start again."

"You don't have to go. You could find what you are looking for with me. I—I would help you," she offered, her voice husky, broken with tears. "I know what it is to grieve, Drummond. To lose those you love. To be cast out of your home. I have lost so much—more than you know. We could heal together. I know we could. Please, Drum. Don't leave me behind. I—I—love you."

"I know." He cradled her face between his hands. His gray eyes tormented, like the sea under a lowering sky, he looked down at her. "I have to go, lassie. Dinna make it any harder than it is. I canna do what you ask."

Her lip quivered. "Cannot stay? Or cannot love me?"

He sighed. "I dinna ken. Since Culloden, I've been half mad with grief and sickness. Try to understand, lass. The wound in my foot was not my only wound—nor yet my worst one. Something inside me died with the clan that morn on the battlefield. I dinna ken if I can ever get it back, not even—not even with you."

She pulled away from him, flinging off his hands. She had laid her pride, her heart before him. His words, however honest, however sincerely felt, had cut her to the quick.

"Then Devil take you, McLeod."

White about the mouth, he turned and left the cabin. When he returned later that day, he found the door locked against him.

It was still locked six weeks later when they entered the Gulf of St. Lawrence, and from there sailed upriver to the wharves of Quebec, New France. Not a word had she spoken to him in all that time.

It was August 15, 1746. A different world and a new life awaited them both.

Chapter Fourteen

United by eagerness to see their new homeland, Rose and the other passengers hung over the rail as the *Salutation* slipped up the St. Lawrence River from the gulf, passing windmills and farmhouses of gray stone clustered along its fertile banks.

Scythers were cutting the golden grain in some of the fields, loading their harvest stalks onto sturdy ox-drawn carts. They waved in greeting as the ship sailed by. The farmers gathered in the harvest under the benevolent eyes of the Blessed Virgin, who gave good Catholics her benediction from the little shrines the passengers could see from the vessel's decks.

"Praise be! 'Tis the promised land—and a good

Catholic land, at that," Mistress McNab exclaimed, her face shining as she crossed herself.

Hamish McKinnon had told them the government would not allow Protestants to settle in New France. But whether it was the number of shrines that filled the woman with such joy, or the sight of such abundant crops, Rose did not know, although she silently agreed with her.

From here, at least, New France seemed everything the captain had promised. The sight of those flourishing farms, the snug stone houses, the fruit trees and forests, resurrected the optimism she'd often thought dead since that fateful moment when the *Salutation* slipped her moorings in the Pool and carried her away.

The town of Quebec—an Indian word that McKinnon said meant "the place where the waters narrow"—was a walled town. It rose from the dark cape like a medieval fortress.

"Up ahead there lies Cape Diamond." The captain gestured with his clay pipe. "And the fortress that rises from it is the Citadel. Twice, the bluidy English—your pardon, dear lady—have tried to capture the town. And twice they have failed." His bright blue eyes twinkled beneath shaggy gray brows. "The Citadel is the reason. Thanks be to God, we are here!"

As the crew secured the ship alongside the wharf and the eager passengers scurried to gather up their few belongings and disembark, McLeod drew Rose aside.

Join the Historical Romance Book Club
and GET 4 FREE* BOOKS NOW!

A $23.96 Value!

Yes! I want to subscribe to the Historical Romance Book Club.

Please send me my **4 FREE* BOOKS.** I have enclosed $2.00 for shipping/handling. Each month I'll receive the four newest Historical Romance selections to preview for 10 days. If I decide to keep them, I will pay the Special Members Only discounted price of just $4.24 each, a total of $16.96, plus $2.00 shipping/handling ($23.55 US in Canada). This is a **SAVINGS OF AT LEAST $5.00** off the bookstore price. There is no minimum number of books I must buy, and I may cancel the program at any time. In any case, the **4 FREE* BOOKS** are mine to keep.

*In Canada, add $5.00 shipping/handling per order for the first shipment. For all future shipments to Canada, the cost of membership is $23.55 US, which includes shipping and handling. (All payments must be made in US dollars.)

NAME: _____

ADDRESS: _____

CITY: _____ **STATE:** _____

COUNTRY: _____ **ZIP:** _____

TELEPHONE: _____

E-MAIL: _____

SIGNATURE: _____

If under 18, Parent or Guardian must sign. Terms, prices, and conditions subject to change. Subscription subject to acceptance. Dorchester Publishing reserves the right to reject any order or cancel any subscription.

"What do you want with me, sir?" she asked him coolly.

"I need t' talk to ye, lassie," he began, drawing her after him to the forward deck, where they could speak privately. "And to do something I should ha'e done long since."

"Oh? And what is that?"

"Ask your forgiveness."

"My forgiveness? But for what?"

"For bringing ye here," he said heavily. "For stealing ye away from all ye held dear. For using ye t' exact my revenge." He squared his jaw. "I know 'tis no excuse but . . . it is my belief that the fever and my grief nigh drove me insane. I still dream of it all. I canna seem t' put it behind me."

He cleared his throat and raised his dark head. His handsome face was tortured. Deep lines bracketed his mouth, and sun-furrows framed his eyes, which were as gray as mist over water. They were so very sad, a knot formed in her throat. Lord, how she'd missed him.

"Anyway, I know ye had no part in any o' that, and I—I want t' make amends. Hamish—Captain McKinnon—has offered ye a berth aboard the *Salutation* when he makes his return voyage to Scotland, if ye want it. Ye could be back in England with your brother by the New Year." He paused. "Or—"

"Or what?" she whispered, unable to believe her ears.

"Or . . . ye can have the land ye wanted."

Her eyes narrowed. "Oh? And how shall I do that?"

He squared his jaw. "How is my business, lassie. All ye have to do is tell me yea or nay."

She stared at him. The choice he was asking her to make was an impossible one. How could she choose between her brother, whom she dearly loved, and the promise of land of her own and a new life here? Besides, the choices he offered her did not include the one she truly wanted. *A future with him.*

She swallowed over the misery in her throat. He didn't want her. He had made that much crystal clear. Not once had he suggested that they stay together—an obvious alternative, considering they were married. But then, he'd never intended to stay married to her. Now that he had no use for her, he wanted to be rid of her and to satisfy his guilty conscience at the same time. The offer of land or a return passage to England was his way of doing so.

She swallowed. Tears scalded behind her eyes. She should be angry. She should hate him—but she just couldn't, no matter how hard she tried. Pride and obstinacy had made her lock her cabin door each night, but behind it she had ached, burned for him.

The same pride and obstinacy padlocked her tongue now.

"Must I give you my answer today?" she asked,

her voice husky with emotion. "I'd like a day or two to think about your offer."

"Of course. Hamish willna sail until he's filled his holds with cargo. Ye have a few weeks to decide, not just days. Now, if you're ready to go ashore, I'd be honored to escort ye into the town. McKinnon has sent a boy ahead to his usual lodgings at the Howling Wolf. I told him to take a room there for us. We willna be going on to Fort Charles until the morning."

"Thank you, sir," she murmured.

Quebec had progressed swiftly from the modest foundations laid by Monsieur Samuel de Champlain 143 years before.

The new immigrants, their sparse belongings carried in shabby bundles, entered Quebec by the St. Louis Gate. Its fanciful turrets, spires and crenellated archway gave the gate a fairy-tale quality.

The charming two-story, shuttered stone houses and shops of the town beyond would have been at home anywhere in Europe.

Small, hooded carriages known as *caleches* whisked ladies with lofty wigs and satin gowns through the bustling town at breakneck speed. Carriage horses competed with oxen or mules drawing laden wagons, dogs pulling small carts, and shaggy-haired, bearded men on horseback. And what men they were!

Many wore skin hats with long animal tails left

hanging down their backs. Their shirts were of fringed buckskin, sewn with beads, and their coats were made of animal furs. They wore them in spite of the sweltering heat, which moistened Rose's brow and upper lip and sent sweat trickling slowly down her spine. They must be the fur trappers McLeod had talked about. The kind of man he soon hoped to become, she thought, wrinkling up her nose.

Shops bellied onto the streets, their windows and stalls offering an assortment of wares that left her amazed. There were poulterers and butchers, hatters and cobblers, blacksmiths and gunsmiths, fishmongers and grocers, churches and cafes, hotels, taverns and chandlers' shops.

All around her, fat bakers and housewives haggled with grocers over the prices of flour or syrup. Convent schoolgirls giggled and gray-robed nuns scolded as a dark-robed Jesuit missionary tripped over the flapping hem of his gown and fell on his beaky nose. French soldiers flirted with serving girls going to the market for their mistresses—and Rose didn't comprehend a blessed word any of them said, for every last one of them spoke French.

She had yet to find her land legs after so many weeks at sea. But for the time being, she forgot her difficulty in walking and let the sights, the smells and sounds of Quebec swirl around her, thinking she'd never stood in the midst of so many people, and been so utterly alone. Before, she'd always had Jim. Here, she had no one.

"There's the inn." McLeod's comment broke into her thoughts. He gestured to a prosperous-looking inn across the street.

Its walls were brick. Red flowers spilled from half-barrels on either side of its door, while trim white shutters framed shining casements, both upstairs and down. A striped gray cat was sunning itself in a patch of sunshine in the stable-yard, and on the swinging wooden sign over the door was painted a gray wolf, howling at the moon.

Rose nodded, feeling suddenly so bone-weary she was close to swooning. Perhaps the inn-keeper would provide a tub of hot water and soap for her use, as well a good meal and a soft feather bed? More than anything, she longed to feel clean, truly clean, again.

"It looks very prosperous," she agreed. "What about Andy? Will he be joining us here?"

McLeod's gray eyes flashed angrily. Was it her tone or that she'd asked after his cousin's whereabouts? For some reason, this hint of jealousy pleased her.

"Not for a while, no. I sent him to purchase clothing and boots for us. Those on our backs, we stole before we threw our breachans down a well."

"I remember your telling me. Why did you not accompany him?"

He hesitated. "Because I wanted to spend the

day with you. In the event you decided to go back to England with McKinnon."

"Oh? And why would you want to do that?" she asked, her heart beating madly.

His expression was carefully blank, emotionless. "McKinnon has advanced me some funds against our future profits. After we pay our respects to the innkeeper, I thought we could find a market and buy ye some new clothes. God knows, ye need some! The clarty rag ye have on can almost stand up on its own. Ye need a new gown—and we'll get ye a new sark or two."

"Sark?"

"I mean a new shift. And a pair of stout brogues that dinna pinch your toes. What do ye say?"

She'd been wondering how she would ever replace her wretched green gown, torn and grubby as it was, for she'd yet to sell Arabella's jewelry. His offer solved that problem. "I would like that very much. Thank you."

It was late afternoon when they headed back toward their cool, whitewashed room above the Hungry Wolf.

Despite the carefully casual way McLeod behaved, and her own circumspect demeanor, hidden currents crackled between them as they toured the market stalls, her purchases carried in a bulging brown paper parcel tucked under McLeod's arm. He was so near—and yet so very far away.

The husky edge to his voice as he urged her to look at this cloth or that item of clothing made her heart race. The slightest brush of his hand against hers was like the touch of a hot spark to her flesh. The way his smoldering gray eyes lingered on her just a little too long filled her with confusion, warmth—yearning.

She closed her eyes just for a moment, aching to feel his strong arms around her. To cradle her cheek upon his broad chest and listen to the steady thud of his heart beneath it. To feel those large, callused hands moving over her body, touching her, exploring every part of her.

A shudder ran through her. Lord, how many nights had she lain awake in the cabin, aching for him to love her? To cradle the wonderful heaviness of his body on her own soft curves. To feel the searing heat as he entered her, possessed her. To know the very moment when the wildness filled his blood and the fire leaped from him to kindle her own desire.

She bit her lip. It was not to be. Never again. Ever since the angry words they'd exchanged aboard the *Salutation*, there was a stiffness between them. A solid wall of pride that neither would scale.

As they crossed the cobblestoned street to the inn, her eyes fell on a black-and-white dog, harnessed between the shafts of a yellow dog-cart piled high with rags.

The poor animal was waiting patiently outside

a haberdasher's, its tongue lolling in the heat, when it suddenly staggered and fell down.

Rose halted, her eyes filling. The poor little thing was dead, surely. But then a pair of golden-brown eyes rolled soulfully in her direction. A hollow flank heaved in utter exhaustion.

"The poor wee brute's been starved," McLeod growled.

At some time, the black-and-white border collie had been a handsome animal. But a cruel master, hard work and too little food had robbed it of its handsome looks. Now a bedraggled heap, it sagged between the shafts of the cart, its long fur matted, its brown eyes dull with misery.

"Poor little thing," Rose whispered, dropping to her knees beside it.

Her concern over the animal's sorry condition became anger when the owner of the dog-cart returned from some errand. Straightway, he began beating the dog over the head with a stick, trying to make it stand.

Trapped in its harness, which was buckled to the shafts, the dog was too weak to stand, let alone escape. It yelped and whimpered in pain—then snarled and flew at its master, biting his ankle in sheer desperation, before falling back down.

Its master roared and pulled a knife from his belt, intending to cut the dog's throat.

Rose could not bear it. Without regard for her

own safety, she flung herself between the Frenchman and the animal.

"Leave him alone, you great bully!"

"How much for the dog?" McLeod asked in French, hastily putting himself between the man and his furious wife. He tore the stick from the man's grasp and pointed at the animal, which had sunk back down to the cobbles. It seemed lifeless as Rosamund tried to unbuckle its harness. He held up a coin. "Here."

The man snatched the coin, testing its gold on his teeth. *"Un autre, monsieur,"* he demanded.

"The devil ye'll have another. Be off with you!" McLeod swore as he flung the stick away.

With a curse, the rag man pocketed the coin and hauled the dog-cart away himself.

"I must hae left my wits in Scotland," McLeod muttered, shaking his head as he picked up the limp animal. "Every penny I have t' my name is borrowed, and what do I do? I buy a dead dog."

But the glow in Rose's shining eyes, the admiration in their depths as she looked up at him, more than repaid him.

Madame Gaspar, the proprietor of the Hungry Wolf, was a trim middle-aged woman with a snowy mobcap. A lace shawl was crisscrossed over the bodice of her immaculate gray gown. Upon their arrival, she had not struck Rose as the sort of woman who would welcome a flea-bitten, dying dog into her spotless inn. She had not given Madame credit for her soft heart, however.

"What do you have there, madame? A baby?" she asked, her handsome face softening.

When she saw it was a dog, swaddled in a piece of old cloth like an infant, she chuckled so hard her ample bosom jiggled.

"Why, it is the rag man's dog, is it not? Ah, that poor little beast! He has not had a good life with Jerome. I fear he will not live till morning, madame. Monsieur," she addressed McLeod, "please, take him out to the stables. Tell *mon fils*—my son, Pierre—to feed and care for him tonight, yes? Tomorrow, if he is still alive, Madame shall take him with her to Fort Charles."

"I've ordered hot kettles brought up for your bath, Rosamund."

She looked up at him in surprise. "Why, thank you."

"I'd like t' use the water after you're finished. My new clothes should be here soon."

"Of course."

Shortly after, McLeod went down to the taproom to speak with Andy and the captain, who had just arrived.

While he was gone, the potboy and Monsieur Gaspar carried an enamel slipper-shaped tub into the room, which they set before the empty hearth. Three chambermaids followed, bearing kettles and pitchers of hot and cold water.

Knowing from experience that McLeod would spend considerable time talking with his new friend, Rose draped her new shift, brown bodice and butternut skirt over a chair. Stripping off her dirty clothes, she lowered herself into the steamy water, groaning with pleasure as it surrounded her.

It had been ages since she'd bathed in a real tub—not since before she and Jim had been ousted from their house in Sadler's Wells by Cumberland's thugs. She'd had to content herself with a basin of hot water and a skimpy sponging every day since then. But this—aahhh, this was *heaven*-ly!

Quickly she soaped herself using the sliver of rose-perfumed soap Madame Gaspar had provided, along with a sea-sponge and linen cloths for drying. She poured the last three jugs of cool water through her hair to rinse out the lather, then piled the wet strands on top of her head. With a contented sigh, she sank back to soak in the steamy water.

Lulled by its heat and by the gentle cooing of the fantailed doves under the eaves outside her window, she tipped her head back, closed her eyes and let her thoughts drift. . . .

She fell into a light sleep and, not surprisingly, dreamed of McLeod.

She lay naked with him on a feather bed strewn with rose petals, their bare limbs entwined. His long black hair was damp, and there was a light sheen of sweat on his body. She stretched voluptuously, knowing from the languid, contented way she felt that they had just made love, and that it had been wonderful.

His handsome face was oh, so tender as he leaned down to kiss her.

"I love ye, my wee Rosamund," he murmured, and she heard her name whispered over and over, like the rustle of the wind through tall grasses. *"Rosamund . . . Rosamund . . . Rosamund . . ."*

Her eyelids fluttered open.

While she dozed, the light had faded. Candles had been lit and placed about the chamber. They cast soft pools of golden light in the dusk.

McLeod stood by the open casement window. He had undressed, and wrapped a linen cloth about his waist. He was watching her from sleepy, hooded eyes that held a sensual expression she knew well. His fine head was framed by the background of amethyst sky, sprinkled with stars, that she could see through the open casement. The sun-warmed scents of sweet peas and honeysuckle wafted into the chamber on a gentle evening breeze.

Immediately repentant, she sat up, shedding water, modestly crossing her arms over her breasts. "Sir, forgive me. The water is barely warm anymore. You should have woken me sooner. 'Tis much too cool for your bath."

"I didna want to disturb ye. Ye looked so

peaceful, sleeping there in the candlelight. Like a wee kelpie, tucked in a snail shell."

"A kelpie?"

"A water sprite. Some folk say the kelpies are water horses with long flowing manes, but I dinna believe it," he murmured. "I say they're wee water fairies with bonnie golden-brown curls and eyes the soft violet of heather. Like yours."

As he spoke, he knelt beside the tub and scooped up the sea-sponge. He squeezed gently, letting water trickle down over her breasts and belly. His gaze followed its glistening passage from the tip of one velvety nipple, down to the tiny goblet of her navel. "Dear God, how I've missed ye, sweeting."

She drew a shaky breath, unable to take her eyes off his mouth as he wetted his lips. Soapy water hid her thatch of golden curls, yet warmth flooded through her, as if every part of her was open, laid bare to his lambent gaze.

"I've missed you, too, my love," she whispered, her voice no louder than a sigh.

She shivered. Goosebumps tingled down her arms, and her nipples stiffened. How swiftly her treacherous body had learned to enjoy the exquisite pleasure Drum gave it. Now his nearness, his voice alone, had the power to arouse her, to kindle a response deep inside her. To make her want him so badly she hurt.

"I should go before I do something we'll both regret—"

"Wait. Don't. I . . . please, don't."

"Rosamund—?" he murmured thickly. He leaned over her. There was a multitude of meanings in the way he said her name.

"Stay here. Stay with me tonight, sir," she urged softly.

"Ye're sure?"

"Yes."

"One more night, then. For auld times' sake. Aye?"

"For old times' sake, yes." She lay back and lifted her face for his kiss. Her hands framed his dark head, then gently pulled him down to her.

His hard, hungry mouth crushed down on hers. Searing, savage heat flashed through her like sheet lightning as he kissed her deeply, lingeringly, touching his tongue to hers until passion blazed up within her and burned as fiercely as his.

He did not stop, not even when she was quivering everywhere. And yearning. Oh, yes. There was the yearning, too.

"May I join ye, lassie?" he asked, his voice thick and sensual as warm velvet.

"Aye, my laird," she whispered.

Dropping the linen cloth about his waist, he stepped into the tub and settled himself behind her. At once, his arms slipped around her, cupping both breasts, drawing her back.

As she leaned against him, he drew each hard little nubbin between his fingers, and playfully nuzzled the side of her neck.

"Hmm. Ye smell as sweet as your namesake, my wee English Rose. Will ye wash my back?" he purred. His eyes were lit by a wicked sparkle as he handed her the sea-sponge.

"I'll do better than that, McLeod. I'll wash your everything," she promised, a husky catch to her voice. Her violet eyes sparkled with mischief—and no little desire.

Unable to help himself, he threw back his head and roared with laughter.

Turning nimbly about, Rosamund straddled his middle. Acutely aware of the hard ridge of flesh beneath her bottom, she took up the sliver of soap and the sponge and slowly lathered him.

Her hands swept down over the curved muscles of his shoulders and upper arms, feeling the carefully leashed power that lay beneath the skin. Her fingertips trailed across his chest. The soapy whorls of dark hair moved with the lapping motion of the water, like tiny sea anemones caught in a current. The motion fascinated her. So did the pebbled nipples that stood up, begging to be kissed, as did her own.

Rinsing the soap from his nipples, she licked her lips and then ducked her head to suck or nip delicately at each one. A delighted giggle escaped her when Drum had to grit his teeth, the pleasure was so intense.

"Come here wi' ye, ye wanton minx," he growled. "Fair's fair, aye? My turn t' devour your wee teats now, lassie." He raised her up a little and then drew her closer, cupping both bobbing breasts, kneading and nipping and suckling on each swollen nipple until she moaned with delight.

Silvery streamers of pleasure sizzled from her breasts to her loins. She was ready. Eager. Wanted him so badly she could not bear to wait, not another moment.

She lifted herself up a little, grasped his shaft and sank down onto it, impaling herself on his turgid sex with a loud cry of pleasure.

Her head was flung back. Her eyes were closed. Her lips were moist and parted. Her damp hair was a mass of drying ringlets that spilled down her back. Her breasts thrust high and round as, with a gasp of triumph, she sheathed him, taking him inside her to the hilt. Another shudder, and she began to move on him, undulating her hips, rising and falling to the rhythms of her inner storm.

Water slopped over the sides of the enamel slipper tub as he grasped her hips and arched upward, pulling her down onto his hard, aching flesh and holding her there.

Her tightness, her wet, silky heat, drove him wild with desire and pleasure. Yet still he wanted more. Wanted her beneath him. Wanted to drive deeper and still deeper into her willing flesh until they were one, without beginning or end.

He had tried to tell himself he did not need her—needed no one. That time and the wilderness would heal what losing Cameron and the others had done to him. But the past few weeks without her had been hell, and had served to teach him otherwise.

During the long sea voyage, she'd become much more to him than a tavern wench. Much more than an unfortunate thief, fated to be in the wrong place at the wrong time. She'd nursed him back to health, had kept him whole and sane by holding him in her arms and comforting him during the dark, tormented nights, when the fever made his mind wander. And then, when he needed her help to keep the shadows at bay, she had given herself to him with a sweet surrender that stole his breath away.

Her love, born of simple affection and caring, had healed him, made him whole again—physically, at least. For that, if for no other reason, he owed her the freedom to do what she would with her life.

He gazed down at the sweet, trusting face turned up to his, and felt a pain as deep and real as a stab wound in his belly. It would be hell to let her go. Akin to tearing out his heart. And yet, he would do it, for he had no right to keep her. She had her own life to live. Her own dreams to make realities. Dreams in which being the wife of a penniless Scottish fur trader had no part.

He had made her his bride for all the wrong reasons. Now, for the right reason—because he cared for her—he must set her free to live her own life. If she chose to return to England, Hamish would see that she reached there safely. Or she could choose the land she'd dreamed of owning, and stay in the new world. He had made sure of that. But whatever she chose, he meant what he said. Tonight would be their last night together. He was determined to make it one she would never forget.

"We need a bed, lassie," he rasped hoarsely. "*I* need a bed. I want to feel ye lying beneath me. I want t' lay ye down and love ye till ye beg me t' stop. And when we're weary, I want ye to fall asleep in my arms—until the next time."

With that he took her up in his arms and carried her, still dripping, to the bed.

The following morning, bathed and well content, if not well rested, they went below to breakfast in the taproom of the inn.

Madame Gaspar set platters of cold herbed chicken, crusty bread and fresh pears dripping with sweet juices before them. There were tankards of foaming milk, coffee and chocolate, too.

They ate and drank greedily, their appetites ravenous after the night's lusty bedsport.

"So. Have you decided what ye will do, Rosamund?" McLeod asked with deceptive casualness when they had finished the meal. Her face was pale, yet her heather eyes had the heavy-lidded, languid look of a woman who had been well loved the night before.

She nodded. "Yes. I've chosen to go on to Fort Charles." She grimaced. "I know Tom Wainwright all too well. When I vanished with the emeralds, I wager he thought my brother and I had doublecrossed him." She shuddered. "Jim's either dead by now or gone deep into hiding, as far from London and Tom as he can get. I've thought about it, and I believe my chances of ever finding him are small indeed. So I've decided to stay here."

"As you will, then. The captain has invited ye to stay at his home, until ye choose where ye will settle. I think he's most anxious for ye to meet his Madeline."

She nodded. The captain's fondness for his wife was well known, and quite touching. Whether she knew it or not, she thought with a pang, Maddy McKinnon was a lucky woman, to be so adored by her husband. "Of course. I'd be very grateful. And what about you? What will you do? Will you leave for the wilds straightway?"

"Not immediately, nay. There are matters I must tend to first. But I hope to be gone before the first leaves fall. If ye're done, Rosamund, shall we be on our way?"

Pierre Gaspar, the son of Marie and François, was a simpleton. But while slow of wit, he was a big handsome fellow, blessed with all the charm of a shy child. His way with animals was little short of genius.

When she and McLeod went out to the stables, Rose scarcely recognized the dog wriggling in his arms as the one she had rescued.

Pierre had cut the thickened ridges of matted black-and-white fur away, combed the tangles from its coat, then bathed and brushed the animal. The dog now smelled better, Rose observed with a sniff, than its former master had. Its eyes were bright, too, and its tail actually wagged.

"Oh, he looks so much better. Keep him, Pierre," Rose urged. "Please. A gift from me to you."

But when Pierre put the dog down, he padded over to her, licked her hand, circled, and then promptly flopped down across her feet. His black nose rested on the toes of the Indian moccasins she had purchased from the cobbler. Almost everyone wore them here, or went barefoot.

Pierre grinned and said something Rose did not understand.

"My son says, like it or not, madame, you 'ave found yourself a dog, yes?" Madame Gaspar translated.

They all laughed.

Rose crouched down to fondle the collie's fringed ears, then scooped him up into her arms and buried her face in his silky black-and-white fur.

She would need all the friends she could get in this untamed land. This little scamp would be her very first.

Chapter Fifteen

Compared to the town of Quebec, the Scottish settlement of Fort Charles was primitive, Rose discovered two days and many miles later.

There were a half-dozen stone cottages and one two-story house scattered along a street of hard-packed dirt. Bushes and vegetable patches flourished behind each garden wall, showing rows of leafy beet and turnip tops, and small dirt hills covered with potato vines. Several log-houses, workshops, trading houses and sheds were scattered about the large square, one of which had been reduced to a skeleton of blackened timbers by a recent fire, judging by the acrid smell that still clung to the place.

Off to one side was a stone well, covered with

a wooden roof, where a number of women and girls wearing aprons over their skirts were drawing water. Split rails enclosed two large pens, one for horses, another for oxen and cows. In the farthest corner of the settlement was a hog-pen, containing a dozen or so plump porkers. The pen had dried to a dust-wallow now, rather than the pigs' muddy delight it would be, come spring. A stout wooden palisade of sharpened logs surrounded the entire fort. There was a wooden blockhouse at each corner, where sentries kept watch for attacks by Indians—there were several tribes in the immediate area—or the English.

The two-story stone house with the dark blue shutters was the captain's own residence. Its mistress, Maddy McKinnon, was a warm, motherly woman who hailed, Rose discovered, from Penzance.

"Penzance! But I was born near there, madam," she exclaimed, delighted by this news.

"My name is Maddy, dear. I'm so happy we have something in common."

Rose smiled. "Maddy it is. And so am I."

"As I was saying, I met the captain when he attended Mass at our family church in Penzance," Maddy explained as she led the way upstairs. "My Hamish was not a man to waste time. He began paying court immediately and soon asked for my hand. Father refused." She laughed. "My father, God rest his soul, had no fondness for the Scottish, you see? But Hamish wore him down, God bless him. In the end, Father gave his permission for us to wed, and here we are." A tall, angular woman with fading blond hair who towered several inches above her shorter, stouter husband, Maddy beamed at Rose from under a spotless lace cap.

"How romantic. But how did you end up here, in the New World?"

"Hamish recognized the opportunities here for a man to make his fortune. My parents had died by then. There was nothing more to keep us in Cornwall. We also had high hopes that in a different climate I might deliver a living child. I'd miscarried several times already, you see. It wasn't to be, alas. We have accepted now that we will never have children."

"Forgive me for being forward, ma'am—Maddy—but surely there is still time?"

"It is possible, aye. But you must admit, at my age . . . well, it is unlikely."

"Then we must hope." Rose smiled. "You were saying?"

"New France is an excellent place to make one's fortune. The only drawback is that, while France and Scotland have been friends and allies for centuries, they are always at war with the English!" Maddy's sea-green eyes twinkled, but then she sobered. "Still, after hearing about Culloden, I must confess I am not very fond of our countrymen myself. What better place to start anew than here?"

"I've come to the same conclusion."

"Here. This chamber shall be yours, for as long as you wish to stay with us." Maddy opened a door at the top of the stairs. " 'Tis very plain and small, but you and His Lordship are most welcome to it. I'm so happy you are here, Rose."

Rose did not correct her. Maddy McKinnon would find out soon enough that McLeod would be sleeping elsewhere. And though she might wonder about it, her innate good manners would prevent her from asking questions Rose was reluctant to answer.

After weeks in the cabin's close, gloomy confines, the room was wonderfully light and airy. It did not seem plain or small to Rose, and she told Maddy so.

There was a wide four-poster bed with a patchwork quilt spread over it. White linen hangings were tied back with tasseled cords. The bare floorboards were of beautifully grained, highly polished wood. In one corner stood a cherrywood rocking cradle that was obviously very old. Beautifully embroidered linens and lace-edged baby gowns and bonnets were tidily stacked inside it. Maddy's fine needlework, she wondered.

"The cradle is a family heirloom," Maddy explained when Rose asked. "It was mine as a child, and my mother's before me. I could never quite bring myself to give it away." She sighed.

"I suppose you're right. I haven't stopped hoping."

Hangings flanked casement windows left open to the air. The view through them was of the Canadian wilderness, vast, green, breathtaking, mysterious. But this time, it was not the promise of rich, fertile land that beckoned to her.

Her eyes—her heart—were drawn to the handsome horseman who sat his mount beyond the settlement's palisades, where the clearing gave way to tree stumps, then virgin forest.

Drummond McLeod rode with his back ramrod straight, his hands light on the reins, moving as if he and the animal were one. His striking profile could have been sculpted from granite as, hair furling on the wind, he stared up at the window where she was standing. Or rather, *seemed* to stare up at her. He couldn't possibly have seen her, not from such a distance, could he?

Still . . . she felt the intensity of his gaze like a physical, sexual force. A wave of intense heat like that from an oven swept over her, almost taking her breath away. And then, very slowly, he turned his gray eyes to the hills, away from her, and rode off.

He didn't look back.

She shivered. The gesture, the turning away from her, seemed oddly prophetic.

"Here, milady. This is for you," Andy said, handing Rose a bundle fastened with string. He looked as if he wished he were anywhere but there, in the kitchen of Maddy McKinnon's neat little house.

"For me?" She carried the bundle to the cherrywood table and unfastened the string bow.

Inside were several yards of patterned cloth, neatly folded, and a white garment, also folded, which looked like a—a bedgown.

She shook it out. It *was* a bedgown! The full skirts fell from a gathered neckline, while the sleeves were gathered at the wrist, so that the last few inches fell in graceful ruffles over the hands.

Such a gown was worn beneath a short-sleeved outer gown for everyday wear, or alone to bed. By any standards, it was an intimate garment. More intimate, perhaps, than her sark, as McLeod persisted in calling her shifts, she recalled, a blush rising up her cheeks.

"I don't understand. Is this from Drummond?" she asked hesitantly, hope rising through her.

"No, ma'am. It isna."

"Then who in the world would send me yard goods?"

"Me, ma'am, I—er—did. Am. I mean, *would*. Do ye not like it, then?" Andy asked anxiously, turning a new black tricorn hat in his hands.

"On the contrary, it's beautiful, truly it is. And of excellent quality." She rubbed the cloth between her fingers. The creamy background was sprigged with tiny purple violets. "The design is one I might have chosen for myself."

Andy stammered, "The yard goods are for a new gown. The—other is to wear under it, aye?"

Understanding dawned. She had suspected for some time that Andy was fond of her. Was he trying to outdo McLeod and the clothes he had bought her? "But I have new clothes, sir," she began gently. "Ones provided for me by my . . . husband. Truly, they are more than adequate for my purposes. Thank you, Andrew, but I cannot accept such personal gifts from you. It would not be right."

"What ye have isna grand enough at all," Andy corrected her with rare earnestness. "After the evening service in the kirk Friday, there's to be a *céilidh*, ye see?"

"A kaylee?" she echoed.

"In the Gaelic it means a visit, aye? Everyone gathers 'round the fire and we all take a turn at singing or playing the fiddle, or maybe the pipes. You'll see. It's a braw bit o' fun, my lady. Here, they welcome new arrivals and celebrate safe voyages by holding a *céilidh*. You'll want to look your best for the dancin', aye? All the lassies will," he added, shooting her a pointed look.

She understood immediately. Andy, bless him, was quite unaware of the offer McLeod had made her and the agreement they had made to go their separate ways.

Here, he was saying, is a new gown in which to dazzle your husband and mend the quarrel between you. All you have to do is stitch it up, and the rift between you will be mended just as easily.

She pursed her lips, seeing Drummond in her mind's eye. Wanting him in still other places with a fierce, physical longing that made her shiver.

Could he be dazzled, now that he'd announced his intention to go his own way and let her go hers? she wondered. Could she induce him to stay with her? She frowned. The other night at the inn, when he'd loved her with such fierce tenderness, she'd been convinced he felt more than desire. More than lust alone.

She was about to refuse Andy's gift when she thought better of it. What harm was there in accepting? It was worth a try, if a new gown would make Drum think twice about leaving her for the wilderness. Pride made for a cold bedmate, she'd discovered—and she'd become very fond of her husband's attentions.

"Yes, you're quite right, Andrew. I do want to look my best. Thank you for thinking of me."

"Ye're very welcome, my lady." The color in his freckled face deepened to the roots of his hair. "Kirsty said—Mistress McLachlann, that is—she said the wee flowers are the color of your eyes, are they no'? She thought ye'd need the . . . the other gown, to go. . . . under."

"Ah. So Mistress Kirsty made it, then?"

"Och, nay, ma'am. One of the fort's women

sewed it. Luckily, she died in childbirth last
month, so her mon put her wee bits and pieces
in the trading house and—Och, I didna mean
'twas lucky for *her* that she died, puir woman
that she was. But, lucky for me. Er, for *you*, that
is, milady. You ken what I mean, aye?"

"I ken very well, thank you," she assured him
gently, trying hard not to laugh. "Your Mistress
McLachlann has a most discerning eye. For
cloth, as well as for men," she added pointedly.

The comment sailed clear over Andy's head,
unnoticed.

"But is there time? For the stitching?" he
pressed instead.

"If I can prevail upon Mistress McKinnon to
help me, I think so, yes."

He looked relieved. "Then I'll leave ye to get
started, aye? A good night to ye, milady."

"It's Rose, Andrew. Where you're concerned, it
will always be Rose, no matter what. Thank you
again, and a very good night to you, too."

Drum and Andy had volunteered to help rebuild the storehouse that had burned to the
ground before their arrival.

They talked as they trimmed the lengths of log,
or carefully set a finished length into its proper
notch with pegs, all without so much as a single
nail.

"If all goes well, I plan to set off early Monday
morn," Drummond told his cousin as they

worked. A part of him was almost relieved that he and Rosamund had slept apart since that night at the Gaspars' inn in Quebec. Whenever he recalled all the nights she had lain beneath him, her body as warm and sated as his own, the guilt returned to flay him.

Why was he still here, alive and well, slaking his lust on a woman's warm body—and an English-woman's, at that!—when the bodies of his kin lay moldering in their graves, their deaths unavenged?

Since they'd reached Fort Charles, the night-mares had returned, too. On more occasions than he cared to remember, he fell asleep, dreaming he cradled Rosamund in his arms. But when he bent to kiss her lips, it was Cameron's gray face that stared up at him and beyond to some place he could not see. It was his brother's cold lips that parted beneath his in a frightful grin, whispering words he could not hear.

When he looked down, frozen by horror, the flesh split and peeled back from his brother's bones, bursting like an overripe plum, leaving only the leering skull.

". . . . with Rose?" he heard Andy ask him.

"What? What's that about Rose?"

"I said, will ye take her with ye?"

He shook his head, surprised to find he could not meet Andy's eyes. "Nay. What about you? Have you changed your mind about coming with me?"

"Never mind me. Let's talk about Rose a wee

bit," Andy repeated impatiently. "She's your wife, mon—in every way. Ye canna leave her behind, not now. It has gone too far for that."

"On the contrary, cousin, 'tis already settled," he said in a tone that discouraged further discussion. "We have agreed that I should leave, and she will stay."

Andy scowled. "I took ye for a man of honor, Drum. A man who meets his obligations, his duties. You're the McLeod. She's your wife, in the eyes of God, and before man. Does that count for naught? Don't ye care what happens to her while ye're gone?"

A thin smile split Drummond's lips. Andy looked ready to clout him on the nose. He'd never seen his cousin so riled up. "I dare say she will find her life much improved, don't ye? After all, the lassie didna want to marry me in the first place, did she? You'd be the first to point that out, I've no doubt."

"Perhaps I would have been, before. But all that has changed now. You're married in more than just name alone. The marriage has been consummated, aye? And dinna claim ye didna want to bed the lass. By then, ye knew full well she wasna Arabella."

"Mind your own bluidy business, Andy," Drum warned.

"And how do ye think our countrymen will treat the poor lassie once ye're no' here to look out for her? And what about our country*women*?

Ye saw how they were aboard ship when they thought her a thief. Do ye want her blood on your hands, mon?"

"Shut up, I said." Drum had a vivid, fleeting memory of McKinnon comparing women to a flock of birds that picked on those different from themselves. He flicked his head to dislodge the image. "It'll no' come to that. And if it does . . . whist, you'll be here t' champion her, aye?" he added pointedly.

Andy flushed. He lifted one end of the log he had trimmed and, with Drummond's help, jockeyed it into place. He looked as if he was considering dropping it on Drum's foot. "I have a bonnie lass of my own I'm courting. As ye'd already know, if ye thought of anything but your bluidy venture with McKinnon."

His cousin was breathing heavily from his exertions—or was it anger? Drummond wondered, bristling as he mopped the sweat from his brow and neck. Holding the axe by the wooden handle, he shook it at his red-faced cousin. "Tend to your own business, laddie, and I'll tend to mine, aye?"

"Nay, I'll not keep my nose out, not if it means standing back and letting you leave her, I willna. I didna stop ye in England, although I should have. I willna let ye hurt her again." His voice had grown quite loud. He glowered at Drum, pugnacious as a terrier, his fists knotted at his sides.

"Hurt her?" Drum sank the axe blade into a log. His eyes were glacial as he turned to Andy. "What the hell are ye saying, mon?" he asked, his tone a dangerous purr. "I've never laid a hand on her or any other woman, as well ye ken."

"You know bluidy well what I'm saying. She cares for ye. Perhaps she canna tell ye, but she cares. Any fool can see it—just as any fool can tell ye care for her. If ye must leave, then leave. But, for the love of God, take her wi' ye. Dinna leave her behind," he urged.

Drum snorted. "It's not a question of leaving her behind. I gave her a choice, aye? Before we left Quebec, I offered her safe passage home with McKinnon, to England. Or the land she's always wanted." His lips clamped in a thin, angry line. "She chose the land."

"Aye? And did ye offer her the chance to be a proper wife to ye? The choice t' settle some land wi' ye—the two of ye, together? Or is she beneath ye? Is that it, Drum? Is she good enough t' warm your bed but not good enough t' be a proper wife to ye, my *laird*?"

Drum's eyes flashed. His lip curled. "It makes nae difference if her Mam's a doxy and her father a chimney sweep! 'Tis the land Rose wants, I tell ye, lad. Not me."

"Then give her what she says she wants—but put a price on it."

"Make her pay for land that's no' mine in the first place?"

"Aye. Strike a bargain. Say you'll give her all the land she's ever dreamed of, but in return, she must give ye bairns."

"Bairns?" Drum stopped trimming a log to stare at him.

For a moment, Andy's suggestion had held a dangerous appeal. He and Rose. Their bairns. A life shared. Days spent working to build something fine together, and the long winter nights . . . and the long summer nights. . . . Och, sweet Lord, the nights!

But, shaking his head, he laughed harshly. "You've lost your mind, laddie. What would I want with bairns?"

"Did ye forget? 'Tis what Cameron asked ye to do, ye bluidy lummox!"

Drum sank the blade of the axe into the log and grew very still. "He wanted me t' have bairns? And how would ye know that? Has Cameron's fetch come vistin' ye here?" he demanded scornfully.

"Nay. I dinna need visits from ghosts, like some. The puir laddie told us wi' his dying breath. Have ye forgotten, mon?"

Drum stared at him, holding his breath.

"When we found the Dunmor laddies that morning, Cameron was already dying. Ye wept and took him up in your arms, remember?"

"I remember. 'Tis what comes after I canna recall—except in my dreams."

211

"Ye held him, and ye asked how ye could help him."

"I did?" Drum asked woodenly, staring into space. Into the past. "I dinna remember. The drums—the shots exploding all around us—the screams—!" He shrugged helplessly.

" 'Survive.' That's what he told ye," Andy whispered hoarsely. His cheeks were wet. His voice was thick with emotion. "He told ye to 'survive, and flourish.'

"At the time, I thought he meant ye, aye?" Andy continued. "That ye should survive and flourish, as the last McLeod of the Dunmor McLeods. But that wasna it. He meant for the *clan* to survive and flourish, *through ye*. And do ye ken why, Drum? Because as long as one McLeod—one single Highland Scot!—survives and flourishes, Cumberland failed. Dinna let him win, Drum. I beg ye. *Dinna*."

Drummond felt the blood drain from his face with Andy's fierce words. The dull thunk of axes against timber, the smell of fresh pine, the shouts of men, the whinnying of the horses—all of it dimmed.

As if by magic, Andy's words returned him to the muddy battlefield of Culloden. To that April morn when Cameron lay dying in his arms, and tears flowed down his cheeks to mingle with the blood and the falling rain.

Survive and flourish.

These were the words he'd struggled to remember. The words Cameron had whispered in his ear. The three words that had haunted his thoughts, his dreams.

The horseshoe nail seemed to burn against his breastbone, pricking his flesh as it pricked his conscience.

Survive and flourish.

"You're telling me to stay with her? To get heirs on a woman I feel nothing for?"

Andy chuckled. "Ye bluidy liar! Ye'd like t' think ye dinna care for her—but I know better."

The knowing grin on Andy's freckled face infuriated Drum. " 'Twas lust, laddie. Not love nor caring. A man—a man needs a woman t' give his body ease."

His cousin's blue eyes twinkled. "Very well. Have it your way. Maybe it isna exactly love, just yet, but it's verra close. God willing, the heart will follow where the . . . cock leads it, aye?"

"The cock!" Drum glowered at him and snorted in disgust. "Whist, mon, ye're full of sh—"

"A good day to ye, my laird."

"—ugar. And a good day to ye, too, Mistress Maggie. Mistress Kirsty," Drummond said, a little gruffly. He inclined his head.

He saw Andy give the McLachlann lass a broad smile. Well, well, now. Was that the way the wind blew? His cousin was right. He *had* been preoccupied.

"It's a bonnie morning, is it no'?" Maggie Stevenson said, addressing him and quite ignoring Andy.

"Bonnie indeed, aye." Drum gallantly inclined his head to the young woman before him. "And made all the bonnier by your . . . er . . . presence, ladies," he added, shooting Andy a malevolent look.

Never one to pass up the opportunity of avoiding Mistress Maggie Stevenson in full manhunting regalia, Andy snorted, set his axe aside and left the work at hand to dip a drink of water from the well.

After a moment's hesitation, Kirsty blushed and followed him. Her grave, kind face was animated as she scooped a dipper of water for herself.

Across the square, out of the corner of his eye, Drum saw Rosamund leave the kitchen door of Hamish and Maddy McKinnon's house, where she'd taken up residence since their arrival. She carried a water pitcher and was headed in the direction of the well.

The group of women congregated about it must have made some spiteful comment as she drew water, for she tossed her bonnie brown head and stormed past them, headed in his direction. Scamp, the little black-and-white dog, trotted at her heels.

What a fierce wee besom she was. A woman with a tongue as tart as vinegar when she wished, he recalled. And lips like honey when she didna, he added, an all-too-familiar heat rushing to his loins.

He frowned. Was it a trick of the light, or had the sun caught the glimmer of tears in her eyes as she turned away from the women? Surely not. He had never known her to cry, not even when her spirits were at the lowest ebb.

Nevertheless, his fists were somehow knotted at his sides, and the urge to rush to her defense was powerful. If Andy only knew how close he'd come to the truth . . .

"Laird Drummond? My laird? Will ye be at the *céilidh* Friday even'?" Maggie asked.

"I'll be there, aye, mistress," he promised, forcing his attention away from Rose and back to the woman before him.

Thief or not, with her glossy black hair swept back at the sides and spilling down her back, her fine figure trimly displayed in a crisp white bodice tucked into woolen skirts, Maggie Stevenson was a handsome woman who would turn any man's eye. There was no hint of the bruised, woebegone creature she'd been after her father's beating.

These were the kind of women he should have bound himself to. Women like Kirsty and Maggie and their ilk. Scottish lassies, born and bred. Like to like, and blood to blood.

"Ye can count on it, Mistress Maggie." He smiled down at her.

She blushed with pleasure and turned to go,

just as Rosamund drew level with them.

As her questioning gaze fell on first him and then a radiant Maggie, Drum turned away.

Maggie tossed her head in triumph. She linked her arm through Kirsty's and the two young women giggled as they hurried away.

"Must you do that?" Rose asked quietly, a brimming jug of water in hand.

"Do what?"

"Shame me."

"Shame ye! I dinna ken what ye're talking about," he insisted lamely.

"Don't play the innocent with me, McLeod. I saw you flirting with the Stevenson wench. Mealy-mouthed Scots, the lot of you! 'Tis a sin to be a Sassenach, but it's fine for that . . . that black-haired sneak thief to be giggling and whispering with another woman's husband in broad daylight."

"Blast ye, woman. I wasna whispering with her," Drum protested.

"No? Well, we'll just see where you're seated at the *céilidh*, won't we, milord?" she said, poking him in the chest.

Water slopped from the pitcher as she marched off, giving him no time to make an excuse. Though why he needed an excuse was beyond him.

Chapter Sixteen

Sizzling sounds and the stench of scorching hair filled the chamber as Maddy applied the heated tongs to Rose's long curls that Friday evening. She deftly tamed the unruly mane into three elegant ringlets that trailed down over Rose's shoulder in the current French fashion.

"There you are, my dear. Perfect," the older woman declared, her lace-capped head cocked to one side as she admired her handiwork. "You look *ravissant*. If this doesn't do the trick, nothing will."

Rose offered no response to Maddy's comment. Convinced the young couple had had a tiff, the dear woman had made several veiled references to Rose and McLeod "mending matters," but not once had Rose confirmed or denied their estrangement.

"Thank you, Maddy. I could never have finished the gown without you." She embraced the woman. "You've been kindness itself."

She admired her reflection in the silver handmirror Maddy passed her, excitement bubbling up inside her.

While she had never considered herself a beauty, she thought she looked almost elegant tonight. A far cry from the tavern wench in mobcap and apron serving ale in the Golden Goose tavern, or the schoolgirl in ruffled pinafore who had carried her slate to Miss Pennington's.

A trio of long golden-brown ringlets cascaded over one shoulder from the lavender ribbon Maddy had given her. The short-sleeved, patterned bodice and skirts they'd sewn from Andy's cloth were in charming contrast to the plain long-sleeved bedgown she wore beneath them, in the current fashion. The full, gathered skirts set off her waist, which, although thicker than before, was still more slender than most.

Maddy laughed and gently patted Rose's cheek. "We Cornishwomen must stand together against these Scots, aye?" She drew a lacy crocheted shawl from a drawer and handed it to Rose. "Here. I want you to keep this. The evenings are often chilly at this time of year." She paused and eyed her archly. "We wouldn't want someone in your condition to take cold, now would we?"

Rose flushed. "How did you know?"

Maddy laughed and embraced her. "Ah, child, there's a . . . look to you. A glow that comes from nothing else. How I envy you! How far along are you, my dear?"

"I have missed my courses twice," she admitted.

"Then it'll be a March babe. The papa doesn't know, I presume?"

Rose shook her head. "McLeod and I have not spoken in some time."

"I see. A lovers' quarrel."

"I'm afraid it's not that simple, Maddy. There was never any love between Drummond and me. Ours was a marriage of . . . convenience. His, not mine."

"Nonsense, Rose. There's certainly love between you. Yours for him, at least. I am not blind, child."

"Perhaps," she lied in a husky voice quite unlike her own. Maddy's kindness was bringing her to tears. Her throat ached, but she refused to cry.

"Tell him about the baby, Rose. The knowledge that you are carrying his child will surely mend the rift between you. Who knows what he will say unless you try, hmm?"

Rose shook her head, swallowing over the knot in her throat. "I just . . . can't. If he does not want me for myself, my pride will not allow me to force myself on him."

Maddy sighed, her hands clasped primly beneath her generous bosom. Her green eyes were serious now. "A babe needs a father, Rosamund, far more than it needs your stiff-necked pride. Swallow that pride and tell him, child."

"Ah, Maddy. I only wish I could."

To her surprise, Drummond came to the McKinnons' house to escort her to the stone church for the evening service. His coal-black hair was clubbed back into a ribbon, and he wore a tricorn hat at a rakish angle. His new frockcoat and breeches had been sprinkled with water, then brushed. The perfectly knotted folds of the linen stock at his throat were stiff with starch—the fort laundress's work, she fancied. His boots were highly polished. All in all, he looked so handsome, so dashing, he could have held his own against any of the gentry in London Town.

Her heart gave a flutter as he bowed over her hand and then offered her his arm. The way his gray eyes ignited as he looked down at her played havoc with her breathing. Her gown seemed suddenly too tight.

"Ye look verra fine this evening, Rosamund," he said, making her a stiff bow.

Fine, he'd said. Not *bonnie*, or *charming*, but *fine*.

"Thank you, milord," she murmured aloofly as he led her across the dirt square. She gritted her teeth, trying to ignore the way her nipples stiffened at the husky sound of his voice, the treacherous surge of heat that pooled in her loins when his fingertips brushed her arm.

They followed Maddy and the captain to the kirk, under the dark, watchful eyes of several Indians—members of the Huron tribe, one of the five tribes belonging to the Iroquois Nation, McKinnon had explained. They wore shirts and leggings of deerskin, decorated with moose-hair embroidery and patterns of dyed porcupine quills. There were also some French trappers, similarly dressed, who had come into the fort to trade pelts for provisions, powder and other supplies.

Even the Indian women had eyes for her tall husband, Rose observed. When he strode past, he nodded a cordial good evening to them, which set the younger maidens to giggling and whispering behind their hands. Rose shook her head. What a ninny she was, to think her husband might be moved to stay at the fort by a fancy new gown that she happened to be wearing. The McLeod was a handsome devil, and a chieftain to boot. He could have any woman he wanted. All he had to do was crook his little finger, and they would come running. Why would he want her, when from the very first he'd meant to make himself a widower, not a husband?

Penelope Neri

Well, she told herself, her chin lifting, it was still worth a try. As Maddy had pointed out, it was no longer a matter of choice. Her baby needed more than a name. It needed a father.

The September evenings were long and golden that year, and so the settlement's elders had decided the *céilidh* should be held outdoors rather than in the barn.

Trestle tables and long log benches were set up around the dirt square in the center of the settlement, then sand was sprinkled over the dirt to settle the dust for dancing.

A groaning trestle table held the platters the settlement's women had spent all day preparing.

There were gigots of pork and whole venison, spit-roasted over glowing hickory logs to a succulent golden brown. Bannocks and scones dripped fresh-churned butter and honey. There was a bubbling cauldron of barley bree seasoned with leeks, tatties and neeps, picked from the settlement's own vegetable patches, and fresh fish tickled from the river by the sandy-haired lads who seemed to be everywhere, darting about like minnows themselves.

The area in the center of the square was given over to the roasting pits and a crackling bonfire.

Flames roared up into the night, scattering sparks and embers against the velvet night like orange fireflies. In its light, and that of flaring pine torches placed at intervals around the

222

square, the settlers sat along wooden trestles and ate or drank their fill.

Afterward, at the urging of the elders, the merrymakers stood up, one by one, and offered some talent to entertain the gathering, just as Andy had promised.

Men, women and children flung themselves wholeheartedly into the beloved dances of their homeland, needing little urging to dance jigs, reels and flings in the sanded square.

Arms held gracefully aloft to represent a stag's antlers, their bare toes pointed, their fringed tartans flying out in a rainbow of red, green or blue plaid, the men and women bobbed and skipped to the skirling music of the bagpipes, played by a rosy-cheeked piper.

Another man, proudly wearing the pleated tartan skirt Rose had heard Andy call a kilt, did an intricate, barefooted dance between the sharp blades of two claymores that formed a steely cross on the ground, risking the loss of his toes.

His performance earned cheers from the onlookers, who saluted his skills with whiskey and Gaelic toasts.

When the dancing was over, another, older piper came forward. Rather than the merry music of before, this piper played a lament. His *pibroch* was a mourning song for the homeland they had left behind, and a way of life gone forever. For old battles lost or won, and for loved ones dead and gone.

Rose did not have the Gaelic, but the low, mournful skirl of the pipes echoed a sorrowing chord in her own heart. She was glad when the piper finished his lament and a lively fiddler took his place to lift everyone's spirits again with a more spritely tune.

"Lady McLeod. May I have the honor?"

"I would be honored, Captain. But alas, I do not know how—"

"I'll teach ye," cut in McLeod's deep voice at her other side. "By your leave, Captain?"

"Aye, aye, laddie. Dance wi' your bonnie bride. I wouldna dream of coming between my partner and his wife." The captain chuckled and inclined his head to her. "Perhaps later, my dear?"

"I'll look forward to it," she promised with a smile.

"You knew I would accept Hamish's invitation, didn't you? But that doesn't mean I'll dance with *you*," Rose said through clenched teeth as McLeod led her into the square. "If we're going our separate ways, perhaps we should start right here and now?"

"Ye dinna mean that, Rosamund. I'm a verra good dancer—as light as thistledown on my feet. One dance. That's all I ask. Ye'll be the envy of every lassie here."

With those sparkling eyes, that grin, that husky tone of voice, he didn't sound as if he wanted a dance at all, but something far more intimate, the rogue.

Under the disapproving eyes of those seated around the square, he took up position behind her, placing the fingers of her right hand on his right palm, planting his left hand firmly on her hip. He jerked her back against him, so that her spine touched his chest and her buttocks brushed against his thighs. None of the other men were holding their ladies anywhere near as closely.

"Just think. The last time I held ye this way, ye were naked. Remember, my *sonsie* lass?" he whispered in her hair.

She blushed. His hot breath fanned her nape and was giving her gooseflesh. "No, I'm afraid I don't."

His grin broadened. "Ye bluidy wee liar."

When the fiddle music started, she gritted her teeth and followed his lead. They skipped forward after the couples in front of them, then back, then retired to opposite sides, lines of men and women facing each other. The women curtsied, while the men made stiff bows.

McLeod proved an excellent dancer, despite the wound he'd suffered. In fact, his grace put his fellows to shame. His black hair shone like a raven's wing in the torchlight, his eyes gleamed, and his striking, arrogant carriage, his masculine grace drew every woman's glance—just as he had teasingly promised. But to his credit, he had eyes only for her. Her heart fluttered and took wings.

"Maddy says the farmers are predicting a hard winter this year, sir," she observed, linking her arm through his when they came together again.

His brow creased in a frown as he swung her around. "And what if they are?"

"Perhaps it would be safer to postpone your departure until you are more familar with the area? The spring, say?"

Taking her hand, he led her from the square into the shadows of the trading post, where they could talk privately.

"I have to go soon," he explained when they were alone. " 'Tis what I must do—for now, at least. A man has his pride, aye? I owe Hamish for the very clothes on my back, the food we put in our mouths—"

"—and for the land you have promised me?"

"That too, in time," he admitted. "I have nothing here that I may call my own, but I willna leech off the people of this settlement," he continued. "Nor will I be a burden. Each and every one of us must do our part here, in New France, and fur trapping is a profitable, respectable venture. Just a few good seasons and, God willing, my debts to Hamish will be paid. Then I shall be free to begin a new life. So, the sooner I leave, the sooner I can pay off my debts. Now do ye ken?"

A new life. One in which she had no part.

"Is there some reason you'd like me t' stay, Rosamund?"

226

Her fingers trembled in his hand. Her heart ached for the closeness they'd shared aboard ship and at the inn in Quebec, however briefly it had lasted. The love that had flowered was still there, in her heart. And beneath it now lay the baby they had created. All she had to do was tell him. To open her mouth and say the words. *You must stay, my love, because we have made a child together.*

And because I cannot bear it if you leave.

But the words that would bind him to her trembled, unspoken, on her lips. Unless he first admitted that he cared for her, she could not bring herself to tell him. Instead, she whispered, tears choking her voice, "Is there anything I could say that would make you stay, sir?"

Again he hesitated. Once again she held her breath.

His eyes changed from soft smoke to steel. His jaw hardened. "Nothing, madam. Nothing at all. My mind is made up. As soon as ye find some land to your liking, ask Hamish t' take a look at it. If he thinks ye've made a good choice, he will help ye file your claim in Quebec." He frowned. "Are ye sure farming the land will prove t' your liking? 'Tis a hard life."

"I know all about life being hard," she flared. "Twice I was uprooted, torn from my home, my possessions taken from me. Then you stole me away and brought me here. Enough. This time I will have something—a home, land that no one can take from me. With or without you," she added vehemently.

With that, she pulled free, picked up her skirts and fled, leaving Drummond staring after her.

It was some time before he realized he was no longer alone. He spun around, his hands closing over the hilt of his dirk, his body tensed for an attack.

Vigilance was a trait he'd acquired when he fled the Highlands. It was one every man needed in this untamed land.

But it was only Maggie, skulking in the shadows like an alley cat. The sly baggage must have eavesdropped on him and Rosamund.

"Ye dinna need to pretend, not with me, my laird," Maggie said, sidling out into the pool of torchlight. The sound of harp, fiddles and pipes carried only faintly here. "I know why it was ye married the Sassenach."

"Do ye now?" He crossed his arms over his chest. His lips thinned.

"My Da heard ye talking with Andrew Lewis. It was a brave thing ye did, sir, stealing the Butcher's whore awa' from him. All of us thank ye for it. And there's not a soul at Fort Charles would reproach ye if ye left Arabella, and chose another. One of your own kind, aye?"

She drew closer as she spoke. Trailing her fingers down his chest, she eyed him archly, leaving him in no doubt as to which of his "own kind" he should choose. *The wee slut hasna learned her lesson since Calum Sinclair . . .*

"Shall we, indeed?" he said, firmly removing her hand. "Then tell the good people of Fort Charles that I was mistaken, aye? That I abducted an innocent woman—the *wrong* woman—from Cumberland's fine town house."

Her jaw dropped. "She—the Sassenach—was never the Butcher's whore?"

"Nay, Mistress Stevenson. She was not. But the Lady Rosamund *is* my wife now—and my wife she will remain. I'll thank ye and the others to remember that, and pay her the respect she deserves. A good night to ye, madam. My compliments to your father."

Tipping his tricorn at the red-cheeked young woman, Drummond followed her back to the square, passing within inches of where Rose was standing.

She had come back to get the shawl Maddy had given her, forgotten as they danced, in time to see Maggie, her face contorted, run by. She could see tears spilling down the young woman's cheeks in the moonlight as she flew past.

Whatever she'd expected when she saw Drum and Maggie standing together in the shadows, it was not this. McLeod's arms were not around the woman. Nor was he giving her one of his not-so-innocent kisses. Instead, he had set Maggie straight, in no uncertain terms.

A giddy euphoria bubbled up inside Rose.

Surely that proved something? Why would he bother to defend her, to clear her name, if he didn't care for her, just a little? That caring, combined with the passion that flared so easily between them, was more than most married couples had.

Maddy was right. A baby needed more than a name. In the morning, she would tell Drummond about his child, no matter how difficult it might be. She would tell him, and then bid him go for the winter while she stayed here, with Maddy, until he returned in the spring. After the child was born, and the wilderness had lost its novelty for McLeod, perhaps they could try again, if he was willing.

The very instant she came to the decision, the anxious knot in her belly unraveled. She felt lighter, more carefree than she had felt in weeks, as if a burden had been lifted from her shoulders. It was the right thing to do. What the innate honesty of her character had demanded of her from the very start.

For the first night in many, she fell asleep as soon as her head touched the feather bolster, filled with excitement, and hope.

She was up with the dawn chorus the next morning, feeling refreshed and eager to carry out the decision she'd made.

Before Maddy stirred to stoke the fire or set the bread dough to baking, Rose washed and dressed herself, then brushed out her hair. It fell in long, loose curls over her shoulders, the way Drum liked it best.

Throwing a shawl about her shoulders against the cool morning air, she let herself out of the kitchen and hurried across the settlement to the barn where Drummond and the other new arrivals slept.

A flush of lemon and salmon pink stained the sky to the east, heralding the sunrise. But for now, the settlement slept on, shrouded in the cool, dewy half-light of dawn. The first cock had yet to stretch its neck to crow. The first of the milk cows had yet to begin lowing to be milked. None of the settlers were staggering, bleary-eyed, to the privy to make water.

Yet to her surprise, she found Andy already outside in the pens. He was furiously forking hay for the livestock.

"Good morning!" she sang out. "Is the McLeod still abed? I know 'tis awfully early, but I need to speak with him straightway. Would you wake him for me?"

Andy plunged the pitchfork into a mound of hay. "I'd be happy to—but ye're too late, ma'am. Ye missed him. The bluidy fool is long gone—begging yer pardon, ma'am."

"Gone! Gone where?" Panic flared inside her. "He can't be gone."

"Trapping. Trading. Whatever ye want to call it. He left a good hour past."

"No, he can't have," she insisted dully. She could feel the slow thud of her heart in her ears, like the hollow beat of a drum. Her belly felt as if someone had driven a fist into it, forcing out the breath in a sickening rush. A wave of nausea swept over her. "I—I have to talk to him."

"Begging your pardon, Rose, but ye canna. He's gone—and he isna coming back."

"Until the spring, you mean." The flat quality of Andy's voice, the finality of his tone, hinted at something more. "That *is* what you're saying? Until the spring?"

There was pity in his face now. Pity for her.

"Nay, my lady. That's not what he said. The McLeod's gone for good."

Chapter Seventeen

"Hey, you! Hey, matey. Hold yer horses, eh? We want a word with you."

Calum Sinclair halted and swung around. Rocking on his feet, he squinted through blood-shot eyes, trying to focus on the couple before him.

" 'S that right?" he slurred. "Well, I dinna 'have words' with the English. Get oot o' my way."

He tried to elbow his way past the tall, dark-haired Sassenach, but the man would not budge. Rather, he clamped a powerful hand on Sinclair's shoulder. The numbing bite of his fingers nearly brought Sinclair to his knees.

"Change yer mind, old son," the Englishman suggested silkily. "We wouldn't want you to 'ave an accident, would we now? A nasty drop inter the river, say?"

Sinclair swallowed. His mouth was suddenly dry, the need for a drink overpowering. There was something in the man's eyes that made the blood curdle in his veins. Something about his voice—not just what he said—that turned his bowels to water.

Instantly sobered, Sinclair darted a nervous glance over his shoulder. There would be no help from anyone 'round here. The wharves were almost deserted, except for the cats that slunk through the shadows, and the water rats that crawled the hawsers from ship to shore.

He wetted his lips, resigned to telling the pair whatever they wanted to hear, so long as they let him live. "Aye, all right then, laddie. What was it ye wanted t' know?"

"There's a cove back there wot says you're the mate of the *Salutation*. 'S that right?"

"Was her mate, aye. Until this last voyage."

"And?"

"An English whore cost me my place, that's what happened. 'Tis on her account I have these stripes on ma back, too, God rot her." Sinclair snarled. He spat on the ground.

"Stripes, ye said?"

"Aye." Sinclair lifted his jersey, showing several tattoos as well as the livid marks of a recent flogging across his back. "Thirty days in the brig with naught but ship's biscuit an' water, and twenty stripes o' the cat."

"What's this wench's name?"

"Arabella. Arabella McLeod."

"Arabella? You're sure?"

"I'm sure."

The man and the red-haired woman exchanged glances.

"I'd like t' buy you a drink, old mate," the man said, grasping his elbow. "Where's the nearest grogshop, then?"

"You, buy me a dram?" Sinclair wetted his lips, salivating at the thought. Still . . . there was that look in the man's eyes. That hint of something awful bad in his voice. "Why would ye do that? Ye dinna even know me."

"Let's just say we're strangers to New France, me and my 'Bella here. But there's every likelihood we might have mutual. . . . friends. Ain't that so, 'Bella, my luv?"

"Right you are, Tommy, love. Mutual friends," the red-headed wench agreed.

Less than an hour after leaving the settlement, Drum found himself in the wild, fertile land McKinnon had described with such eloquence. He discovered an untouched wilderness of river bottoms and valleys, crystal lakes and rushing rivers, over which the mountains loomed in distant, white-capped splendor.

He rode across vast prairies and meadows

where daisies, lupins and poppies nodded bright heads amongst the grass, and through shadowed forests where ancient maple, pine and oak towered all around him and cast their scented shadows. Leafy vines twined between the tree roots, while in places tall grasses reached to the horses' chests.

The woods teemed with moose, elk, deer, squirrels and other creatures with no fear of man. Briers and bushes grew between the trees, hung with berries like glistening jewels. The marshes were alive with wildfowl: honking geese and quacking ducks that swam in the shallows or filled the sky with their whirring wings. The rivers and streams were the home of the playful otter and the plentiful, fur-yielding beaver, as well as silver sturgeon and bass.

Even the sunlight was different here. It fell through the leaves to dapple his hands with coins of green and gold as he followed the winding river up hill and down dale.

It was a wild, beautiful land, he thought, inhaling the grass-scented air. One in which he was now alone, an Adam without an Eve in the Garden of Eden. Except for an occasional glimpse of bear, panther, elk or moose—animals he'd seen only in drawings, until now—he saw no other signs of life.

As the day wore on, tired muscles and a chafed backside made themselves known, yet he was still eager to see what lay beyond the next crest, the next valley, the next bend of the river.

Sometimes he found that only more of the same verdant green forest awaited him, or a grassy meadow. Other times, the land fell away in sudden deep gorges—knife wounds made by a giant's blade—where torrents of icy water hurtled over vast boulders. The force of some cascades was so great that the spindrift dashed up became a fine, damp mist which drifted like phantoms over the roaring falls.

The mountains rose in daunting splendor before him, their uppermost peaks craggy and capped with snow, their lower slopes cloaked with still more woods of fir and pine.

This new land was more lovely than he'd ever imagined. In certain places, it so resembled his beloved Highlands, it brought a lump to his throat. The black of fertile earth, the dark green of the deep forest—mile after mile of virgin timber—spread as far as he could see, in every direction. It was there for all with the courage to claim it, tame it, build their dreams upon it, as Rose would build and dream without him.

He sighed. He had left Fort Charles far behind but, God help him, he had not left sweet Rosamund. He carried her with him in his heart. Perhaps he always would.

Three pack horses plodded after his hardy gelding, heavily laden with traps, snowshoes, blankets, wampum, beads and other trade goods which he would give to any Indians he happened upon. Or who, God forbid, should happen upon him.

The Iroquois people he'd met at Fort Charles had done nothing to inspire his fear. On the contrary, he'd decided that, apart from their obvious physical differences, their tattooed faces and guttural language, the Indian people were much like white men: fiercely proud and protective of the land they called Earth Mother, their gods and their women and children. In fact, many of the Scottish settlers had adopted the buckskin shirts, breeches and moccasins worn by the Indians, while Scottish women braided their hair in the same fashion as the Iroquois women.

No, it was the chilling tales he'd heard about Indian war parties or bands of renegade braves who massacred entire families in their cabins that made the blood run cold in his veins.

At the first inkling that a raiding party was abroad, runners were secretly sent from the fort to outlying homesteads. They hastened from cabin to cabin, warning the settlers of the danger approaching, risking their own lives to spread the alarm. The alerted families immediately rose and fled into the night on foot, traveling silently, swiftly, and taking nothing with them but the clothes upon their backs and whatever weapons they could carry.

He had an unwelcome image of Rose as such a settler, her face pale, her eyes wild with terror as she tried to fend off an attack by hostiles.

Angry at the direction in which his thoughts kept turning, he thrust the image to the back of his mind. He told himself Hamish would never let Rose leave Fort Charles without a proper escort. A lone woman was physically incapable of clearing trees and stumps, raising a cabin and doing the million-and-one tasks of carving a living from the wilderness. Of course, Rose would need laborers to help her work the land. But what sort of men would they be? And what if they expected more from her than a chance to work the land?

He tried to squelch the voice that said what Rose did was no longer his business. Andy and Hamish had both been right. If he wanted to know what Rose was doing, he should have been the one to choose that land. He should have been the one to clear those trees, raise that cabin, break that ground.

From what little she had confided to him, she had spent her entire life in search of a place to call her own. One that no one could take from her. He could have provided that home. And in return, she and the children they made together would have replaced the family he'd lost. Or if not replaced them, eased some of the pain of their loss.

Out here, on New France's western frontier, where the wind had a savage bite and where the deep shadows could hold bear, cougar or savage warriors, a wise man respected his enemies, seen or unseen, and cherished and protected those he loved. There was no telling when they might be taken from him.

The fourth day after leaving Fort Charles, Drum made camp on the bank of the river, lighting a fire as soon as the purple gloaming began to fall over the glen, as he'd done the first three evenings.

At this time of day, the light faded fast and the slender column of gray smoke from his fire would not betray his presence. After piling rocks around the fire to contain the blaze, he shouldered his flintlock musket and melted into the dense woods.

But unlike the first three days, he did not go deeper into the woods to hunt. He went only as far as the tree line. There, he crouched down to wait.

True night fell like black velvet over the wilderness, its hush pierced with the trill of cicadas and the sleepy twitter of birds as they settled down to roost.

Soon after, the moon rose, climbing high into the heavens, and stars came out, one by one, to add their flickering lights. Still he did not return to the fire or to the bedroll he had spread beside it. Instead, he crouched as still as a statue in the cover of a massive oak, his eyes trained on his campfire and the surrounding area.

As he had the past three nights, he heard

wolves howling in the distance and the occasional eerie screams of a cougar close by. Yet he remained as still and silent as when he and Cameron had hunted the red stag through Glen Dunmor.

For two days now, he'd been aware that someone was following him, keeping his distance, stopping when he stopped, moving on when he moved on. Who was his unknown stalker? he wondered. A lone brave of the Five Iroquois Nations who saw a single white man as easy prey, and coveted the trade goods carried by his pack horses? Or was it a war party, out for his small keg of whiskey, his weapons and his scalp?

Either way, gut instinct said he would soon find out. . . .

His long wait was rewarded when, moonlight glinting off the blade in his fist, the stalker slipped between the trees, heading toward his little camp. A lad, Drum guessed by the light-footed way he moved. Young and lithe, but lacking the seasoned woodsman's skills needed to make a stealthy advance on his quarry. Still, even green lads were capable of killing.

Just before reaching the spot where he had built his fire, the stalker hung back and looked about, obviously wondering where he had gone. He must be able to see the string of pack horses hobbled beneath the trees, Drum thought. Abandoning the flintlock, he silently circled around and came up behind the youth, rising up from

Penelope Neri

the shadows like the bogle Aunt Flora had warned them about.

"Aaggghh!"

The surprised cry strangled in the stalker's throat as Drummond hooked his arm around his neck. His weighty forearm was braced against the youth's windpipe, effectively cutting off the supply of air. Drummond jerked the stalker back against his chest, holding him so tightly the lad's feet left the ground.

He dug his chin into his captive's temple, replacing his brutal forearm with the cold sting of a sharp blade across the soft white throat.

"Who are ye? Why are ye following me?" Drummond rasped through clenched teeth. "Talk, damn ye!"

Chapter Eighteen

"It's—it's me," the stalker croaked. "Rosamund."

"*Rosamund?*" he growled incredulously.

"Aye," she whispered.

"Bluidy hell, woman." He swore foully as he released her and spun her around. His eyes searched the pale face, noting the wide, frightened eyes, the hair shoved up beneath a battered, broad-brimmed hat, the men's breeches. "I almost killed ye."

"Nay, laddie. I wouldna have let ye do that," insisted a third voice.

Drummond groaned and released her as Andy stepped out from the cover of tree, Scamp padding silently at his heels.

"Sweet Lord, mon," he growled. "All of ye?"

*   *   *

"Well, ye found me. What now?" McLeod demanded later, after they'd supped on a sparse meal of half-raw ash-cakes and black coffee.

"I don't know," Rose said miserably, her good intentions flown.

Somehow he seemed more formidable out here in the wilds than he had at Fort Charles. Three days' growth of black stubble had lent him a swarthy, disreputable look. The long midnight hair that fell loose to his shoulders only added to his savage appearance. He looked dangerous, sinister, unpredictable as any cutthroat pirate or rough-and-ready highwayman, just as he had the first time she'd seen him, in Arabella's looking glass.

How could she tell this brooding stranger that she loved him beyond all reason? Or that she was carrying his child? To do so, she would have to disclose her deepest feelings; to lay her heart bare once more, and trust that he would not break it in return. With this mood upon him, she was not sure that she dared. He seemed so gruff and angry, did everything with such vicious, consummate skill, she thought he might eat her alive if she spoke out of turn.

"Ye followed me for four days and ye dinna ken why?" His eyes were withering, his tone scathing.

"Of course I know why! I want you to—to help me. To find a good place to settle, I mean." It was the truth, she realized, but she could not bring herself to say more, not without some indication, however small, that he felt more for her than desire.

His nostrils flared. "Ye'll need somewhere a wee bit closer t' the fort than this, lassie. Even a day's walk is too far when ye're desperate. Living way out here—!" He eloquently gestured at the wilderness that ringed them, " 'Tis folly."

His scowl deepened as he turned to Andy. "What the devil were ye thinkin' of, mon, t' let her come traipsin' after me? Or did ye think at all?" he added caustically.

"What was *I* thinkin' of? Whist, it wasna up to me. When did either of ye two blockheads ever listen to me? And your lady, my laird, is every bit as stubborn as yersel'," he ground out through clenched jaws.

"Oh? How so?"

"She traded that—that tight-fisted old skinflint, Alistair Johnston, her gold trinkets for his last horse, the wagon, a freshened cow, and everything else, and then rode off with the lot of them before I could stop her. Sweet Lord, mon, I was hard put t' catch up with her, she left the fort sae blessed sudden. Strikes me the two o' ye deserve each other!"

Glowering at Rose and grumbling under his breath, a bristling Andy stomped off, leaving them glaring at each other over the fire.

* * *

The following day, they traveled for several hours across rolling meadows and then entered deep woods of maple and oak where sunlight barely penetrated the leafy treetops, and where the wagon had little room to maneuver.

The light that fell through the boughs dappled their hands and faces with wavering patches of green and topaz. It was as if they were riding through an underwater grotto, Rose thought, patting the neck of her trusty "kelpie" or water-horse.

Scamp gamboled along beside them, taking small circuitous side journeys every now and then to explore intriguing scents, before returning faithfully to dog her horse's heels.

"There's a fey feeling t' these woods, is there no'?" Andy observed as she returned to ride alongside the swaying wagon. He addressed his question to no one in particular. "I keep expecting t' spy a wee fairy or a goblin peeking out from behind a tree."

Rose had been thinking exactly the same thing. She laughed softly. "Me, too. It's as if no one has ever been here before. As if we were—"

"—Adam and Eve in the Garden of Eden," Drummond supplied gruffly from the other side.

Rose looked over at him, surprised that he was listening. "Yes," she agreed softly, and then quickly looked away as his smoky gaze rested thoughtfully on her face.

Andy snorted. "What does that make me, then? The bluidy sairpent?"

" 'Tis either that or the apple," Rose suggested cheekily.

They both laughed, and even Andy had to smile, until Drummond added, "If there's really anyone in these woods but ourselves, 'tis more likely t' be Indians than the wee folk. We'd best keep our ears and eyes peeled, aye? We dinna want t' walk into an ambush."

It was a sobering thought, and for a while the three of them rode on in watchful silence.

At mid-afternoon, they left the magical forest behind and came out into an open area drenched in mellow sunlight. From somewhere nearby they could hear the noisy rushing of water.

Drummond rode ahead, leading the way in the direction of the sounds as if he had been there before.

They reached a broad, swift-flowing cataract that flung itself off a high cliff to the valley floor below. A rocky promontory to one side commanded a breathtaking view in every direction.

Drum sprang down from his horse. Planting a booted foot on a convenient rock, he leaned on his knee and gazed out over the land that swept to the distant, hazy horizon.

Before him, the river plummeted in frothy white torrents over black boulders, spilling into a huge whirlpool below before rushing on.

From the falls, the river wound its way through a beautiful valley with a broad flat floor that was covered in more forests and grassy meadows.

Willows and berry bushes hung low over the river further downstream, while reeds and rushes grew in shallower areas.

The river would guarantee a year-round, plentiful supply of water, while the sheltering bluffs would buffer the valley against the fierce winter blizzards that came howling down out of the north.

"Well, cousin. What do ye say?" Drum asked softly.

Andrew dismounted and came to stand alongside Drum. He shaded his eyes against the bright afternoon sunlight and slowly turned his head from left to right, taking in the lovely vista that spread out below and before him.

" 'Tis Glen Dunmor," he whispered, as if unable to believe his eyes. Then he laughed and whacked his cousin across the back with a resounding thump. "Whist, laddie, 'tis almost home!"

Rather than wait for one of the men to explain—not that they seemed as if they intended to—Rose slithered down from her horse's back unaided, groaning as the feeling returned to her numbed legs. "What are you two talking about?"

Andy turned to her, a merry grin splitting his freckled face almost in two. "Ah, Rose. Just look

248

at this valley. 'Tis the spitting image of where we lived in Scotland, lassie. Glen Dunmor reborn."

"Is this where you were leading us, McLeod? I thought we'd turned back, but I wasn't sure. You looked as if you knew where you were going."

McLeod nodded, a faraway look in his gray eyes. "Aye, lass. I did. I passed this bonnie valley two days ago and couldna put it out of my mind. 'Tis as if God picked up Glen Dunmor in the palm o' His hand and set her down here in New France. All that's wantin' is the keep itself. Were I intending t' settle some land, this valley would be the place for me, Rosamund," he told her seriously.

" 'Tis a wee bit farther from the settlement than I'd like, but ye canna have everything. And besides, Quebec's growing, as is Fort Charles. I wager before too long, there'll be other settlements springing up, much closer than the fort. As it is, ye've several thousand acres of meadow pasture for the grazing of flocks and herds."

He dropped to one knee and picked up a clod of black earth, crumbling it like cake between his fingers. "And look at this. Rich, fertile soil in which t' plant your crops for a fine harvest. The forests will supply all the timber ye could ask for. They're teeming with deer, elk and other game. The river will provide both men and beasts wi' all the water they'll ever need, as well as fresh waterfowl and a wee fish or two for the pot, aye?

Ye were right about what ye said earlier, lassie. 'Tis the Garden of Eden!"

She smiled. His enthusiasm was contagious— and the valley really was every bit as beautiful as he claimed.

They found a way for the horses to slither down into the valley, and then spent what was left of the daylight exploring.

Rose picked daisies and wove them into a chain; then she discovered briers weighted down with blackberries, and a tree that was covered in wild plums. She picked one and ate it greedily. It tasted tart but good, and she laughed as purple juice ran down her chin.

"Hmm. Just think of all the jams I could make with these. And the blackberry pies and preserves with the berries. Oh, and what jellies we'd have! What wines and liqueurs!" she declared. Arms outstretched, she whirled around and around until she was giddy, laughing in sheer delight. Her long, loose curls flew out around her as she twirled.

"Oh, I just love this valley! Mmm, smell the air. Taste the wind. Feel the warmth of the sun on your face. It's so beautiful here—and soon it will all be mine, God willing."

She suddenly halted and smoothed down her hair, standing demurely before them now, her hands clasped primly before her.

"Gentlemen, may I welcome you to my humble abode? My laird Drummond, dear Master

Lewis, welcome to. . . . New Dunmor!" She swept them both outrageous curtsies, laughing at their stupefied expressions.

"Then I take it we're staying for the night?" Drum asked dourly, but there was the suspicion of a twinkle in his eyes, and the corners of his mouth were twitching.

"A night?" She laughed. "I don't know about you, sir, but I intend to stay for a lifetime," she said softly.

He grinned and shouldered the Brown Bess. "Then ye'll be needing a bite to eat, aye? Andy, see to the beasts. I'll see what I can find for the mistress of New Dunmor's first supper."

"And what shall I do?" Rose asked eagerly. She was willing to do anything that didn't involve riding. They had ridden so hard and so far since they'd caught up with McLeod, she'd almost become a part of her wretched saddle.

"Build us a cooking fire. If ye remember how." He slung a powder horn across his chest. "One without smoke. Ye'd best—"

"Gather only dry kindling. I know," she cut in before he could finish.

"Aye," he said gruffly. "We dinna want ye t' smoke us out."

Their eyes met for an endless moment, her violet to his fathomless charcoal.

She could feel heat rising up her cheeks like boiling milk rising up the side of a pot. *Say it,* a tiny voice urged her. *Forget your foolish pride, and have done with this charade. Tell him you love him. That you're carrying his child.*

But try as she might, the words remained locked inside her.

He seemed about to say something, too, but then he abruptly turned away from her.

She thought she glimpsed a flicker of regret, of frustration in his eyes as he slung a leather satchel over his arm. But he said nothing more as he shouldered the long-muzzled flintlock and plunged into the undergrowth.

"He's a proud man, is Drummond," Andy murmured after he'd gone. "A man who considers his word sacred, once given. It still eats at him, that he couldna keep his sworn oath to Cameron. He canna forgive himself, and move on from it."

"Perhaps. But what has that to do with me?"

Andy paused. "To Drummond's way of thinking, 'tis a sin t' love ye, want ye, to dream of ever being happy with ye, when his kin lie mouldering in their graves. For as long as their murders remain unavenged, he believes that he has failed them. That he has broken his word. A man who breaks his word doesna deserve happiness."

Rose sighed. "His vow was made to dead men, Andy," she reminded him, moving stiffly about the perimeters of their campsite. Every muscle in her body ached. "They have gone beyond caring what happens in this life, to a better world."

She forced herself to keep moving, tucking fallen pine cones and small branches into the pouch of her hiked-up skirts. If she were to stop, even for a moment, she doubted she could go on. But she would rather die of exhaustion than ever admit that she was tired.

"Which matters most? Tell me! Oaths made to the dead, or vows given to the living?" she continued after a weighty silence had yawned between them.

"You forget, lassie. A man has his honor to uphold. His good name depends on it. And Cameron was—"

"Cameron! Cameron! Cameron!" she cut in, whirling to face him. "I have heard enough of Cameron McLeod to last me a lifetime! What of James Trelawney, the brother I shall see no more? Or of you, Andy Lewis, who lost all you held dear? And what about me, torn from land and kin by your wretched laird—forced to wed a stranger who wished *me* dead, and himself a corpse?

"Enough, I say. Enough! We cannot bring back the dead, nor change the past. We can only go on, and make the most of our future. Life is too short to squander in sorrowing for all we've lost. McLeod should tend to the living and let the dead rest in peace."

Andy cleared his throat. Too late, she caught the warning in his expression and spun about.

McLeod was standing just a few feet behind her. His hands were knotted into fists at his sides. With beard-shadow darkening his upper lip and jaw, his expression was unreadable. But his eyes were hard and cold as flint.

"Is that what ye really think, Rosamund?" he asked softly.

"Aye," she replied without hesitation, looking him square in the eye. Her chin came up. " 'Tis the reason I followed you."

Without further ado, she bent to gather more kindling. Anger had revived her, given her energy, so that her skirts were soon filled with firewood. But when she turned around, ready to continue their argument, Drum was gone.

She scraped a small depression in the dirt, then knelt down beside it and carefully built their cooking fire, using only dry leaves and twigs. Despite hands that shook on the tinderbox, a tiny flame soon licked at the kindling. A curl of woodsmoke rose up into the treetops.

"I'm thinkin' ye care for him powerful bad or ye wouldna be sae riled at him. Ye love him, do ye not, lassie?" Andy asked gently, his hand on her shoulder.

When she did not answer him, he drew his hand away. Shaking his head, he went to settle the horses for the night.

The gloaming had already fallen when Drummond returned, carrying a dead rabbit by the ears. He must have snared it, for they'd heard no shot.

All light had faded and the moon had risen by the time the coney was skinned and roasted.

They wolfed it down in silence, along with the soda bread Rose had baked in the ashes of the fire, and tin mugs of black tea, sweetened with honey drizzled from an earthenware crock.

Rose eyed Drum over the rim of her cup as she sipped. Lost in thought, he was staring into the flames of their campfire.

What did he see in them? she wondered. Mayhem and murder? His brother and the clan McLeod as they lay dying? Or . . . was he considering what she'd said?

"What did ye mean earlier?" he demanded suddenly, as if he had read her thoughts. "What was the reason ye followed me?"

Her lips tightened. "I came because you made a vow to me, McLeod," she said, her chin up, her eyes fixed on him. "One I've decided to hold you to."

"What vow? I made ye no vows."

"Nay? What of our wedding vows? Like it or not, we are bound together by those vows for as long as we both draw breath. The Roman Catholic Church will not sanction a divorce between us. Nor are there any grounds for annulment," she added, blushing and looking away. "So, since I am unlikely to become a widow in the near future, I have decided to hold you to them. Andy insists you are a man of honor. I shall expect you to uphold the promises you made me, as you endeavored to keep those made to your brother."

Penelope Neri

His dark head came up. His pewter eyes narrowed. Face darkening with anger, Drummond looked from her, then across at Andy. His cousin needed no second hint. Picking up his bedroll, he hurriedly left them alone.

"What more do ye want of me?" Drum ground out when they were alone. "I told ye, this valley is yours. I'll have Hamish file the claim on it, just as soon as ye—"

"Devil take Hamish," she cut him off. "What I want is my lawful husband beside me. For the two of us to work this land together—as husband and wife. 'To cherish and keep her,' that's what you promised. 'Until death do us part.' Remember?"

"Nay, it canna be, lassie."

"It can—it must. You have sworn it before God."

With an oath, Drummond turned on his heel and stomped off into the night.

A panther screamed close by. The horses milled about, whinnying nervously. Scamp's head came up. He growled deep in his throat, but did not leave her side.

She heard a twig snap underfoot and looked up to see Andy returning to the fire.

"That hard-headed fool. Ye're the only woman he wants, if he'd only admit it. If he willna come t' your bed, lassie, then ye must go to his."

"So he can throw me out of it? No, thank you, sir."

256

Andy clicked his teeth. "Whist, lassie, ye're as bad as he is."

Drum hauled off his boots, shucked his breeches and dived into the river, gasping in shock as its icy flow surrounded him, cooling the heat in his blood.

A cold dunking was as good a means as any to cure what ailed him, he thought as he clambered back out onto the bank to dry off in the breeze. Truth was, he wanted her, day or night. Wanted her so badly he could taste her. Thoughts of her consumed him, eating him up from the inside out.

The sight of her moving about their camp each evening drove him to distraction. Curling golden-brown hair floated about her exquisite flower face, tanned a mouthwatering gold by the sun. Her breasts rounded out the cloth of her brown bodice, lusher, fuller than he remembered. When she bent to stir the contents of the kettle hanging over the fire, the voluptuous shape of her bottom beneath gathered butternut skirts filled him with such raw, raging lust, he could not stand it.

His hands itched to lift her petticoats. To turn her beneath him, part her thighs and drive deep into her tender flesh. To love her with a wild, mindless fury that would exorcise both their demons, once and for all.

During his few days of solitude in the wilder-

ness, he'd thought long and hard about what
Andy had told him at the fort.

Survive and flourish, Cameron had urged him
with his dying breath. But the only possible way
his line could flourish now was through Rosamund, who was his lawful bride. He was the last
McLeod, the sole survivor of the Dunmor branch
of his proud clan. Surely he owed it to them, to
her, to father legitimate heirs on his lawful wife?
Strong sons who would carry on the McLeod
name, and bring it strength and honor. Beautiful
daughters to enrich it with their pride and grace.

His mind made up, he dressed and pulled on
his boots, then headed back upstream to their
camp.

Rose had already rolled herself into her blanket, he discovered. The little dog had tucked itself as close to her as it could get. He strode over
to her bedroll and towered over it, looking down
at her. A low growl rumbled from her guardian.

"Whist, dog. Down wi 'ye," he cautioned softly.

Rose's eyes were closed, but in the moonlight,
he could see her lashes quivering like velvety
moths against her cheek. The wee minx was not
asleep, he knew.

"Ye were right, Rosamund. I am honor bound
t' keep my wedding vows to ye, if that's what ye
want," he began. "However, I have some conditions of my own. If I am to be a husband to ye
in every sense of the word, then I shall expect
you to be a proper wife in return. I want ye in

my bed, lassie, and I want bairns of ye, too. A litter of bairns. Agreed?"

"Aye, my lord. Agreed," she whispered, sounding as if she could not believe her ears.

"Then it's settled. Now, get some sleep, lassie. At first light, we begin cutting timber for our cabin."

Chapter Nineteen

Having chosen the perfect site for the cabin—close to the river, yet far enough away and on high enough ground that a spring flood would not take them unawares—Drum and Andy set about felling the trees, splitting the timbers and hewing the notched pine logs from which the cabin would be built.

Raising a cabin was difficult, exhausting work when several neighbors worked together. For two men alone, it was a backbreaking undertaking. But by working from dawn to dusk, they raised the main cabin in just two weeks.

Large by New World standards, it measured a roomy seventeen by twenty-one paces and smelled gloriously of pine sap and new wood. In the coming weeks, any gaps in its log walls would be chinked with moss mixed with mud. The latter, Rose brought up from the river in their only bucket, a little at a time.

It was an exhausting, backbreaking time for them all, yet when they were done, they had a snug, handsome shelter that was half log cabin, half Highland croft. In it they could comfortably pass even the harshest of winters.

Too exhausted that first night to do more than drag their bedding inside its four sturdy walls, Rose spread her feather bed on the planking, while Andy filled his ticking pallet with straw and hauled it up the new ladder to the small loft where he was to sleep.

That night, they bowed their heads over the first supper that Rose cooked for them over the first fire ever lit on the new hearthstone.

"Will ye say a few words, Drum, or shall I?" Andy asked uncertainly. Since Culloden, Drum had made little secret of the fact that his faith in God had wavered.

"Nay, I'll do it, laddie, if ye'll both bow your heads."

Andy flashed him a pleased grin.

"Dear Lord," Drum began after clearing his throat. "We thank ye for giving us strong bodies and sound minds wi' which t' build this fine house, and beseech ye to watch over us, and keep those within these walls safe from harm."

In a loud voice, his smoky eyes intent and fixed

heatedly on Rose, Drummond added, "And while we're asking favors, Lord, I'm also asking that ye make my bride, Rosamund, verra fruitful, so that our numbers at New Dunmor may soon multiply."

Rose squirmed and looked down at her moccasined feet as both Drum and Andy added a robust, "Amen!"

So be it, indeed. Though Drum did not know it, their numbers were going to multiply somewhat sooner than he expected.

In the days following the cabin's completion, the men built a simple open shed attached to the side wall for the livestock and the woodpile. The sloping shingle roof would keep snow and rain off the beasts and ensure that the winter's kindling remained dry. A roomy pen, enclosed with long log rails, provided room for the animals to move around when fine weather permitted.

To her surprise, Andy and Drummond showed considerable talent in wood-carving—a common enough pastime among men, but one in which very few showed any real artistic accomplishment. After a few evenings by the fire, Andy proudly produced a handsome rolling pin, the handles carved to look like blackbirds with their necks extended to warble.

"Can ye bake a berry pie for us, Rose?" he asked hopefully after he presented his gift to her. "I've a powerful fondness for a crumbly crust filled wi' sweet berries." He grinned. "Och, my mouth's all water, just thinking about it."

Poor Andy! There was such a wistful expression in his eyes.

"I can—and I will, very soon. Promise," she told him, laughing. "Lucky for you, the brambles are just loaded with berries this season."

Not to be outdone by his cousin, Drum fashioned a box bed like the one in McKinnon's cabin aboard ship, as well as three stools and a trestle table of white pine that could be erected when needed, then taken down when it was not.

The problem of their immediate shelter and comfort solved, Rose settled down to the task of making the cabin more than just a crude dwelling.

For the first time since she and Jim had been ousted from their little house in Sadler's Wells by Cumberland's lackeys, she had a home to call her own. And now she had land surrounding it for as far as she could see.

In her mind's eye, she saw the trees cleared, the stumps burned out, the rolling acres of dark earth plowed under and planted with corn and wheat, the grassy pastures grazed by herds of cows and horses, or flocks of sheep. New Dunmor cows and horses. New Dunmor sheep.

Next spring she would plant vegetables and flowers behind the cabin, and in the summer the area would be green with turnip and carrot tops, pea-vines, potatoes, beets and rows of maize, or Indian corn.

She'd traded two of Arabella's gold chains and a signet ring for all of her purchases, including seeds and livestock, from the shrewd old Scottish trader at Fort Charles.

Under her direction, Drum and Andy passed an entire day unloading the wagon, which was piled high with her purchases, everything from provisions to household goods and reading materials. There were barrels of flour, and others of cornmeal, each with a large flitch of bacon stored inside to keep it from spoiling. There were sacks of beans and dried apples, too.

Rose smiled when she saw them hefting the latter into the cabin.

When they were children, her brother had told her the shriveled, brownish slices of dried apple were murderers' ears. And, silly little goose that she was, she believed him! She'd cried and squeezed herself into the farthest corner, refusing to eat or look at anything their Granny made with dried apples, including apple pie.

Of course, Jim had then persuaded Granny to give him Rose's share of the pie, too!

There were also several smaller sacks of brown sugar, tea and coffee; earthenware crocks of salt and lard, and squat jugs of vinegar and molasses, stoppered with corks. There were farm tools, including a plow, an auger, a spade and a hoe, as well as her homemaking tools, which included a sewing basket and lengths of unbleached muslin, a quilting frame and a spinning wheel.

She ran her hand over the spinning wheel, which Andy had set close by the hearth. She looked forward to spinning during the winter months, once they had some sheep to shear for wool, or found some flax plants. Mam had always said she was a very fine spinner, and it was no more than the truth. Her flaxen thread and wool yarns were always evenly spun, with no ugly lumps or tangles to mar the texture of the finished piece. She enjoyed weaving, too, and had a project in mind for which she would need a loom, but . . . first things first.

At her request, Andy erected shelves on either side of the narrow window to hold her white-enameled tinware, which included plates and mugs, horn spoons and wooden bowls. Another rack of white oak beside the enormous fieldstone hearth held her cast-iron pots and fry-skillets. A kettle perched on the spider in the chimney nook. He'd also fixed several pegs in the knotty pine walls, on which to hang their clothing.

In one snug corner, out of the drafts, Drummond placed the sturdy box bed he'd made with planks taken from the wagon's sides, then strung with crisscrossing strips of rawhide.

On top of it, Rose spread her precious feather bed, stuffed with warm, fluffy goosedown, then threw linens, woolen blankets and patchwork quilts over it.

" 'Twill be a fine warm nest for us come Christmas, aye?" Drum murmured, pointedly eyeing the bed, then Rose. "Come, lassie. Sit here beside me. We'll try it out for size."

He fell backwards across the bed and lay there with his arms and legs outflung, laughing as she muttered "Later" and skittered nervously across the cabin, away from him.

That night, Rose crawled into the downy softness of her feather bed alone. But despite its comfort, she could not sleep.

She lay there wide awake listening to an owl hooting in the deep woods, and the distant scream of a mountain lion as she stared up at the rafters, her body taut with desire.

After Drum's invitation to try the feather bed, she fully expected him to join her. To lie down beside her, sweep aside her meager protests, and claim his husband's rights.

The thought made her curl into a ball and hug herself, she wanted him so much.

It was long after moonrise when she heard him leave his bedroll and stride across the cabin to stand beside the bed.

She quickly closed her eyes, pretending to be asleep. But the image of him standing there, his midnight hair silvered by moonlight, remained imprinted on her eyelids.

When he looked down at her, his expression was one of such dark longing it stole her breath away. But then he moved to the door and went out into the night, leaving her awake and wanting him more than ever.

The following day, she went to pick berries for Andy's pies along the banks of the river.

Picking her way through deep drifts of autumn leaves, she heard a honking sound.

Shading her eyes, she looked up to see a gaggle of gray geese against the bright blue. They were flying south to spend the winter in warmer climes.

"See you in the spring," she murmured, coming out of the woods onto the riverbank.

Here, the bramble bushes grew thick and were laden with plump, glistening blackberries for her blackberry pies, jams and throat cordials.

Her basket was already heaped high when she heard the low, insistent rattle of drums. Drums? Way out here miles from the nearest settlement?

Pah-rum-pah-rum, pahrum-pom-pom!

Convinced she must be hearing things, she started clambering over rocks, following the sound, weaving her way between long grasses and thorny bushes until she came out onto a high ridge above the river. From her vantage point, she could see clear across the valley—and what she saw made her eyes widen.

Redcoats!

A small platoon of English dragoons was marching up the valley, flanked by their officers, who were on horseback. The red of their uniform coats, the snowy white of their stocks, the dense black of their hats, breeches and polished boots could be seen for some distance, if the rattle of drums and the jingling music of their horse-harnesses had not advertised their presence. The sunlight winking off bayonets, buttons and braid made them impossible to miss.

She frowned. What on earth was an English military platoon doing way out here, in French territory, she wondered?

"They'll have come doon from the north," a voice hissed softly in her ear, as if its owner had read her thoughts.

Startled, she turned to see Drummond lying on his belly in the long grass beside her. He must have moved as silently as a seasoned back-woodsman, for she had not heard him when he crawled up through the long grass and loose rocks to reach her.

"But why?" she wondered aloud. "What business have the English in New France?

He shrugged, yet his eyes held a cold, distant light. She knew that when he looked at the soldiers, he did not see men. He saw Culloden Moor. Captain Harry Williams. "Butcher" Cumberland and his dying brother. . . .

"Spying business, I dare say, lassie. Yon Sassenachs are greedy bastards, aye?" He smiled grimly as she flinched. "Hudson's Bay Company is no' enough for them, by the looks of it. The clarty English will be wanting every bluidy piece of fur-trapping territory there is!"

Her head came up. Her lips clamped in a thin line. "And the French don't?"

His scowl softened to a grin. "They do. However, the French have sensibly allied themselves wi' the Scottish over the centuries."

"And that makes them the better people?"

"Nay, lassie. It makes them the devil I know, as opposed to the one I dinna ken at all." His eyes narrowed. "Thinking of running off and joining your countrymen, were ye, my lass? Ye could lead them to a wanted man, aye? A Highlander wi' a reward of five hundred guineas on his head. Ye could buy several acres wi' that sum, lassie."

She turned and cast him a withering look, irritation sparking in her eyes. "I probably could, yes. But I never gave it a moment's thought. And if I had . . ." She shook her head but didn't go on.

"What, lassie?" he purred. His sensual change of tone made the skin at her nape tingle. He dragged his thumb down the curve of her cheek. "What if ye had, hmm?"

"I just wouldn't. I have no intention of letting you off as easily as that, McLeod."

"Nor I you, my *sonsie*," he breathed. Catching her by the back of the neck, he drew her down into the long, sun-bleached grasses and held her hands above her head while he kissed her full on the lips.

"My God, woman. Ye make my bluidy stones

ache," he murmured. For a long moment, he gazed deep into her eyes. Then he slithered back down the way he'd come.

The wretch left her lying there with the sunlight warm on her face, the sweet taste of his kisses still tingling on her lips, wanting him more than ever.

"Drummond! Wait for me." Calling after him, she quickly slithered down the steep, rocky ridge to where he waited.

"Keep your bottom down, else the Sassenachs will see ye," he called to her in jest. " 'Twould make a fine target, aye?"

Catching up to him, she laughed and said, "You just worry about your own bottom, McLeod."

At the foot of the ridge, they dropped to their knees in the grass to catch their breath. While he lay back, she leaned against a tree trunk and watched his strong chest move up and down with every breath. Dear God, how she wanted him—here, now. It had been so long. Too long.

She reached over and ran her fingers through his long midnight hair. Surprised by the affectionate gesture, he rolled over and, to her surprise, he kissed her again. A quick, hard kiss.

The warmth of his tongue sent tingles down her spine as he swept her hair aside and very slowly kissed the nape of her neck. Gooseflesh covered her skin. A delicious shiver eddied through her as his lips traced the blades of her delicate shoulders, then lazily fingered the laces of her bodice.

Drawing her bedgown down to uncover her breasts, he caressed their soft white skin, his tongue finding her raspberry nipples.

"Beautiful. Sae beautiful," he breathed.

As his tongue swirled around each swollen peak, wonderful sensations filled her body.

He teased a lock of her long, loose curls, murmuring how lovely she was.

"Look at your curls, lassie. In the sunlight, they look like spirals of antique gold."

But as she reached to unfasten the laces of his breeches, he pulled away. Her fingertips brushed his rigid manhood as he rose to his feet.

"I canna wait t' sample your berry pies. Will they be ready for supper this even', lassie?" he asked innocently, a smile tugging at the corners of his mouth. It was all he could think of to say, his mind was so flooded with thoughts of her, and with the need to have her. But not here. Their child would be conceived on a feather bed, not in the open, with only the hard ground beneath them, like a tinker's bairn. His gaze flickered back to those perfect ivory mounds, steepled with crimson nipples, and his groin tightened. The thought of making love to Rosamund here, in the deep grass, with the autumn sun beating down on their bare bodies and surrounded by the scents of dried leaves, woodsmoke and mist held a certain appeal. . . .

"Pies?" she demanded, sitting up. She gathered the open bodice fronts over her bare breasts, vexed and confused by the way he was staring at her. The heat in his eyes was at odds with his abrupt change of subject. Did he want her or not? she wondered. "What pies?"

"The ones ye promised Andy ye'd make."

"Oh, those."

"Aye. Blackberry's my favorite, too. I'm thinking we'll be needing one pie apiece. Maybe more. Ye'd best make haste and get started on the crust, lassie. It's already past the nooning, is it no'? I'll see ye back at the cabin."

And with that, the wretch left her high and dry, wanting him so badly it hurt.

The Redcoats had clearly marched away toward Montreal. The sound of their drums had faded to a muffled rattle. She could hear it only faintly now, like the crackle of distant thunder.

"Good riddance," Rose muttered without a twinge of guilt. "Bloody Sassenachs."

Scrambling to her feet, she brushed herself off, lifted her heavy basket over her arm and headed down the slope toward the cabin.

As she skidded down a grassless incline, scattering small pebbles and loose dirt as she went, she almost stumbled over a huge mountain lion.

The great cat was crouched behind an outcropping of huge boulders. Long blond grasses camouflaged its tawny gold pelt until she was just a few feet away. It was devouring a deer carcass with noisy ripping sounds.

She froze, swallowing a startled cry as the lion's huge, cobby head came up. Its ears pricked. A ferocious growl rumbled deep in its throat as its unblinking golden eyes caught and held hers.

For what seemed an eternity, she stared into their shining depths, frozen in place by a mixture of fear and awe. The cat's elongated black pupils were like slitted windows into the beast's savage soul. The golden irises brimmed with strength, intelligence, life, like bubbling molten gold.

In those moments, she could see every detail of the cat's tawny face in exquisite, terrifying detail. The quivering whiskers that sprang from its jowls. The muscles that rippled beneath its sleek golden pelt. The massive chest . . . the lean flanks. . . . the huge clawed paws . . . the tail that flicked back and forth in anger at her intrusion.

And then, in a golden shimmer, it abandoned the bloody deer carcass and vanished in a single svelte bound, melting into the long grass like a tawny shadow.

Rose was left standing there, wondering if it had been real at all, or if she had imagined staring into the golden eyes of the mountain lion.

The eyes of the mountain lion. The Eyes of the Tiger.

As she hurried toward the cabin, trembling in

reaction to her brush with death, she wondered if the encounter with the mountain lion had been a sign. A nudge to revive an almost forgotten memory. For the incident had reminded her of Arabella's emeralds, and her plan to dispose of them.

While still aboard the *Salutation*, she'd had an idea that, while it would not return them to their rightful owner, would put them to a far, far better use.

Tonight, after delicious blackberry tarts with fresh cream, she would share her idea with the men.

Chapter Twenty

The days had grown shorter, the nights longer and cooler since the cabin was finished. With the coming of October, summer had melted into fall, turning leaves scarlet and gold and sending evening mists to wreath the valley like smoke.

"I've been thinking," Rose announced as the three of them sat around the trestle table that evening. The remnants of the savory stew, fresh-baked bread and blackberry tarts they had enjoyed for supper lay between them. Firelight flickered over the cabin walls, and candles had been lit despite the early hour.

"Be careful, lassie," Drummond cautioned with a grin. "Thinking might be dangerous on a full belly."

She shot him a scathing look.

"What about?" Andy asked.

Rose held out her hand. "These," she said softly.

The emeralds winked in her palm, reflecting the light in firebursts of brilliant green.

Andy had seen the emeralds before, but still gave a low whistle. "Surely they canna be real, not sae big as that?"

"Come, now. Would His Grace, the Duke—the Prince of Wales—buy paste for his lady-love?" She shot Drum a pointed look.

He dismissed the jewels with a brief, disparaging glance. Getting up, he poured himself a dram of whiskey from the keg and then drained it in a single draft. "Two worthless lumps of green glass. That's all they are here."

"True. But in Europe they are worth a king's ransom, are they not?" she pressed.

"So they say. But ye canna eat emeralds," Drum growled.

"No," Rose agreed, her eyes shining. "You can't." She leaned forward, her eyes bright, her lips parted in her eagerness. Firelight gleamed in her hair and eyes and glistened on her moist lips. "But you *can* eat the bread bought with them."

He frowned. "What are ye getting at, lass?"

"I want to send the emeralds back to Scotland, where they can do some good."

"Scotland!" both men exclaimed together.

She nodded. "If Arabella's emeralds were sold, hundreds—thousands—of Highlanders could be saved from starvation with the proceeds. Think about it, Drum. All the Scottish widows and children with no man to support them since Culloden would have food for the winter. Perhaps even longer." She shook her head. "So much good could be done with these two 'worthless pieces of glass,' could it not? 'Tis criminal to hoard them here, where—as you so rightly said—they are quite worthless."

"She's right, Drum. It's a grand idea, don't ye think?" Andy asked, his tone excited.

"Who would ye get t' sell the stones for ye?" Drum asked, playing Devil's advocate. "Who could ye trust not t' rob ye—and the Scottish people—blind?"

"Hamish McKinnon," she shot back straightway. "A more honest, decent fellow than Hamish I've never met, Scottish or English. Present company excepted, of course," she added, favoring Andy with a warm smile that did not extend to Drummond. "Besides, as a merchant, the captain would probably know a jeweler on the Continent who could be trusted. One who would not question the jewels' true origins."

Catching the affectionate grins Rosamund and his cousin exchanged, Drum scowled, smothering the jealous urge to hook Andy out of his seat, punch him in the nose and toss him into the river.

Obviously, she had given the matter of the emeralds considerable thought before broaching the subject with them. Still, if he were honest with himself, he had to admit that her plan had an ironic justice to it that pleased him.

"She's right," Andy agreed before Drum could think of any objection to raise. His blue eyes shone. His freckled face, ruddy from the heat of the fire, glowed with enthusiasm. "It could be done, could it no', Drum?"

"There. I knew *you'd* see the possibilities," she crowed, sounding relieved. "Someone should ride back to Fort Charles first thing in the morning. There's no time to waste. Maddy told me that Hamish was sailing for Scotland again as soon as his holds were filled or the winter set in, whichever came first. The St. Lawrence is frozen for five months of the year, you see, so he cannot wait indefinitely. Unless someone rides to Fort Charles straightway, we could miss him."

Andy nodded slowly. "The cabin's raised and chinked, and the animal folds are finished. If ye think ye can spare me, Drum, I could leave tomorrow morn. And while I'm at the fort, I could fetch us some extra provisions, aye? Is there anything ye need, Drum?"

"I need ye to stay here, that's what I need," Drummond growled. "There's plenty of work needs doing before winter sets in. There's kindling to be split, and I'll be needing help with the hunting. Then there'll be meat to smoke and dry,

God willing. For that, we'll need smoke racks made. . . ."

Andy's neck stretched in indignation like a wild turkey's. It also turned bright red. "You said yerself this morning, all that remains is to dig ourselves in for the winter. What more would ye have me do, mon? Besides, I've had my fill o' watching the two o' ye circling each other like scrappy dogs, both waitin' for the other t' make the first move."

Drum bristled. "Then go, damn ye," he growled. "I'm no' your nursemaid, t' bid ye hither and thither. But make haste, aye? With that bite to the wind, the first snow will be falling any day now. Ye dinna want t' be snowed in at the fort till spring, do ye, now?"

"Nay," Andy agreed, casting first Drum, then Rose a long, calculating look. "I dinna want that."

They bade Andy farewell just as the first ray of daylight fell through the long-needled pine boughs the following morning. Any hard feelings between the two men had evaporated during the night. They exchanged bear hugs and much back-slapping before Andy finally took his leave.

He rode off mounted on the best of their horses. A pack horse followed on a leading rein. One of the long-muzzled flintlocks was carried across his shoulder, while in the satchel fastened to his saddle Rose had tucked a two-day supply of smoked venison and the ash-cakes she'd baked for his journey while it was yet dark. They were still warm from the Dutch oven.

The precious emeralds were safe in a suede drawstring pouch, which hung on a cord about his neck, beneath his long shirt. Andy carried the jewels close to his heart, as was the cause to which they'd soon be put, God willing.

As he vanished over the hill, Rose closed her eyes and offered up two silent prayers; the first, that Captain McKinnon had not yet sailed, the second, and more fervent, for Andy's safety. While at the fort, she had heard the Scots talk about savages attacking innocent travelers. Of hostile Indians looting and burning settlers' cabins. She could not help worrying for his safety till he returned.

"While ye're sighing after my cousin, wife, I'll be splitting the winter's kindling, aye?" Drum murmured, glaring at her. Bad enough his bride looked with such dewy-eyed affection on his cousin. That she made no attempt to hide her fondness for him made it even worse. Had the wee besom no shame at all? he wondered. He'd never seen that wistful, worried look on her face for him, for all that he was her husband. Nor had she given any indication that she intended to warm his bed in the near future, her promise notwithstanding.

Stripping to the waist despite the frosty bite to

the air, he tossed his shirt over a nearby bush, spat on his hands and hefted the axe.

Warm breath and body heat rose from him like steam into the chilly air as he swung the axe with ferocious skill, sending white wood chips flying. He grunted in satisfaction. If he did not lop off a hand or a foot, or a few toes here and there, there was something to be said for hard labor when the days turned cold. Or when a man was vexed. Or when he lusted after a lassie who just happened to be his bride. . . .

The moment Drum turned his back to her, Rose snatched up the full linen shirt he'd draped over the bush.

There was a fine dry wind blowing this morning despite the cold snap in the air. She could have the grubby thing laundered, dried and back in place before he ever noticed it was gone.

But as she reached for the garment, she froze, her hands loosely caught in its folds. Wide-eyed, she stared at the half-naked man before her.

Though always acutely aware of him, she'd not seen him unclothed since the Howling Wolf Inn.

Now his sinewy muscles, strengthened by long hours of vigorous physical labor outdoors in all weathers, danced beneath the smooth pale-gold flesh of his shoulders. Beads of sweat gathered across his brawny back and then trickled slowly down his spine or the shadowy T of dark hair that bisected his broad chest.

She followed the drops' snaking descent over his abdomen, down over his washboard belly, until they reached the belt that rode low at his waist.

"Ouch!" She yelped with surprise as fingers like manacles closed around her delicately boned wrist and squeezed.

"Was there something ye were wanting, Rosamund?" he purred, thrusting his handsome, wicked face into hers.

She slowly released the breath she was holding, ashamed of the sudden heat that leaped through her loins. "Just your—your shirt. Look. It's filthy." Throwing off his fingers, she grabbed the garment and tossed it into her basket.

His huge hand hooked over the edge of the wicker, preventing her from flouncing away with it. With the other hand, he took back his shirt and tossed it over the bush again.

"Dinna bother yoursel' with my dirty laundry, lassie. I'll wash it myself by and by," he informed her, his cool gray eyes meeting hers in silent challenge. "There's only one duty I'm askin' of my wife, for the time being. You'll recollect what that duty is, I'm thinking?"

Oh, Lord. *Did* she! She stared up at him, into irises the cool hue of woodsmoke, rimmed with charcoal at their outer edge. They were the mysterious color of ashes. Of smoke and fog, or mist over water. A woman could lose herself in those eyes. Could lose her very soul.

But, outwardly unmoved, she gave him a non-committal shrug. "As you will, then."

The very instant he turned back to his wood-chopping, however, she snatched up the shirt, tossed it into her basket and bolted.

Wading through rustling drifts of colored leaves, she headed down to the riverbank.

As she looked back over her shoulder for Scamp, who bounded joyfully at her heels, she saw that Drum had stopped working to watch her.

His head was cocked to one side. His eyes were narrowed, heavy-lidded and sensual as he watched the basket bouncing against her swaying hip.

Heat and a queer, jittery excitement filled her belly. He was watching her the same way that some of the men who came to the tavern had once watched her. Like a starved cat watching a plump mouse. She smiled to herself. Let him watch all he would, for the good it would do him. He'd have to do more than watch, if her part of their bargain was to be met. Looks alone did not make babes, that she knew of.

She had high hopes that with Andy, God bless him, gone for the while, her husband would be moved to do more than merely look at her. And once he'd made the first move—

She shivered with anticipation. It wouldn't be long in coming now. She could feel it. Could feel herself—sensed *him*—wanting it more with each passing day. Could feel her body softening and straining toward his when they were close. A rush of sensation filled her breasts and loins when he chanced to touch her, be it ever so lightly. She shuddered. As far as she was concerned, it could not be soon enough.

Down by the broad, swift-flowing river, she scrambled over rocks and exposed tree roots, working her way farther and farther downstream until she found a spot where a trio of flat boulders formed a perfect natural scrub-board. It was several yards below where they drew water, too, so that her washing would not sully their drinking supply.

Kneeling, she rolled up her sleeves, then took Drum's shirt from the basket, intending to spread it over the rocks. Instead, she lifted it to her face. Her nostrils flared. The shirt smelled like him. A mixture of salt and sweat, an earthy male scent that was uniquely—tantalizingly—his own. She felt heat flare, deep in her belly.

"Fool!" she hissed under her breath.

She threw herself into her work, scrubbing strong lye soap into grimy seams and ruffled cuffs. As she worked, she thought about Drum's strange reluctance to let her wash his clothes.

She believed she knew why the proud, obstinate brute had refused her offer. To have her do his washing would make her seem more of a wife than he was ready to acknowledge.

*   *   *

Unused muscles protested as Drum swung the axe, deftly splitting dry logs into neat sticks of kindling.

As he chopped, a pair of furry red squirrels chased each other about the woods, ignoring him as if he were just another tree. Their amusing antics made him think about the other wild creatures he'd seen since they came to the wilderness.

The pelts of the wolves, bears and panthers were thick and heavy, a sure sign that the snows were deep, the winters long and harsh, in these parts. More bitter, he believed, than Highland winters.

A satisfied smile curved his lips. That difference aside, the valley continued to remind him of Glen Dunmor, lacking only a fine stone keep to overlook the bonnie land he'd chosen for his own. And there was a perfect site for such a dwelling. A high, flat bluff at the head of the valley offered a breathtaking view of the falls, the woods and the valley spread out below.

It was there he planned to build the fine house in which they would raise their children. And some day, this foreign glen—so far from the Highlands he loved—would ring with the laughter and shouts of a new generation of McLeods, just as Cameron had wanted.

When his first child was born, he would adopt a new motto for the Canadian branch of his clan, too. No longer would his battle cry be "Hold

Fast." From here on, the McLeod motto would be "Survive and Flourish."

He'd tried—many times since they came here—to imagine Rosamund as the mother of that new generation, but he could not see his wee lass as the mother of anything, unless it were the collie, which followed her like a shadow. He smiled to himself. God help him, he had no difficulty imagining himself conceiving those children with her, though!

Night after night he lay awake, reliving the times he'd bedded her. He remembered the feel and shape of her beneath him. How warm she'd felt. How sweetly curved. The taste of her on his lips and tongue. Her tantalizing, feminine scent.

Annoyed at the erotic direction in which his thoughts seemed always to stray of late, he fell to splitting the stack of logs with renewed vigor.

Sweat rolled off him when he finally paused to catch his breath and wipe the stinging sweat from his eyes. He looked around the small clearing, which was strewn with drifts of colored autumn leaves, struck by how much they'd already done; by how much they had still to do.

He was a man who prided himself on doing what he did well, and it pleased him that the large, sturdy cabin they'd raised had an undeniable air of permanence. It was squarely hewn and soundly built, the gaps in its logs well chinked with moss and river-mud to keep out chill drafts. Not far from the cabin was the broad tree stump he'd hollowed out, to form a sort of basin where Rosamund could grind her grain into flour with a stone pestle—once they had crops to harvest and grind. For the time being, it would serve as a handy mortar in which to grind acorns into coarse flour, or to make medicinal powders or teas from the dried leaves and seeds Rosamund gathered. Aye, and the love potions and aphrodisiacs she must surely use to keep herself in his thoughts, he added with a grin.

He shook his head. The lassie was driving him mad, she was. It was a miracle he hadn't chopped off a part of himself, he gave so little thought to the task at hand—and so much to the matter of Rosamund.

He hadn't heard her come back to the cabin. She must still be down by the river, at her washing. His eyes darkened as he imagined her bent over her laundry—including the shirt she'd filched from him—her full breasts and sleek rear jiggling with her movements. *God, how he loved that wee arse. . . .*

One such lusty thought led to other, similar thoughts, and to a now familiar stirring at his groin. He remembered the way she'd looked the evening before, her long damp hair spread over her hands, to dry by the fire. Her cheeks had glowed with its heat, and from her nightly wash.

He shook his head. And her washes every evening bewitched him, too. The blessed ritual of it all was destined to drive a man to madness—if his imagination didn't!

First she filled the kettle with water and hung it on the crane over the fire to heat. Then she brought out the precious scrap of scented French soap—Madame Gaspar's parting gift—which wafted rose perfume to his nostrils; the linen drying cloths; the sea-sponge. Then she made a small but charming fuss of shooing him out of the cabin for a short while so that she might have her privacy.

And when he was again permitted entry, the torture began in earnest, for the fresh, sweet scent of her carried across the cabin to his bedroll all night long. Her tantalizing scent... along with the image of her standing, naked as Eve, before the fire, squeezing a soapy rag over her breasts... the drops of water trickling down her pale curves, poised on the very tips like dewdrops clinging to a rosebud... kept him hard and sleepless most of the night.

Come to think of it, he spent a good part of his days as hard and randy as a buck during the spring rut—and it was all her doing, the minx. This morning, just the sight of her with her skirts hiked up to bare her pretty ankles and calves, and that withy basket jouncing saucily against her hip, had brought home what his body already knew. He wanted her. Lusted for her.

Even now, remembering, seeing her in his mind's eye, he knew there was a marked bulge in his breeches. He only hoped she hadn't noticed it.

Uttering a string of ripe Gaelic curses, he set his jaw and turned back to his wood-chopping, swinging his axe with renewed vigor. Loud thunking sounds rang through the small clearing, drowning out fluting bird calls, scattering the squirrels to their holes.

White wood chips flew and the sweat dripped from him as the pile of kindling grew.

When he'd split several dozen logs, he carried armfuls of kindling to the woodpile against the side of the cabin. There he stacked it neatly beneath the overhang, where it would keep dry.

He was on his way back to the flat tree stump he used for a chopping-block when he heard a terrified scream, followed by Scamp's frenzied barking.

The urgent sounds made his blood run cold. Had it been a panther's snarl—or a woman's frightened cry?

Savages!

Grabbing up his flintlock, he raced down to the river, leaping over tree stumps as he went.

There it was again, that dark flash. It wasn't an animal at all, Rose saw, flicking wet hair from her eyes as she lunged forward and dragged the tiny body toward her. It was a child, strapped to a cradleboard!

She plunged into the river without thinking of

the dangerous, swift current. Ignoring the freezing water, she battled the river's powerful, icy tow to reach the dusky infant that bobbed face down in the shallows, bluish limbs flailing weakly against its beaded turtleshell.

Pulling the cradleboard toward her, she quickly turned it over and tucked it snugly under the crook of her arm. The baby gave no sign of life as Rose battled her way across the current, fighting to reach the bank she had left.

Good swimmer that she was, she was still no match for the powerful river. Slowly, surely, the cold was sapping her strength. Leeching her energy. The powerful current taunted her, letting her gain a little ground and then sweeping her farther and farther into midstream. The rushing white water carried branches and other debris along with it on its headlong flight to the sea.

Drained of strength, frantic for some lifeline, she spotted a willow tree that had fallen into the river and wedged itself between some rocks. It was her last chance.

Just as they were about to be swept past it, she clawed for a handful of its slender branches and hung on tight, letting the river race on without her.

"Help! Heeelp!" Teeth chattering uncontrollably, she clung to her fragile handhold with all her strength, holding the unwieldy cradleboard above water as she screamed.

On the distant bank, Scamp ran back and

forth, barking furiously. *Please God, let Drum hear him, before the babe and I are swept away.*

And then, suddenly, she saw him. He exploded from the forest like a dark arrow, loosed from a bow; tall, bare-chested, his lean, powerful frame silhouetted against the forest. A moment later, he tore off his boots and dived head first into the river, his arms outstretched before him.

His black hair was plastered to his head like an otter's when he resurfaced, breaking through the rushing flow like a ball from a pistol. His sinewy shoulders rippled with muscle as, arm over powerful arm, he cleaved the water, battling the forceful, freezing current to reach her.

His eyes widened when he saw the child. Without a word, he took the cradleboard from her. "Hang on to my belt," he yelled over the river's dull roaring.

She needed no second urging. Fingers hooked over the broad band of leather, she kicked her legs and did what she could to help him tow them back to the shallows.

It took every remaining ounce of their energy to clamber up the shingled riverbank, beyond the water line to safety. Drum appeared little less exhausted than she as he flopped down.

Side by side, they lay on the shingled bank like beached fish, panting heavily. Their chests heaved, and muddy water spewed from their mouths.

As soon as Rose had caught her wind, she

pulled herself up to see to the baby's welfare.

Still breathing heavily, she scrambled to her knees and lifted the child from the cradleboard into her arms.

"Open your eyes, baby. Please, open your eyes," she urged, yet the poor mite was cold and blue in her arms. As limp and lifeless as any rag doll.

"Oh, God. He's drowned," she whispered brokenly. She chafed his plump, chilly little arms, pinched a pudgy cheek, but the tiny face remained bluish beneath the dusky complexion. There was no sign of life whatsoever in the cold, wet little body.

"Is he dead?" she asked Drum anxiously as he pulled himself up, onto his knees.

"I dinna ken, lassie. We'll find out soon enough, aye?"

He took the baby from her and, gripping both of its tiny ankles in one huge hand, upended the infant and slapped it smartly across the buttocks, like a newborn. Once. Twice.

"It works wi' newborn lambs sometimes," he said by way of explanation.

Following each slap, there was a moment of agonizing silence in which Rose held her breath. Her heart almost stopped beating as she waited, waited. And then—miraculously, the infant mewled. Spluttered.

Bubbles of muddy water spewed from its little mouth and ran down its tiny chin. It coughed, then sneezed like a kitten. More water and muck streamed from its nostrils. Two small, furious fists waved, then it turned dark red all over. Its first, kittenish howl quickly became a loud, tigerish bawl of outrage.

About to sniff the newcomer, Scamp yelped and darted backward in surprise. He cocked his ears and barked, his plumed tail wagging.

Rose laughed aloud with joy and relief. "He's alive!"

"He is that. Here. Take the wee salmon." Drum handed the squirming infant to her, grinning despite himself. "Or shall we call him Moses?"

"Moses?" She wrinkled her nose in distaste. "Why on earth would we call him Moses?"

"Because ye took him from the river, did ye no'?"

"Oh! That's right, I did—though I didn't see a single bullrush." Laughing, she hoisted the baby over her shoulder, patting its little bottom to soothe it, cuddling it close to warm it.

The small body squirmed against her own, full of life and vigor.

Scamp growled low in his throat, jealous of the infant who commanded all her attention. The collie pushed closer to her, resting his dappled muzzle on her wet thigh.

"I was scrubbing the clothes when I saw his dark head among the weeds," she explained, wondering why Drum was staring at her so. She felt a sudden need to say something to fill the crackling silence between them. "I—I thought it must be a beaver or an otter at first. Then I saw his little arm waving." She shrugged slender shoulders, shivering uncontrollably as a gust of cold wind blew off the river. "I j-jumped in without thinking."

"Where did ye learn to swim? Not many can, especially not the lassies."

"In Cornwall, as a little girl. Our farm lay close to the beach. Me and my brother used to gather bunches of kelp. The farmers use it to feed the soil, you see. We spent so much time in the water, my Granny used to say my brother and I were half seal, half human."

"Silkies," he murmured with a half smile that transformed his stern, handsome face into something wonderful.

"What did you say?"

"Nothing. Go on."

"Well, I was trying to swim back to shore when the current caught me. Luckily, I managed to grab a willow branch and hang on." She was forced to shout over the baby's wails and Scamp's excited barking.

The red-faced child locked chubby fingers over fistfuls of Rose's wet hair and crammed it into his mouth. Making little coughing noises, he burrowed his head against her shoulder. Despite his strident wails, not a single tear ran down his face.

Drum stared at Rose and the wean, unable to

look away. He had never been able to imagine her as the mother of his children before. But he could now, very well. She looked like the paintings of the Madonna and Child he'd seen in Edinburgh. Radiant. Glowing—though in her case, he fancied it was the cold, rather than the child, that had caused that ruddy glow. This was how she'd look with his child cradled against her. With their bairn tugging at her breast.

An overwhelming tenderness filled him.

"He's after his mam's teat," he observed softly. He had seen bairns at Dunmor rooting against their mothers that way.

"Yes," she agreed. Heat filled her cheeks. She jiggled the infant up and down as she patted his bottom. "There, there. It's all right. Shush, do, dearling. We'll find your mama, never fear."

Drum stiffened as Scamp growled again, his tufted ears pricked, his hackles standing up. The dog was looking at something or someone behind him. He held the dog's collar to keep it from rushing at them and in a low voice ordered, "Turn around, verra slowly, lass. His mam's found us."

Chapter Twenty-one

A Huron brave, an old man, a woman and a little girl, all of them dressed in buckskin, stood shyly by the line of trees where the forest proper began. Like their own, the woman's hair and clothing were wet. They looked startled to see him and Rosamund sitting there.

Slowly Drum stood, bare-chested, with water streaming down his body. He smiled at the party in greeting, extending a hand to the oldest man.

Long gray hair fell loose past the old one's bony shoulders. From a single narrow braid hung metal dangles, pony beads and feathers. The lines in his seamed brown face were carved as deep as knife wounds. But despite his advanced years, his dark-brown eyes were bright with intelligence as he raised his hand to return Drum's greeting.

Drum gestured for Rose to give him the infant. She handed him the squalling baby and watched as he stepped forward and placed it gently in the old man's arms. The grandfather then handed the child to the anxious-eyed woman, uttering a few guttural words as he did so.

As the infant rooted at the woman's breast, his wails became low cooing sounds. His obvious contentment left no doubt that she was his mother.

"Etes-vous français?" the old man asked Drum in a reedy voice.

Drum shook his head.

"Anglais?"

"No, sir. My name is Drummond McLeod. I'm Scottish. *Ecosse.*"

"Ecosse?" The old man nodded sagely. "Your tribe is well known among my people. The Scots, they are takers of furs, neh? But you speak the English tongue. That is good, for I, Two Bears, also speak English. I am grateful to you for the life of my grandson, Red Moon."

The woman must be the old man's daughter. "It is my wife who deserves your gratitude, monsieur. It was she who saw the bairn and pulled him from the river. Not I."

The old man nodded sagely. His rheumy gaze shifted to Rose. He looked her up and down, his lined face expressionless, then grunted approval.

"The heart of Make Clouds Woman is good."
He uttered a guttural command and then nodded to one of the Indian hunters. The bairn's father, most likely.

The brave stepped forward. Close up, he was
even more imposing than from a distance. Most
of his head was shaved. The small circle of hair
that remained had been scraped back into a
horse-tail and divided into long, black braids,
decorated with feathers and beads. His arms and
chest were bare, except for a woven pouch slung
across it, and woven bands worn high on the upper arms. His only garments were a fringed
buckskin breechclout, leggings and moccasins.
But it was his liquid dark eyes, the keen intelligence and fierceness in their depths, and his
striking, hawklike features that riveted Drum's
attention.

With a nod, the brave lifted a small doe off his
shoulders and placed it at Drummond's feet.

"A fine kill, sir. I thank you," Drum said for-
mally, making a small bow. He extended his
hand to the man in thanks.

As the brave clasped it, his snapping black
eyes met Drum's. A thrill ran through him. A
powerful connection had been forged between
them in those few, brief seconds, though the
warrior had said nothing.

The Indian woman approached Rose, the baby
carried on her hip. She clasped Rose's hand in
her own, drew it to her lips and kissed it. "*Merci,*

madame. Merci bien," she murmured shyly. Snatching up the cradleboard, she ran off into the forest. Her father and little daughter followed her.

With an almost imperceptible nod of farewell, the brave turned and followed his little family.

When Drum turned back to Rose, he caught her staring at his bare chest with a strange look on her face. His nipples hardened in response as she quickly looked away, but not before he'd noticed that her cheeks were bright pink.

"Do ye know how t' dress a deer, Rosamund?" he asked casually.

Wrinkling her nose, she grimaced and shook her head. "No."

"Then 'tis time ye learned. And dinna look so down in the mouth. We've enough meat here for a fortnight. That's something t' smile about, aye? Now hand me my shirt, lassie."

"I—um—can't." She looked away, unable to meet his eyes.

"Canna what?"

"Hand you your shirt."

His eyebrows lifted. "And why can ye no', pray?"

"Because I don't have it, that's why," she snapped.

He grinned. "Ye teasing wee besom, hand it over. I ken that ye took it when ye thought I wasna looking."

"I'm not denying that I took it," she hedged,

hugging herself against the chill wind that blew off the river. "In fact, I was scrubbing it when I saw the babe." She swallowed. "I—er—I'm afraid I lost it when I jumped in. Your—your shirt's downriver, McLeod," she finished in a rush.

His gray eyes darkened. His lips thinned. His former good humor vanished like smoke as the day's chill began to seep into his bones. "My shirt's *where?*"

"Down—er—downriver," she repeated in a whisper. It was all she could do to keep from laughing.

"Ye lost my only shirt?"

"Aye! But I didn't mean to. Honestly. It was an accident." Before he could react, she gathered up her sodden skirts and fled upriver to their cabin, cold rat-tails of wet hair slapping behind her as she went. Scamp raced after her.

Once inside the cabin, she shucked off her wet clothes and draped them to dry over stools set before the hearth.

Shivering in only her sheer wet shift, which clung to her like a second skin, she furiously rubbed her hair dry on a linen towel. Her teeth chattered as she moved about the cabin, adding fresh logs to the fire, stoking embers so the flames curled up to lick at the logs.

When she had a fine blaze going, she peeled off her wet shift and draped it over her quilting frame to dry. She was about to wind a blanket around herself when Drummond burst into the cabin.

He came inside to dry off and find something else to wear, expecting Rosamund to be ladling broth into bowls for them both, or perhaps slathering ash-cakes with the butter she'd churned yesterday.

What he had not expected was to find her as naked as Eve in the Garden of Eden, her skin warmed by dancing flames, an invitation in her soft violet eyes.

Take her, a small voice urged. *Lay her down beneath ye, mon, and take her. 'Tis your right, as her husband. 'Tis what she agreed to. Take her. Plant your bairn deep in her belly.*

But instead, he only scowled at her, demanding, "Have ye no decency, woman? 'Tis the middle of the day—and you naked. Dress yersel'." With that, he turned on his heel and left her alone.

"You wretched hypocrite!" she muttered under her breath, but her disgusted expression quickly became a grin. He'd be back—she just knew it—and soon, unless she'd been mistaken.

Drawing her stool closer to the fire, she put on the now dry shift and took up some sewing to do while she waited.

Chapter Twenty-two

When Drummond returned to the cabin a scant half-hour later, she was still perched on the stool by the hearth, wearing only her sheer sark and a blanket draped around her like a shawl. Her skirts and other laundry were hanging over her quilting frame, steaming as they dried.

She must have been staring into the fire before he came in, for her eyes had a fey, dreamy look to them. The heat in their depths made the fire in his loins flare.

Flustered by the naked desire she saw in his face, she quickly looked away.

The flames on the hearth writhed as the autumn wind followed him into the cabin. He halted on the threshold, taking his time in barring the door, uncertain if he should speak, and what to say if he did.

She said nothing. Neither did he. He simply turned and stood there, waiting. His fists were knotted at his sides, his chest rising and falling like a green lad's as he fought to control his breathing. It was thick and unsteady with a mixture of hot, unbridled lust and a fierce hunger too long denied.

When he raised his head, he found her eyes upon him once again, large and luminous as a cornered doe's in the ruddy gloom and the dancing firelight.

"Rosamund," he murmured.

"Oh, Drum," she whispered on a shiver.

He stepped forward. She met him halfway, the blanket falling as her arms went around his neck. Taking her by the upper arms, he pinned her against the cabin wall.

"I want ye, lassie. God help me, I want ye, and I want ye now," he ground out, his handsome face dark with desire.

"But it's the middle of the day, remember?" she teased.

"I dinna care. I must have ye."

"Then take me," she urged, breathing as heavily as he.

She uttered a small cry as he stepped closer and took her in his arms. His hard flanks pinned her against the rough log wall at her back.

"Hold me," she urged, a shudder moving

through her. "Hold me tight. Never let me go again."

She arched her head back, baring her silky throat to his lips, pressing hips and belly against his flanks with the earthy abandon he'd dreamed of.

"Rosamund. Ah, my sweet, sweet lass . . ." Twining a fist in the thick rope of her hair, he drew her head back and feverishly kissed her open mouth, her throat. Tasted her salty sweetness on his lips.

As his tongue danced down the vale between her breasts, his hands stroked her hips, then cupped the taut swells of her derriere.

With a groan, he drew her against him, fitting her silky curves against his aching shaft.

In the firelight, he could see how her breasts had blossomed under her shift. The hard nipples made tiny hillocks in the sheer cloth. There was a dark shadow at the base of her belly, too, where her thighs joined.

Dear God, how he ached to touch, to taste her down there. To feel her writhing beneath his tongue, his lips. To sheath himself deep in the silky heat and wetness he remembered. Unless he had her soon, he'd go mad!

Dropping to his knees before her, he grasped the hem of her shift and slid it up, until the fabric was bunched over her thighs.

Somehow he seemed bigger and stronger, pressed against her this way. Everywhere she looked, everywhere she touched, he was all springy hair, all fiery male heat, all smooth unyielding muscle stretched over bone.

Firelight played over the planes and angles of his rugged face as he knelt at her feet, his forehead pressed against her mound, his hair as dark as spilled ink where it pooled over her pale flesh.

His warm breath fanned her skin. What he was doing with his tongue, his teeth and lips sent shivers shimmying through her.

"Ah, 'tis bonnie ye are, my lass. Aye, and the taste of ye is like clover on my tongue," he murmured.

One hand pressed to her belly, he nuzzled her navel, then her thatch of curls, her silky inner thighs, until her knees went weak with rising passion and threatened to give way.

He must have sensed she could not stand, for he drew her down onto the heap of woolen blankets and furs she had piled before the hearthstones.

"Rosamund," he whispered, pressing her down onto her back. He planted tiny kisses on her knees, the silky flesh of her inner thighs, the moist, velvety petals between them.

Just the low, husky way he said her name made her shiver with delight.

"Do ye ken how much I want ye, lassie? How much I love the taste of ye?" He planted a tiny kiss in the soft nest of golden curls before him.

Darted the tip of his tongue at the exquisite jewel hidden just below.

She flinched as if he'd touched her with a red-hot ember. "Stop. Not there. You must not . . . not again."

Yet she arched up, off the furs, at the first hot dance of his tongue over the trembling flower of her sex. She knotted her fingers in the thick strands of his hair as he drew on that hidden jewel. Whimpers escaped her, trilling like bird-song in the smoky hush.

"Ahh, but ye've a fine wee arse on ye, woman," he murmured in a wicked, husky voice. He splayed his huge hands over her buttocks and squeezed, then slid one hand between her thighs and eased his finger inside her.

"A fine, firm arse and a quim like velvet," he growled huskily. "Warm, wet velvet. I wonder, ma bonnie? If ye dinna want me t' kiss ye here . . . and here. . . . why is it ye're so blessed wet?"

He began to work his finger in and out of her, each time deepening his entry, strumming his thumb over the tiny, swollen bud just above it. He would not stop, not even when she cried out and begged him to take her.

"Ye told me true, did ye no'? Ye were a virgin when I had ye the first time?"

"Yes," she panted, too caught up by what he was doing to care what he was saying. "Oh, God, there, right there . . . *yes*."

"Och, and me too bluidy stupid and blind t'

306

cherish ye for it. Ah, well, then, we'll take it a wee bit slower this time, aye?"

."Slower? No! Don't you dare, McLeod—"

"On your back, now, there's a good girl. Open your legs for your mon, aye."

Smoldering, she lay back. Her curling hair spilled over the blankets. Her shift was rucked up, her thighs spread like a wanton's. Honeyed heat and moisture welled against his fingers when he eased his hand between them.

"Och. I'd say ye're wantin' me awful bad. Are ye no', lassie?" he breathed, stroking in and out. His voice was thick and dark. Potent as whiskey. Smoky as peat from some Highland moor.

"Yes . . . oh, yes . . ." she whimpered.

"I forget, Rosamund. Are ye sharing my bed because you made a vow, or because ye want me, and the pleasure I bring ye?"

"*You*, damn you. You and the—and the pleasure."

With a roguish chuckle, he shoved down his breeches, then peeled her sark off over her head and tossed both garments aside.

"There, now." Braced on his knees between her legs, he looked down at her naked body, his senses bewitched by her beauty all over again.

She shivered under the heated blaze of his smoky eyes and tried to hide her breasts with her hands. But he held her wrists above her head and would not let her.

"Dinna cover yersel', my heart. 'Tis bonnie ye

are, in every part the good Lord made."

Flames danced over her body, turning her glistening nipples to rubies, stroking her flawless skin with shadows of topaz and rose.

His warm breath had made the gooseflesh rise down her arms, as he swept aside her golden-brown curls to bare the tender flesh where throat met shoulder. He kissed and growled and bit her there until she moaned with pleasure. Ducking his head lower, he sucked hard on each carmine peak, his hair pooling like black ink over her breasts. His caresses made her shiver and squirm beneath him.

When he felt the pulse rising from deep within her, he lifted her hips and spread her wide with his sinewy thighs. Hooking her legs over his shoulders, he entered her in one smooth, deep thrust that made her cry out with pleasure.

She kneaded the soft pelts beneath them as he rode her harder, faster, deeper. He maintained the same powerful rhythm until his shaft pulsed. He reared back, his gray eyes closed as he caressed the tiny bud of her passion. Then a great shout escaped him.

Seconds later, she felt the surge and heat as his seed sprang into her, and the pulse of her own climax shimmered through her like summer lightning.

For a moment, neither one of them could speak, they were so short of breath.

"Whist! That was more of a marriage than any

McKinnon spoke over us, aye?" Drum said, panting as he rolled off her. "You're mine now, Rosamund McLeod. My wife in every way."

"Yes," she agreed happily, snuggling against him. "McLeod . . . ?"

"Whist, lassie, you'll call me Drummond hereon or I'll know the reason why."

"All right. Drummond it is, then. May I ask you something?"

He grinned, idly winding one of her curling ringlets about his finger. The way the coil sprang back upon itself once he released it fascinated him.

In the firelight, she had the blurred, rosy look of a woman well loved by her man. To see her that way filled him with pleasure. Aye, and with pride, too, by God.

"Drummond?"

"I heard ye, lass. And right now, with my knees weak and my short-sword spent, ye may ask whatever ye want." He tweaked her nose. "However, I canna promise I'll have strength t' answer ye. Ye near killed me, woman."

She laughed softly at his outrageous claim and softly punched his chest. "Do you always shout when you . . . ?" She blushed. "You know."

His dark brows cocked in surprise. "Why, Mistress McLeod. Did I do that?"

She giggled and leaned up on one elbow to look down at him. She liked what she saw very much, if that pleased little smile she wore was anything to go by. "You wretch. You know you did."

"Naaay, I dinna recall it," he denied, his lambent gray eyes dancing beneath sleepy lids. Grasping her hand, he placed it over his spent shaft and said, "But if ye'll stroke ma short-sword a time or two, we'll find out, shall we no'?"

"Hmmm. Let's," she murmured, and her lashes swept provocatively downward.

A low groan escaped him. "Rosamund?" he whispered, capturing her chin between his thumb and finger, and tilting her face up to his.

"Aye?"

"For myself, I pray 'tis a verra, verra long winter."

"So do I, sir. Oh, so do I."

"Drummond. I have something to tell you," Rose began the following morning as they sat facing each other over the trestle table.

The bowls before them were empty now. They had both wolfed down generous helpings of the oatmeal porridge she'd cooked. Now they were enjoying tin mugs of strong black coffee while the morning's bread baked in the Dutch oven beside the hearth, filling the cabin with a delicious aroma.

"Can it keep till later on, lass? I've a mind to teach ye to shoot this morning, while the weather holds. Ye never know when it'll come in handy. Ye must know how t' defend yerself while I'm off hunting, aye?"

As he spoke, he took up his flintlock, powder horn and everything else he would need for her lesson, and led the way outside. Seconds later, she heard him exclaim in surprise.

She hurried outside and saw that he was holding a fringed buckskin tunic up to his chest. It looked much like the ones the Huron family had been wearing the day before.

"Where did you get that?"

"It was just lying there on the tree stump, neatly folded. This knife and the sheath were with it."

"Is it a gift, do you think? From Two Bears and his family?"

"I believe so. I canna think who else would leave such a thing, can you?" He pulled off the black frockcoat and waistcoat he had put on, lacking any shirt to wear, and pulled on the buckskin shirt, belting it about the waist and tying the knife in its beaded sheath to the belt.

He looked like a woodsman, with his long hair worn loose and the fringes of the shirt fluttering in the breeze.

"Do you think they knew I lost your shirt?"

He grinned and shook his head. "No. It's more likely they pitied the proud white warrior whose woman canna flesh a hide, nor dress a deer, nor sew him a bonnie buckskin shirt."

She punched his chest. "Indeed? Then mayhap the proud white warrior should find himself a beautiful Huron woman to warm his bed," she suggested sweetly.

"Ye dinna mean that. If I did, ye'd be jealous, aye?" he countered. He was laughing as he crowded her up against a convenient tree. Its trunk prevented her escape as he dropped ticklish kisses on her face and neck.

"Me? Jealous? Not in the least."

"But ye would miss me?" He gave her a smoldering look and cupped her breast. Her nipple surged to tingling life beneath the ball of his thumb. "Just a wee bit?"

She swallowed and shook her head. "N-not in the least." Her tone was unsteady, yet her violet eyes shone with laughter. "I'd find myself a handsome Huron brave to take your place."

He slipped his arm around her waist, drew her against him and smiled. "I dinna care t' boast— for I'm not a boastful mon by nature," he explained, his breath hot in her ear, "but I sorely doubt any mon could be better than I was last night. Aye?"

She laughed softly, color filling her cheeks. "Braggart! I hate to admit it but . . . you're right. Nothing could be better than you were last night, sir—except what I have to tell you. Here."

Taking his heavy hand, she placed it over her rounded belly and held it there. "Can you not feel a difference?" she whispered.

He frowned. His dark brows rose. A strange expression filled his face.

"Are ye telling me you're breeding?" He looked as if he would have liked to laugh but was reluctant to hurt her feelings.

"Och, lassie," he began gently. "Did yer mam never explain such things to ye? It takes longer than a night for a lassie t' ken if she's breeding. All in good time, sweetheart." He patted her bottom in patronizing fashion.

She snorted her disgust. "I know enough to know that this babe's been growing in my belly for three whole months now."

"Three months?" His fingers splayed over her belly. A look of wonder crossed his face as he felt the curving fullness beneath the gathers of her skirt.

His heart began to race as his mind acknowledged what his hands had already confirmed. Her roundness was caused by the bairn she carried beneath her heart.

His bairn. Their bairn.

He swallowed. Tears smarted behind his eyes. A part of him that he'd thought dead since last April flickered to life, like a guttering flame on a moon-dark night.

"Say something. Are you happy?" she asked anxiously, her own hand pressed to her belly now, as if to protect their child from his answer.

"Aye, lass. Verra happy," he whispered thickly, gathering her into his arms. "More happy than I ever thought possible." He paused. "Did—did Andy ever tell ye the legend of our fairy flag?"

"Your fairy flag?"

"The fairy flag of the McLeods. 'Tis an old story about an ancestor of mine, one of the McLeods of Dunvegan, it was. He fell in love with a fairy, and had a bairn wi' her."

Her tawny brows arched delicately. "With a fairy?" She laughed.

Eyes twinkling, he nodded. "Aye. And when it was time for the fairy lassie t' return to her magical kingdom, she left behind a wee silk blanket for their bairn. It was made of shimmering gold threads, and was sprinkled with crimson 'elf marks' that had the look o' blood to them. 'Tis said the scrap o' silk had special powers. Ones that the McLeods could use three times t' save the clan from destruction, if it were waved in times of great and genuine peril.

"I'm thinking one o' my clan must have been waving that fairy flag when I stole ye away from London."

"How so?" she asked huskily, moved by the sentiment behind his tale.

"Because if I hadna stolen the wrong lassie and made her my bride, the Dunmor McLeods would have died wi' me."

"That's not true. You would have married someone else."

"I dinna think so, Rosamund," he insisted gravely. "If not for you, I would have ridden off into the wilderness and never come back. I would have steeped myself in a broth of sorrow and never come oot of it. Such men as I was are not long for this world."

Overcome by emotion, he ducked his head and kissed her, holding her so fiercely, so tenderly, she thought she would die from her happiness and the sweetness of it all.

As they kissed, feathery flakes of snow began to fall, blanketing their clearing and the roof of the cabin and powdering the long-needled pines.

Autumn was over. The long, deep Canadian winter had begun.

Drummond's prayer was going to be answered.

"Put up your pistol, sir. 'Tis Maggie Stevenson from the fort. Good evening t' ye, sir."

"Well, well. Look who's come calling, 'Bella. Welcome to our humble abode, mistress. 'Tis Maggie—our old friend Calum Sinclair's sweetheart, is it not?" Tom acknowledged with a smarmy grin, stuffing the pistol back into his belt.

"Aye, sir, it is. I couldna speak wi' ye this morning. My Da'—well, he was none too fond of Calum, aye?"

Tom's smile broadened as he took her hand. "Think nothing of it, my dear. But may I inquire as to the nature of your call upon us?"

She thought she detected an edge to his tone

that filled her with unease, but she was too nervous to consider what it might mean.

"This morning at the fort, before my Da' sent ye packing, ye were asking about an English woman named Rose or Arabella, were ye no', sir?" Maggie breathlessly asked the foxy-faced Englishman. Her plaid shawl drawn up over her dark hair, she darted a glance over her shoulder to make certain no one—especially her father or that nosy Andrew Lewis—had followed her from the fort to where the dark-haired Sassenach and the red-haired woman had made their little camp outside its log walls. She'd get a good walloping from her Da' if he discovered what she'd been up to. Although an ill-tempered man with no liking for the McLeod or his Lewis cousin, he drew the line at betraying a Scot—or his wife—to the hated Sassenachs.

"Aye, luv. I was," the Englishman confirmed.

"This woman you are looking for, is she your wife?" she asked hopefully.

"Me wife? Gawd, no, luv! Rosie's my . . . sister. My very dear, long-lost sister. In't that right, 'Bella?"

"That's right, Tom," the red-haired woman agreed.

She was very beautiful, Maggie decided, but a cold fish by the looks of it. She had an unkempt, unwashed look about her, coupled with a calculating gleam in her hard green eyes. Something about her put Maggie in mind of the prostitutes and doxies she'd seen strutting their wares in Edinburgh.

"Well, I know where she is. I'll—I'll tell ye, for a price."

"A price, eh? How much are you after, girl?" Tom snapped.

"Och, it isna silver I'm wanting. Just for you t' take me back to Quebec with you. So I can be with Calum."

Tom's brows rose. "Miss him, do ye, love?"

"He said . . . he said he loved me," she admitted in a rush. "That he wanted t' marry me. But then . . . something happened. My Da' found out about us, and we were separated. I—I'm carrying his bairn, sir. My Da' will kill me when he finds out, but I canna hide it much longer. Did Calum—Mr. Sinclair—did he send any messages for me?" she asked hopefully.

"God bless you, of course he did, luv. His very last words were to tell his Maggie that he loved and missed her."

"Last words?"

"Before we bade him farewell. And why wouldn't he miss a pretty girl like you? Come over here beside me, luv. Set down and warm yerself while we talk. Hey, you! Move over, you bloody great cow. Make some room for my pretty Maggie here. In a delicate condition, she is." Tom jerked his head, indicating the red-haired woman should move.

'Bella cast Maggie a foul look but shifted herself without protest, while the Englishman sat down beside her.

She was dimly aware that his arm was around her. That he was fondling her backside as she talked.

"The woman and Drummond McLeod have settled some land to the northwest of here. I heard Andrew Lewis describing the valley to Captain McKinnon. He said it's to the north of the river. There's a waterfall just a quarter mile from the cabin with a high ridge, shaped like the prow of a ship."

" 'S that right, Maggie?" Tom said thickly when she was done. His arm was around her now, and he was kneading her right breast. His fingers dug cruelly into her soft flesh "Why don't you and me go inside the tent, eh? You can give me the rest of the directions while I give you the rest of Calum's message, eh?"

"Tom!" the woman warned, shooting him a furious look.

"Shut your yap, 'Bella," Tom growled. Taking Maggie by the hand, he led her toward the tent.

In the opening, she balked. "Please, sir, I dinna think I should—"

"Shouldn't what? Shouldn't go in the tent with me? But I've a message t' give you, remember? From your Calum. A very special . . . very private message, if ye know what I mean." He winked.

"Oh. Then I suppose it would be all right. But only for a little while. My Da'—"

"It'll be more than all right, luv," Tom promised, his eyes hot and rapacious. "You'll see."

Andy's eyes narrowed when Margaret Stevenson returned to the barn, where he and Kirsty's wedding celebration was in full lively swing.

The guests were dancing to the music of fiddles, fifes and drums, and there was a great quantity of good food and an excess of strong drink. While no one was overly fond of Angus Stevenson, no man could accuse him of pinching pennies when it came to his niece's wedding.

Father Andreas, the Jesuit priest, had married Andy and Kirsty earlier that evening. He was looking forward to his wedding night, and eager for the high-jinks of the revelers to be done with. Still, there was something about Margaret's furtive departure from the barn an hour ago, and her reappearance a few moments ago, that made him give her a second glance.

The lass had a dazed, crushed look to her, like a whipped hound. Her eyes apeared glazed, while her mouth was swollen and turned down. Even her clothing had a rumpled air to it, as if someone had . . . Nay, surely not?

"Your wee cousin's awful quiet t'night," he murmured to Kirsty. They had just concluded a lively reel, their first as man and wife, and had retired to the buffet tables for a well-deserved cup of punch.

His bride was red-cheeked and glowing as she

sipped. Her strawberry blond hair had escaped its neat coil and the pretty lace cap to frame her grave, sweet face in shining tendrils. "Perhaps she's up to no good," he suggested.

Kirsty sighed. " 'Tis possible, but she's probably still sulking."

"About our wedding?"

The new Mistress Lewis frowned. "It's not just that. Maggie wanted to talk to the English couple this morning."

"What English couple?"

"The ones who rode in from Quebec this morning. But you know how my Uncle Angus is. He told the poor thing to tend to her own business, and wouldna let her speak with them. He has been so stern with her since that business with Sinclair." She sighed. "I don't know how she'll endure keeping house for Uncle with me gone."

"Whoa, lassie. Say again. What English couple?" Andy persisted. "Do you know who they were?"

"I don't believe they gave their names. They came to Uncle's blacksmith shop looking for your cousin's wife."

Andrew's head snapped around as if jerked on a chain. "They asked for Lady Rosamund by name?"

"Aye. Rose, they called her. The man said he was her brother, I do believe. I think the woman was his wife."

Rose's brother must have come in search of her! What had his name been? "Was his name Jim? Jim Trelawney?"

"Forgive me, Andrew, but I really couldna say," Kirsty apologized. "They were here for only a few moments. If I remember correctly, they asked after Rosamund, then inquired where they might find Maggie. They said they had a message for her from Calum Sinclair in Quebec. Well, of course, the mere mention of the man's name was enough to set off my uncle's wretched temper. He bade the pair get back on their horses and be gone in no uncertain terms."

"And they left? Just like that?"

"Aye. They could be anywhere by now. Uncle Angus said that their sort were not welcome at Fort Charles. That if they knew what was good for them, they'd leave, Calum Sinclair's messages be da—. Well, I expect you can guess what my uncle said," she amended hurriedly with a pretty blush.

"Och, I ken," Andrew admitted with feeling, his sudden scowl softening as his bride favored him with another of her sweet, shy smiles. "I still remember how the auld devil bellowed when I first asked him for your hand."

"And I. You were very brave, Andrew. A veritable St. George braving the dragon."

"I was, wasn't I?" he agreed, grinning. "But then, look what I had t' gain. It was well worth braving the old dragon, t' claim the bonnie princess as my bride."

She laughed. "What a flatterer you are, Master Lewis."

"It's not flattery, Mistress Lewis. It's the truth. I still canna believe we're marrit, my love," Andy murmured, taking her hand in his and looking down at her. "I love ye, princess."

"I love you, too, Andrew."

He was about to steal a kiss from his bride when a tipsy James Gordon hooked him roughly by the arm and swung him around.

"Whoa, laddie! Watch yersel'!" he protested, trying to throw off Jamie's hold.

A young woman had also grabbed Kirsty by her arm, and was dragging her away to where a crowd of other young women awaited.

"Whist, now, Andrew. 'Tis high time the happy couple were tucked snugly into their marriage bed—and who better than their good friends t' escort them to it, aye? Another dram for the bridegroom, Alistair, you old skinflint. Aye, and some watered wine for the bride. 'Twill lend her the courage for the bedding—and God knows, the lucky lass will need it," Jamie said with a bawdy wink. "'Tis said all the Lewis men are most generously endowed. Is that not so, Andrew?"

Andy laughed, Maggie and the English couple quite forgotten as he gave Kirsty a shrug and a grin.

He and his bride were lifted up onto the shoulders of the noisy revelers and paraded around the torchlit barn.

Soon, my love, he promised silently as his eyes met Kirsty's. *Let them have their sport. Soon they will leave us alone. After tonight, we'll have the rest of our lives together. . . .*

Chapter Twenty-three

As November became a bitterly cold December, Rose and Drummond were forced to accept that, for whatever reason, Andy would not return until the spring. It could be March, or even April, before they saw him again.

"He should ha'e been back long ago," Drum murmured, his face grave with concern. "I pray to God he wasna killed by hostiles."

Rose slipped her arms around his waist and pressed her cheek against his back. "I'm sure Andy's fine, my love." She smiled. "And he'll be even better when he finds out that we're together, with a baby on the way. Your cousin is something of a matchmaker, I believe. He enjoys playing Cupid, as my dear Miss Pennington would have said."

"Who's Miss Pennington?"

"My former teacher. Don't you remember the way he looked at us that last evening? You said he'd surely want to be back at New Dunmor before winter set in. But when he looked from me to you, the strangest expression came over his face."

"It did?"

"Aye. I think he decided not to return until the spring right then and there. He wanted to give us the chance to be alone here together. To get to know each other."

"And perhaps he planned to do a wee bit of courting of his own while he was at the fort, aye? The lovely Mistress Kirsty McLachlann willna wait forever, after all. And pretty young lassies are in short supply at Fort Charles." He grinned.

She nodded. "He would never have left Kirsty in the first place if not for his loyalty to me."

"I dinna ken what the laddie was thinkin' of, lettin' you traipse after me. But I'm verra glad ye found me," he murmured, slipping his arms about her waist and drawing her against his chest.

She murmured agreement. She had cherished these months spent alone with Drummond. The past and their stormy beginnings were firmly behind them now, where they belonged. Their affection for each other was gradually deepening into a love that would, God willing, last a lifetime, and be strengthened by both the joys they shared and the adversity they endured, side by side.

Rose had never been happier. She had a man she loved, a baby on the way, a snug home and the beautiful land she'd always dreamed of. What more could she ask for? If Drummond had never said he loved her, it did not mean that he didn't care. Just that he could not bring himself to say so aloud. Besides, he showed his love for her in so many other little ways, she did not need to hear him say the words.

When she heard the cabin door open at dusk two days before Christmas, she was stirring the pot of stew she always kept simmering over the fire now that winter had drawn in. A cold current of air eddied about her ankles.

Thinking it was Drum, who'd gone up into the hills to find a wild turkey for their Christmas supper, she gave a shudder but didn't look up from her task.

"Welcome home, my love. Brrr. It's freezing out there. Come in and warm yourself," she urged over her shoulder.

"Don't mind if we do, Rosie."

She spun around, dropping the ladle in her shock. The blood drained from her face.

A man and an auburn-haired woman stood on the threshold, snowflakes swirling around them.

The man wore a battered hat pulled down low over his eyes, and a ragged bearkskin coat that reached to his ankles. Despite the heavy black stubble on his jaw, she would have known him anywhere.

"Tom. Tom Wainwright!" she breathed, her tone incredulous.

"That's right, luv. Good old Tommy boy, all the way from London Town." His eyes were wet black stones in the cabin's gloom. "Happy t' see me, are you?"

"O-of course I am. I'm just . . . surprised. How . . . how ever did you find me?" she asked breathlessly. Forcing a dazzling smile, she prayed that she looked and sounded happy to see him.

"How did I find you?" He snorted his disgust. "Don't gimme that, you lying, thieving little slut, not after I followed you halfway around the bleedin' world! You didn't want me t' find you, ever. You thought you and yer fancy man could rob ole Tommy blind an' get away with it, didn't you, Rosie, gel?"

"Don't talk daft, luv. Of course I wanted you to find me," she insisted. "Why wouldn't I? I always had a soft spot for you, Tommy, luv. You know that."

Wainwright snorted. "You, soft on me? Not bloody likely. I know you, my gel. I know what you're trying to do now—and it won't work. You always thought you were too good for the likes of me, didn't you, Mistress Rosie?"

His hand came out like a striking snake. He stroked her throat, making her flesh crawl—then splayed his fingers across it and cruelly squeezed. "Where are the Eyes of the Tiger, you thievin' little bitch?"

"Timbuktu, for all I care!" she lied, abandoning her act and trying to twist free of his grip. "Truth is, they were gone long before I boarded that ship back in London. So if you came for the emeralds, you've wasted your time."

With a shriek, the red-headed woman suddenly lunged across the cabin. Her voice was as harsh and coarse as a costermonger's in the market as she rounded on Rose. Her eyes were colder, harder than the emeralds.

"Don't gimme that. We know you got 'em somewhere. You told Kitty O'Brien you had the goods, before you scarpered. If they weren't at Riverside, then they must be here, with you. So, either you tell us where you've hidden 'em or your fancy man dies."

"Just like poor ole Jim, eh, 'Bella?" Tom taunted with a gloating sneer. "Kicked the bucket, Jim did, Gawd rest his soul. So did your friend Calum Sinclair. Took a looong swim off a short pier, poor Calum did. Of course, we helped 'em."

Again that sly, quick grin.

"So. If you don't tell us everything we want ter know, Rosie Posie, me and 'Bella will 'help' you and yer fancy man, too. *Promise*."

After his casual comment about Jim's death, she heard nothing more Tom said. They had killed her brother. Jim was dead. *Oh, God.* She had suspected he could be, but a part of her had hoped she was wrong. That Tom had spared him.

Her heart began to beat very fast. She was trembling uncontrollably, but somehow she managed to get her limbs under control. Forced them to obey her. She couldn't let Tom or the woman see how deeply they had wounded her. *Put it aside for now, Rosie. Put it aside,* she told herself. *Think only of the baby. Think of Drum.*

"What did you do to my husband?" she asked Tom, her voice breaking.

"He's taking a nap, luv—for the time being. Whether it becomes a permanent nap depends on you, and whether we find the stones," he rasped. "So sit your arse down!"

Tossing caution to the winds, she made a mad dash for the door. But before she could get past him, Tom's arm shot out and hooked around her. He jerked her up against him, his forearm braced across her windpipe, cutting off her breath.

"I won't tell you anything. Not until I've—"

"Sit, blast ye!" Tom snarled. Releasing her, he shoved her down onto a three-legged stool.

She had no choice but to sit there and seethe as she massaged her swollen belly. No choice but to watch helplessly while the pair methodically ransacked the cabin she had worked so hard to make a home.

They plucked her and Drum's clothes from the wooden pegs where they were hanging and rummaged through them, tossing them down and trampling them carelessly underfoot when they did not find what they were looking for.

They slashed open the sacks that held their precious provisions. Dried meat, grain, flour, salt and dried apples spewed out onto the planks. They emptied barrels of cornmeal and flour, sifting through the powdery contents for the emeralds.

While Arabella kept a pistol trained on her, Tom climbed the ladder to search the tiny loft where Andy slept.

Bits of straw drifted down like snow as he emptied out the ticking pallet and sifted through its straw stuffing, wisp by wisp.

Rose hugged herself about the arms, well aware of the baby's sudden burst of activity in her belly. Poor little baby. It was frightened, too. But the pair could search all they wanted. They wouldn't find the emeralds, no matter how hard they looked. Once they'd convinced themselves she was telling the truth, and that the emeralds weren't hidden anywhere in the cabin, what would they do? Would they leave, and not come back? Or would they be so angry they would . . .

Swallowing, she left the thought unfinished, trying not to think about Jim and what they'd done to him. Nor how easily they could do the same to her, if the fancy took them. If she thought about that, she knew she'd panic, and she couldn't afford that. She didn't dare become reckless, not when she had the baby and her husband's safety to think about.

Dear God, please let Drum be all right.

The woman gave a low crow of delight when she found the jeweled rings in the deep pockets of Rose's old petticoat. Those pockets were where she'd stowed the loot from Arabella's jewel coffer so many months ago.

"Still no sign o' the emeralds, luv?" Tom asked, tearing into a biscuit as he slit the tick covering of Rose's prized feather bed with a knife.

Goosedown billowed from the bed like snowflakes, one curling feather caught incongruously in Tom's sooty hair, she noticed. It took all of her willpower to sit there and not spring at him. In her hurt, her fear and grief, she wanted to strike out, to claw his face and pound her fists against his chest. To hurt him as deeply as he had hurt her. This must be what Drum had felt, she thought. This burning rage. This unquenchable fury to avenge a loved one's death.

"Nah. Not a one," the woman confirmed angrily. "Just some rings and earbobs. I reckon she's stashed the emeralds elsewhere." Arabella scratched her hennaed head, the ends of which had grown out, revealing roots of a muddy brown shade. " 'Strewth! When I think of all the bleedin' nights I lay beneath that ugly, fat pig. Of all the times I shared His Grace's bed, pretending I enjoyed his attentions—and for what? For nothing, that's what! If that little slut's hidden the emeralds here, I can't bleedin' find 'em, Tommy. You think she's telling the truth?"

"Yes! I told you the emeralds weren't here," Rose repeated.

Quick as a flash, Tom's cruel fingers knotted in the neckline of her clothing. The force of his grip lifted her off the stool. She hung there by her gown, the cloth twisted about his fist. It was wound so tightly it cut off her breathing.

"Damn you, Rosie." Tom's black eyes blazed. He thrust his swarthy face—no longer handsome, but contorted in fury—full into hers. His spittle sprayed her cheek when he spoke. "I should bleedin' kill you for doublecrossing me, gel!"

"I didn't doublecross you. I was *kidnapped*," she croaked. "At pistol point. What was I supposed to do?"

"That's a load of cock and bull! You expect me to believe that?" Tom snarled, squatting down beside the stool. "When it's the same bloke you're with now? And like as not, his bastard in yer belly? Don't make me laugh, Rosie Posie. Old Tommy's no fool—and only a fool 'ud believe that. You and him planned it from the start, didn't you? Come on. 'Fess up, my girl!"

"Believe what you want. I told you the truth.

Hey, you wretched harpy! Get out of my things!"

The woman was holding the violet-sprigged gown Rose had sewn for the *céilidh* up to her own buxom figure. When she started unfastening her sorry cloak to put it on, Rose wanted to leap at her and wrest the garment from her paws.

But Tom's grip did not slacken. In the end, she was forced to sit there, silent, sullen and fuming, her throat sore, while his woman stole her gown.

"Ye'd best guard that sharp tongue o' yours, my gel," Tom cautioned. He waggled a finger at her as he straddled one of the two straight-backed chairs Drum had made. " 'Bella's quality. She ain't used to being spoke to that way."

" 'Bella? *Ara*-bella? You mean, she's Cumberland's wh—"

"*Was*, love. Was," he cut in, grinning like the old Tom she remembered. "Right after she was mine."

Suddenly, understanding dawned.

"You used us, didn't you?" Rose exclaimed softly. "I—or maybe Jim?—was meant to take the drop for the Riverside robbery all along. You and she were supposed to get away with the emeralds, but we were to be the ones hanged for it. That's why Andy saw you with the guard that evening. You needed a—a thief to divert suspicion from her," she cried, "after I'd given the emeralds to you."

"Clever gel," Tom approved, jerking the long

muzzle of the flintlock in her direction. "Now, instead of yapping, dish us up some grub. And look lively about it, ducks. Ain't no telling what I might do to your man if I get angry. Or to you, either, come to that."

In short order, the pair had slurped down half the Dutch kettle of savory rabbit stew she'd made for Drum's supper.

Although it was an effort to swallow over the painful lump in her throat, Rose forced herself to eat, too. She'd be stronger, faster, more alert, with a little food in her belly. Besides, when Tom and Arabella saw her eating too, they'd know she hadn't tried to poison them. Perhaps that would encourage them to eat more. And with full bellies and a warm fire, there was a good chance they'd fall asleep, and then . . .

After they'd eaten, the pair drew closer to the warmth of the fire, as she'd hoped. One kept a desultory watch over her as she lit a stub of tallow and bent her head to some sewing. The other dozed.

The candle stub seemed to burn down very quickly. Time stood still as she sewed and waited, sewed and waited.

The side seam and hem of the infant gown were almost finished and her eyes ached with strain when she heard Tom snoring at last.

She waited until Arabella was also sound asleep, her jaw slack, before standing.

Heart in her mouth, she gingerly tiptoed between the sleeping bodies, edging her way to the door.

She was about to lift aside the wooden bar that Tom had replaced when she remembered the flintlock. Drum's Brown Bess.

Edging back to where Tom sprawled, deeply asleep, she saw the firearm's muzzle. Oh, no! The weapon was wedged solidly beneath him. There'd be no moving it, not without waking him up.

Abandoning her efforts, she crept back to the door. First she'd find Drum, she told herself, and then they could decide what to do with the pair.

She'd unbarred the door and was about to lift the latch when Tom's menacing voice rang out so suddenly she flinched.

"Stop right there, Rosie. Twitch a bloomin' muscle and I'll blast yer bleedin' head off. So help me, I will!"

She froze.

"Stir yourself, 'Bella. I've had enough of this. If Rosie Posie won't talk on her own, it's time we helped her out." His eyes glittered. "I know some tricks that'll make her sing like a bloomin' nightingale."

Chapter Twenty-four

Rose was licking his face!

Drum groaned and tried to move his head to escape her rough, persistent tongue. Demons were hammering nails into his skull. The pounding was making him feel sick and dizzy.

"Whist, lassie, have done wi' ye. Let me sleep for a bit, aye?" he grumbled.

But the wee rascal wouldna stop. Rather, she whined low in her throat, entreating him to wake up, then licked him again.

Whined? He opened an eye just as Scamp's long tongue swiped across his face again.

Groaning, he opened both eyes, startled to see a frosty, star-studded sky above him. His teeth chattered. Blessed Mary, it was so bluidy cold!

And what the devil was he doing here, in the snowdrifts between cabin and barn? Had he and Rosamund quarreled? Had she tossed him outside on his arse t' sober up?

Belatedly, he felt the bloody gash at his temple, the pounding ache in his badly bruised shoulder, and remembered a glimpse of a handsome lass with red hair and eyes as hard as emeralds. Seconds later, lights had exploded in his skull and everything had gone black.

He must have been clouted from behind. That meant there had been two of them, at least. He looked around for his flintlock, but it was nowhere to be seen. They had taken it.

The snow-covered clearing was sparkling white, ringed by dark-green forest. It was lit as brightly as by day, thanks to a full moon.

The white terrain lurched as he struggled to stand up, rocking on his heels as he stared at not one, but two cabins. Mercifully, the pair came together and blended into one as he stared at them.

Not a sound escaped the sturdy dwelling. It was as silent as a tomb. *Sweet Lord, what had they done to Rosamund?* If they'd hurt her—if they'd harmed the bairn she carried—he'd kill the bastards with his bare hands, inch by inch, he swore.

Scamp lay at his feet. His brown eyes were dulled. His sides heaved. Muffled whimpers of pain escaped him.

The game little collie must have tried to protect him. His attackers had injured the dog badly, probably by kicking it. But somehow the game collie had managed to revive him. He was not about to leave him out here to die in the snow.

He pulled himself up and carried Scamp into the shed where the horses and two strange mounts were stabled. Then, taking two empty grain sacks, Drum sprinted back to the cabin, drawing a long, sturdy log from the woodpile as he went. It wasn't Brown Bess—the intruders had taken the flintlock—but if his idea worked, it would serve.

Rose coughed. Her throat burned and her eyes watered, but with her wrists tied behind her back, she could not rub them or shield them.

Tom reached for the poker. The end was red-hot, where he had heated it in the fire. He shot her a look of eager anticipation and stirred the fire's glowing embers.

Sparks showered over the hearth as a log dropped down.

"So. What's it to be, Rosie? Will ye tell me what you've done with the emeralds, or will I have to hurt you, eh?"

He held up the poker. The last three inches glowed reddish orange. He reached out, bringing the red-hot tip so close to her cheek she could feel the heat it gave off from several inches away.

"I can't tell you what I don't know," she whispered, closing her eyes.

"Don't gimme that. You know where they are. Did you sell 'em—is that it?"

Thick billows of smoke poured from the fire.

"What's all this bloody smoke, then?" he growled, turning back to the fire. He coughed. "Do something, gel! A body can't breathe in 'ere."

Arabella was coughing, too. They both were. Like Rose's, their eyes streamed.

"What do you want me to do? My hands are tied," Rose reminded him. "Something must be wrong with the chimney. A bird must have fallen down it or something. It's not drawing. I might be able to clear it if you untied my hands." She doubled over in another coughing fit.

"Never mind her. Open the bleeding door, Tom. I'm choking to death in here," Arabella rasped.

"So the gel can scarper? The devil I will," Tom said, but he soon had no choice in the matter. Arabella was complaining loudly that her lungs were afire, her eyes burning. He couldn't draw a decent breath himself, nor open his streaming eyes, the acrid smoke in the cabin was so thick.

"Let's get out of here, Tom. I—aaagh! aaagggh!—I've had enough o' this smoky hole," Arabella said, tears streaming down her cheeks.

"All right, love. Grab them blankets and let's go. You! On your feet," he ordered Rose, gripping her wrist so cruelly she thought the delicate bone would snap. "You're coming with us."

He unbarred the door.

Arabella spilled blindly from the cabin, drawing greedy gulps of clean, frosty air as she staggered out into the snowy clearing.

As Tom followed, dragging Rose after him, a log arced down from the sky. It landed across his skull with a noisy "thwack." He grunted and then toppled sideways, dropping the heavy flintlock and releasing her as he fell.

Drum leaped down from the roof after the weapon as Rose wrenched her arm free of Tom. He leveled the flintlock's muzzle at the pair, before Tom could scramble to his feet. Blood trickled down his sooty cheek as he swayed there.

"I should blow your bluidy heads off!" Drum ground out, his features hard in the wan dawn light. "But I willna waste my shot on your miserable carcasses. Take your nags and go, before I change my mind!"

The pair needed no second urging. Casting Drum wary looks, they hastily mounted up and rode from the shed. Within moments, they'd vanished into the wintry night as if they'd never been.

"And a bluidy good riddance, too," he yelled after them. "Blessed Mary, will ye look at you, lass!" he exclaimed as Rose flung herself into his arms.

Her face was black with soot, except for the two white rings of her eyelids. Laughing, he licked the ball of his thumb and tried to wipe the smudges from her cheeks.

"Ye look like a bogle, lassie!"

She punched him in the chest. "You! What's a bogle?"

"Somethin' ye might see in a kirkyard on All Hallows Eve."

"Never mind that. Oh, Drum!" she cried. "Thank God you're all right." She went up on tiptoe to plant kisses all over his face. "I was so afraid they'd hurt you."

"Ye're telling me, lassie. It was so blasted quiet in there, I thought the bastard had killed ye," he whispered raggedly. "Smoking them out was the only thing I could think of." He grinned. "It works with bees. Lucky for us, it works wi' Sassenachs, too."

She stuck her tongue out at him, silly with relief. "They wanted the emeralds. That man was Tom Wainwright, the one I told you about, remember? The woman—the woman was Arabella Slater." Her smile faded. "She's the one you were looking for, Drum. Cumberland's mistress. The woman you thought—the one you mistook me for. I—I—"

To his dismay, she burst into tears.

"Shoo, shoo, lassie. Never mind Arabella, or whatever her bluidy name is. She's no' important. You and the bairn, ye're all that matter t' me. What's wrong wi' ye, lovie?" He grasped her chin and tilted her face up to his. "I've never seen

341

ye greet like this before. Did they hurt ye, is that it?"

Her lower lip trembled. She blinked back tears. "Tom killed him, Drum. He killed my brother. Jim's dead."

"Ah, God. The clarty bastard," he said vehemently, drawing her close. He held her, gently stroking her hair and rocking her till she'd cried herself out.

She was shivering from a combination of shock and cold when he shook her gently. "Go on inside and get warm now, love. It's freezing out here."

"B-but the fire's not drawing," she told him through chattering teeth, hunching her shoulders.

He grinned. "I ken it isna. The smoke was my doing, aye? It'll be fine when I take the sacks out of the chimney. Go on now. I'll be right in."

As soon as he barred the door behind him, she fell into his arms. "Oh, Drum." She shuddered. "Hold me. Never let me go again."

"I'll do better than that, woman," he promised. Pulling her into his arms, he kissed her with an ardor that left her breathless, backing her across the room and down onto their ruined bed.

"Oh, Drum. I never thought I'd see you again," she whispered as she lay beneath him amidst drifts of fluffy down feathers, stroking his dear, cold face. There was a trickle of dried blood on his brow, but other than that and being chilled, he seemed unharmed. She would warm him, she promised herself. They would warm and comfort each other for the rest of their lives, no matter what.

"No more did I. Dear God, how I want ye, lassie. I want ye powerful bad." His gray eyes blazed.

"I want you, too." She lay back and drew up her skirts. "Hurry," she urged, holding out her hands to him. Her eyes were deep, dark violet with desire as he knelt between her thighs. "I can't wait. I want you inside me *now*."

Shucking off his breeches, he spread her thighs with his knees and eased into her.

His powerful, sinewy shoulders blocked out the flickering play of the firelight as he began to thrust, rocking back and forth to deepen his entry. He filled her sight, her senses, as exquisitely as he filled her body.

With a low murmur of pleasure, she curled her arms about his chest, crying out as he buried himself to the hilt inside her.

This would be no leisurely mating. She knew it, welcomed it, wanted it that way. Fast. Fierce. Hard. Deep. He ached for her. She ached for him. Her blood sang, swift and hot, to his lusty blood. Soft flesh yearned for his hard flesh.

They came together in a dance as old as time, desire heightened by the danger they'd escaped, and by their fear of losing each other. Their fierce coupling was an affirmation of lusty, vigorous life by those who had felt death's breath upon their necks, yet had lived to tell of it.

Their heavy breathing, the slap and slide of flesh against naked flesh, pervaded the smoky gloom. Their murmured endearments grew huskier, thicker, as Drum thrust into her time and time again.

Sometimes he leaned back and slipped his hand between her legs to tease the tiny coral jewel that lay hidden within the swollen petals of her womanhood. She sobbed and begged him to hasten her climax. Implored him to hurry, to bring her to speedy release.

Instead, he slid his hands under her delectable bottom to lift her higher, to hold her fast. And with every powerful thrust, he drove harder, deeper, into the slick, hot sheath between her legs.

He filled her, stretched her to the limit, until she arched upward, bent like a bow beneath him. A low moan escaped her as her body spasmed in pleasure.

The smoke and pine-scented gloom fractured. Colored lights shattered across her closed eyelids. Fireworks splintered the shadows.

"Drum! Oh, Drum—!" she sobbed.

A liquid pulse ripped through her body with all the force of a whirlwind, yet left stillness and bone-deep contentment in its wake.

Her name fell like a hoarse prayer from his lips as he reached his own climax, buttocks clenching as he pumped to fill her one last time.

In the quietness that followed, he rolled from her and pulled a blanket up over their damp bodies. Drawing her against him, he pressed her lips to her shoulder.

"Did I hurt ye?" He splayed his hand over her swollen belly. "Or the bairn? I was so afraid I'd lost ye, I couldna think past havin' ye."

"We're both fine." She placed her hand over his. "There. Do you feel him moving? He's strong. Like his Da'."

"He?"

"Our son." The words trembled on the darkness between them. Golden. Honey-sweet. *Our son.*

He smiled. "Or daughter."

She shook her head, smiling mysteriously in the shadows as she snuggled against him. "It's a boy. I feel it here," she explained, touching her heart.

The baby chose that moment to kick. They both felt the sudden movement and laughed.

He drew her earlobe gently between his teeth. "Clever laddie. He agrees with his mam."

"What name shall we give him, Drum?"

He pursed his lips in thought. "In my family, the firstborn lad is named for his dam's kin. My mam was a Cameron, Catriona Cameron. So my brother was Cameron McLeod. I was named for my father's mam, my Granny Janet Drummond."

"You mean our son must be Trelawney Mc-Leod?"

"Aye. 'Tis a bonnie name, I'm thinking."

"For a girl, mayhap. But not for a man—and that's what he'll be, some day." She wrinkled her nose. "I think we should name him after our two brothers. Cameron James. Do you like that?"

"Aye, I like it fine," he agreed softly, seeing the tears that glistened in her eyes.

For several moments, they lay curled together in companionable silence. As their breathing slowed to normal, he could feel the babe moving in her belly, fluttering beneath his hand. The wonder of that new life, hidden yet undeniably real and alive, awed him.

Rose broke the drowsy silence first.

"Drum?"

"Aye, my love?"

"Do you think Tom and that woman are really gone for good?" She sounded doubtful.

"I hope so. But we'll be extra careful till we're sure, aye?" He enveloped her small hand in his large one and squeezed.

"They ruined so much of our stores. It was all my fault. You told me to bar the door behind you, but I didn't. I—I thought you'd only be gone a short while," she blurted out.

"I'm t' blame, too. I should have been on my guard. But, thank God, they didna kill us and they didna take everything we had. We'll manage, lassie," he soothed her.

She sniffed, and he knew she was close to tears again. The coming bairn made her prone to bouts of crying.

"Och, hinny, dinna cry. Dinna fash yerself. The bairn's unharmed. We're unharmed. It could have been worse, aye?"

He asked himself what more he could say or do to comfort her, and knew, in his heart of hearts, that there *was* something more he could say—but did not.

Those three dangerous little words were locked deep inside him. And, try as he might, he could not force himself to utter them.

Tomorrow, he promised himself, drawing her into the curve of his body. He wrapped his arms tightly about her and buried his face in her hair. *Tomorrow I'll tell her how much I love her.*

Chapter Twenty-five

"Rosamund, we need t' talk," he began one bitterly cold morning.

"Aaah. That explains the scowl you're wearing," Rose said with a smile that hid the sudden sinking feeling in her belly.

Setting a large wooden bowl and a horn spoon on the table before him, she straightened and kneaded the small of her back as she went to fetch the honey and cream for her own porridge. Unlike Drum, who wolfed down vast quantities of porridge seasoned only with salt, she preferred hers sweet and creamy.

Dawn had hardly broken, yet she had been up for over an hour already, cooking the morning porridge, bundling up to go outside into the frigid morning to milk their cow. But unlike other mornings, her back was aching today. A nagging ache.

For a moment, her fears surfaced. How could she think of giving birth to their child all alone, out here in the wilderness, with only Drum to attend her? Her mother had died of complications following childbirth, even though she'd had an experienced country midwife in attendance.

Fears crowded her mind like dark moths fluttering to a flame. She tried to thrust them away. Surely acknowledging such fears was dangerous. It served only to make them more real. Confidence, that was the secret, she had decided. She would think only good thoughts, strong thoughts, and nothing bad would happen.

"Eat your porridge," she fondly urged her husband, dropping a kiss on his hair. As usual, it was neatly clubbed back in a queue. She sniffed and smiled in pleasure. He always smelled of soap, for like her, he washed himself every morn and night, despite the hour and despite being tired, and regardless of whether the water in the jug was cold. Cold? Ha! As often as not, it had a layer of ice on it, now that they were nearing the end of January.

They had welcomed in the New Year—*Hogmanay*, as Drum called it—with a dram of whiskey for her husband and a mere drop of the same swimming in a hot milk posset for herself, she remembered as she brushed an unruly lock off his brow.

"If that dark expression is aught to go by, I'd sooner hear whatever you have to tell me on a full stomach."

"Our stomachs are what we need to discuss, lassie," Drum began gravely. "As you know, Wainwright and his woman destroyed more of our provisions than we could afford to lose. By my figuring, what we salvaged will last only a fortnight more. I dinna want to leave ye, but it would be best if I went now, rather than wait until you're closer to your time, aye?"

"You're going back to the fort?"

He nodded, grateful she'd said it for him. "Aye."

"Without me." But even as she said it, she knew what his answer would be. What it *must* be. In her condition she would slow him down. He had to go alone.

"Aye." He reached across the table and squeezed her hand. "You're in no condition t' travel, love. The snow's too deep. It'll be hard enough for me and the horse, as it is. For a lassie sae heavy wi' child . . ." He shrugged broad shoulders.

She nodded. "You've no need to explain yourself to me, McLeod. I understand. Besides, I have Scamp to keep me company, don't I, boy?" she added brightly, forcing a smile as she patted the dog's silky black-and-white head, which was resting, as always, on her moccasined foot.

The little collie never strayed far from her side now. Nor did he often leave the warm nest of wood shavings she'd made for him in a basket beside the hearth. Tom Wainwright's vicious kick had broken something inside the poor little beast. It was a deep hurt that neither time nor her sparse healing skills had been able to mend. She had resigned herself to keeping him comfortable until the end came, and to asking Drum to put him out of his misery if he ever seemed in pain.

"When will you be back?" she asked levelly, fondling Scamp's silky ears.

"If I leave tomorrow morning, in about ten days, God willing." He reached across and placed his hand on her swollen belly. It was as round and taut as a drum with the vigorous new life they'd created, and doubt filled him. "Ye said the bairn willna be born for over a month yet. Are ye certain of that, love?"

"As certain as I can be, aye."

"Then I should be home in plenty of time for the laddie's birthing. There's a wee bit of smoked venison and a bit o' bacon in the cornmeal bin. More than enough t' feed ye for twice that long. Ye willna panic if I'm a day or two late?"

"Me, panic? Sassenachs never panic, didn't you know that?" she challenged, and forced a bright smile. "It's the ice in our veins."

She forced another smile as he drew her down

onto his lap. Her breathing quickened when he gently fondled her breast, cupping the soft mound and finding the nipple even through her thick layers of clothing. He rubbed it while he gently nibbled and bit those few inches of her neck that were left exposed. His warm breath down the collar of her bodice made her shiver with anticipation. "W-what had you in mind for the rest of the day?" she asked unsteadily. Her nipple hardened between his fingers.

He grinned for the first time that morning. His gray eyes glinted with a devilish gleam. "Weell, there's no work to be done, not in this weather, aye? And we have all the dry kindling we could ever need. So . . . I shall spend the day pleasuring my bride."

As he spoke, his voice dropped to a husky growl. He slipped his hand up her skirts. But his heavy-lidded, smoky gaze and expectant grin faded to annoyance when he felt all the impediments to his explorations. Three sarks? Two layers of petticoats? Two pairs of hose?

"Whist, lassie, ye've more layers to ye than an onion," he grumbled. "How's a man to find what he's after, beneath all these petticoats and fol-de-rols?"

Gently taking his earlobe beween her teeth, she sank her teeth into it. "Peel away the layers, milord," she whispered in his ear. "One . . . by . . . one."

*　　*　　*

Much later, they lay on their sides, her back curving against his chest. His hands were clasped gently over her swollen belly. They were watching the flicker of firelight over the log walls of their cabin as they made love yet again.

He was still hard, still lodged deep inside her, moving strongly, rhythmically, yet with such gentle care for her comfort, she could have wept at the warm cocoon of pleasure and sensation in which his body cradled hers.

His chest and thighs were deliciously rough. She could feel the springy hairs rubbing against her back and bottom. His sinewy arms encircled her as he dropped feathery kisses over her throat and shoulders.

Her breathing quickened. Sighs became gasps of delight as his hand slipped down over her swollen belly, to plunder the nest of curls at its base. His nipples were hard little buttons against her back as he teased the sensitive bud within the soft folds.

"Aye, lassie, aye," he crooned against her ear when she began to quiver and moan.

She arched helplessly against him, pleading and exposed.

"That's the way of it. Let it come, love. Let it take ye. Nay, nay, dinna fight it, ma *sonsie*."

"Ah! Aaah!"

"*There*. Aye. And there again. Aye, that's my good lass."

He drew her back, onto him, holding her fast,

rocking with her as his own climax shuddered through him. The two of them were one as he emptied himself inside her.

"I love you, Drummond McLeod," she whispered fiercely as he pressed his lips to the side of her throat. "I love you so much. Promise me you'll be careful. That you'll come home safely to us."

"I will." He turned her to face him and kissed her lips, tasting the salt of her tears on his own as he did so. Their eyes met. "I swear it, on my brother's grave."

He'd given his word, and she knew he meant it. That his honor and pride, if nothing else, would ensure that he came back. But the words she longed for him to say remained unsaid, hanging unspoken in the air between them.

"I promise," he said again.

Even to his ears, the words sounded empty.

Chapter Twenty-six

Drum had been gone ten days on the bitterly cold morning Rose awoke to find that, during the night, Scamp had died.

Her back beset by a nagging ache, she bit back her tears, gently wrapped his stiff body in some sacking, and then bundled up to go outside.

Shivering despite a heavy cloak and several layers of clothing, she milked the cow and gave the horses their nosebags of grain. Carrying an armful of firewood, she staggered back inside, stacked the kindling beside the hearth, and then carried the little collie's body outside.

The fir trees' evergreen branches were spangled with flakes of sparkling snow. Like angels robed in glorious white, they ringed the area

Drum and Andy had cleared for the herb and vegetable garden she planned to plant in the spring.

The earth was iron-hard beneath its mantle of white. Far too hard for the digging of a grave, however shallow. But beneath the trees, she found what she'd been looking for: a deep depression in the ground. It would have to do.

Kneeling down, she gently placed the stiff little body in the hollow, then gathered rocks and stones to heap over it.

When she was finished, she was exhausted but satisfied with her work. The heavy layer of rocks would keep wild animals from disturbing her faithful companion's resting place. Two sticks of kindling and a bit of string formed a crude cross, which she placed at the head of the small grave as a marker.

Whether animals, like people, went to Heaven, she did not know. But, her teeth chattering, her tears freezing on the frosty air, she murmured a hasty prayer anyway. If any dog deserved to go to Heaven, Scamp did.

After wishing him a multitude of unsuspecting rabbits and all the bones he could ever hope for in his animal paradise, she hurried back toward the cabin.

She had reached the woodpile when she skidded on a patch of ice. As she flung out her arms to break her fall, her body twisted. A sharp pain knifed through her belly. Doubling over, she saw bright splashes of crimson in the snow.

Blood. *Her* blood.

Oh, God . . . the baby.

"McLeod!" she screamed as a second pain hit. *"Drummond!"*

Her knees buckled. The ground rushed up to meet her, and then everything went black. . . .

"Drummmond!"

He was starting to imagine things. He'd heard of it happening to men in the desert. Why not out here, in this desert of blinding white snow, where the endless white of mountain, land and sky, the seemingly endless silence of the snow-bound world, could drive a man to madness?

But he could have sworn he heard Rosamund cry out for him, her voice keening on the wind like the mournful cry of a seabird.

He reined in his weary horse and cocked his head to listen.

Nothing. Only the low moan of the wind, the jingling of the pack mule's harness—sounds he'd grown so accustomed to, he hardly heard them anymore.

He should have waited another day. He knew that now. The elders at the fort—both Scottish and Indian—had warned him he should not leave this morning. They'd looked up at the white sky, sniffed, and foretold a blizzard before nightfall.

He'd looked and seen only the promise of another crisp, if bitterly cold, day. Had he, in his eagerness to get back to his wife, to tell her that he loved her, seen only what he wanted to see?

He feared so.

Whatever his reasons, he'd chosen to ignore the old men's warnings. To load up horse and mule and set off.

But now the first flakes were beginning to fly, swirling like goosedown on the wind. It was too late to turn back. All he could do was ride on.

Rose stirred. Opening her eyes, she found herself lying on her back in the snow. She was staring up at the tops of the pines and the pale sky far above them.

She frowned. What had happened to the charcoal and lemon skies of dawn? Had she been lying here that long?

She shuddered. No wonder she was so cold. Or that her hands and feet had gone numb. Or that her head felt so heavy she could hardly lift it. When she tried to shout for help, only a feeble whimpering sound came out.

Perhaps she was dead and did not know it. Was that possible? She thought it might be. It would certainly explain why she felt so weak.

She tried to sit up, to call out, but the effort was too much for her. Slowly, she sank back and surrendered to the snow's cold embrace, drifting back down into the velvety black fog of blissful unconsciousness.

When she awoke again, the sky above her had darkened to the pale lavender of early afternoon. She could hear voices nearby. Men speaking in a guttural language that she recognized as the Iroquois tongue, spoken by the Indians who had come to trade at Fort Charles.

She had to hide. They would kill her if they found her!

After several attempts, she managed to roll over, to drag and push herself up, onto her knees. Inch by exhausting inch, she crawled into the woods like a baby, leaving a long smear of dark-red blood in the snow behind her.

She came to again with a feeling of utter terror. The savages had caught her. They had strapped her to a crude board of some kind. Her arms and legs were tied down. Fur robes were heaped over and under her, cocooning her in warmth. Her hands and feet were no longer numb. God, no. If only they were! Now that the feeling had returned, they hurt. Burned. Oh, Lord, how they burned.

Her extremities were the least of her problems right now. What mattered was that she was being carried swiftly through the forest, taken farther away from the cabin with each passing moment. Farther and farther from Drummond. When he returned from the settlment, he would find her gone.

Somehow, she had to get away. . . .

*   *   *

Curled deep in a womb-like cavern under a hill, Drummond dreamed. . . .

He saw Rose standing on the high promontory that rose over the valley of New Dunmor like the prow of a great sailing ship.

Her bodice hugged her high, round breasts. Her violet-sprigged skirts were pressed flat against her slender hips by the wind. About her shoulders she wore Maddy's fringed ivory shawl. Her golden-brown ringlets twisted like sea anemones tossed on a current, and her eyes were as dewy as the purple gloaming that crept through the glen with the coming of twilight.

"Wake up, Drummond," she whispered. Her voice echoed in the chambers of his mind. Arms slender and graceful, she reached out to shake him, her lips curved in a tender, loving smile. "Wake up, my love! 'Tis far too cold for you to sleep. Soon we shall be together again. . . ."

"I love ye, Rosamund. I love ye with all my heart," he shouted, but she was fading away, becoming one with the mist.

"Rosamund! Dinna leave me. I love ye! Come back!"

He awoke with a gasp and a start to an eerie stillness.

Something had changed while he slept, but for the life of him, he could not think what it was.

His horse and the pack mule were still there in the cave he'd found, carved from the side of a steep hill. So were his provisions. The deep wall of snow that had been hurled against the cave mouth during the blizzard still sealed his exit. In fact, that very wall of snow had saved his life. It had kept out the killing cold, and conserved the heat given off by the animals.

The silence, that was the difference!

He could no longer hear the dull moaning sound that had been his constant companion for the past two days. The blizzard had finally passed.

It took him a long time to dig his way out, with only his hands for tools. The wintry sunlight, reflected off the snow, was blinding when he crawled out of the cave through the low tunnel he'd made. He had to shade his eyes to see.

It took him another two hours to make the opening large enough to lead the animals outside.

The going was bitterly hard all that day. He waded through deep snow that came up past his knees in some places, drifted up to the horses' bellies in others.

It was getting dark and he had yet to make camp for the night when he spotted a party of Indians, gliding like shadows between the skeletal black trees. They called back and forth to each other, their strange tongue interspersed with bursts of raucous laughter.

They wore wicker snowshoes over their moccasins, like those Drum had seen the French trappers wearing at the settlement, as well as fur hats. Heavy fur robes—of bear, buffalo or wolf-skin—were draped around them.

He considered showing himself or calling out to them in greeting, perhaps offering to trade some of his provisions for one of their warm fur robes or a seat at their campfire. But in the end, he decided against it.

The Indians were heavily armed. Trade tom-ahawks, long-bladed knives and hefty wooden war clubs dangled from their belts. There was no sign of the bows and arrows used by harmless hunters. Furthermore, they were passing a small keg of what could only be whiskey from man to man. He did not know if they'd come by it hon-estly, in trade, or had stolen it on one of their bloody raids. Either way, he fancied their laugh-ter had a dangerous, drunken edge to it and kept his distance.

Ducking out of sight, he led his animals into the cover of some low-hanging fir trees and a huge outcropping of rock for the night, and let the renegades move on.

Chapter Twenty-seven

While still a mile from the cabin, Drum spotted a column of dark smoke rising above the leafless fretwork of the woods. The sight of it, hanging like a funeral pall of black crepe against the white sky, made the blood turn to ice in his veins.

He kicked the horse, forcing a burst of speed from the weary beast. He kept on kicking it until the horse finally burst from the forest into the clearing.

There he flung himself down from its back, devastated by the sight before him.

Where their cabin had once stood, there was now only a hollow shell of blackened log walls. The lean-to had fared no better. Lazy ribbons of dark smoke were still unraveling into the frosty sky.

"No! Dear God, tell me it isna happening," he whispered hoarsely. Forcing reluctant limbs to obey him, he staggered across the clearing.

"Rosamund!" he roared. His anguished cry was like the howl of a crazed animal, ripped from deep inside him. Like a man possessed, he searched the gutted ruins, terrified of what he might find.

Smoldering charcoal burned his fingers. Soot and grime blackened his hands and cheeks. He rummaged through the ashes and the ruins until he found a feathered war club, the charred remnants of a whiskey keg, quite empty now. But her body was not in the burned-out ruins, as he'd feared.

Hope—relief—welled up inside him.

Rosamund must still be alive or he would have found something, surely? The war party that had attacked the cabin must have finished his small keg of whiskey, then carried Rosamund off to their village as their captive, along with the livestock.

If he could overtake them, there was a chance he could still save her.

As he stumbled away from the smoldering ruins, he tripped over a small mound in the dirt. It was covered over with stones and rocks, and by a layer of powdery snow.

Two sticks of kindling, bound together to form

a crude cross, leaned drunkenly over one end of the tiny mound. Or rather, over the grave, he amended, for what else could it be but a wee grave?

The sight of it chilled him to the marrow. But, although his chest ached with sorrow, he could not cry.

At some time between his departure and the savages' attack, Rosamund must have lost their precious wee bairn. She'd scraped a hole in the hard ground to bury the poor mite's tiny body here, beneath the wee mound of earth at his feet.

Tears clogged his throat. Dear God. Was there to be no end to this nightmare? No ease from this pain?

Kneeling down, he bowed his head and uttered a hasty yet fervent prayer for the soul of the babe he had loved and lost, without ever seeing its dear face or hearing its cry.

When he rose stiffly, his eyes were still dry, but a cold, dark rage had pervaded his body. He felt a bone-deep chill that had nothing to do with the weather.

Hauling himself astride his exhausted horse, he followed the tracks of the raiding party in the snow. They led away from the cabin and on through the deep woods.

It was mid-afternoon of the following day when he stumbled across a trappers' camp a short distance from the banks of the river. There were several sleds piled high with beaver traps, pelts and trade goods, as well as a few shaggy horses and pack mules.

A half-dozen whiskery trappers were standing on the riverbank, looking down at something and grimly shaking their heads.

"Bienvenue. Welcome, stranger," an olive-skinned man greeted Drummond as he emerged from some leafless bushes nearby. He wiped his mouth on the sleeve of his long fur coat. There was a greenish, sickly look about him as he nodded at the huddle of men down by the water. "It is a tragedy, *non?* I would not go any closer, unless you 'ave a strong stomach, *mon ami.* As you can see, I have not."

"What happened there?" Drum asked, cutting him off. A chill had settled over him, like a cold, creeping fog. "What are your friends looking at?"

"A band of Mohawk renegades surprised some white travelers who had camped on the riverbanks last night." The trapper shrugged. "They scalped and killed the woman, then took the others captive and burned their wagon, from what we can tell. Monsieur? Monsieur, wait—! Come back here!"

Drum heard nothing after the man had mentioned the woman. If there was a chance, however remote, that the dead woman was Rosamund, he had to know.

He ran toward the river, taking great strides that seemed to go nowhere. Each breath he drew felt torn from his lungs by ripping talons.

"My wife was captured by an Indian war party," he told a sad-eyed Frenchman when he reached the line of trappers. "They burned our cabin to the ground. Let me through. I have to see that woman. I need to know if she's my wife."

"Per'aps you could describe something she wore . . . a ring, or a necklace?"

"No, nothing. Besides, I dinna have time for that." With an impatient snort, Drum shoved his way between the beefy shoulders of the men, but they refused to let him any closer.

Brought up short, he stood stock-still, and stared at what looked like a pitiful bundle of rags, huddled on the muddy riverbank before him.

Nay, not rags. It was a dress. Rosamund's dress. Ah, God. Ah, God in Heaven. It was she.

"Noooooo!" he roared, his knees buckling. "Noooooo!" Poleaxed by grief, he knelt in the snow, his head bowed, his shoulders heaving. Tears coursed down his cheeks like rain.

She lay on her side, her face and scalp covered with blood. Some of her golden-brown hair had been lifted. What was left of it was soaked dark-red with old blood. So was her cloak and the violet-sprigged gown she wore. The calico gown she'd sewn for the *céilidh*.

Tears filled his throat, his chest. More scalded his eyes. What a son-of-a-bitch he was. What a cold, uncaring bastard. She'd deserved so much better than him. He'd never told her how bonnie she looked in that dress. Not once. Just as he had never told her that he loved her.

Instead, he had ridden off, leaving her alone and defenseless. Had abandoned her, left her to be captured and killed, without ever telling her that she meant more to him than life itself.

You should tend to the living, and let the dead rest in peace, she had said once.

And she was right, ah, God, so very right. He'd been too absorbed by his grief, too caught up in losing Cameron, to consider what it would mean to lose her. He should have told her. If only he could have her back for one more day—another hour!

"Our deepest condolences. We will see that your wife is given a proper burial, *mon ami,*" a trapper reassured him, pity in his eyes as he patted Drum's shoulder. "Jean-Louis here will say the words over her himself, will you not, Louis?"

"It would be an honor, sir. My brother, he is a priest in Montreal, *non?* It is better you remember her as she was, *n'est-ce pas?*"

"You see? Come along now, *Ecosse.* Come away. . . ."

Dry-eyed and stumbling, Drum let the Frenchmen lead him back to their campfire. He moved slowly, woodenly, like a man in a deep trance, doing whatever they told him. For the time being, the trappers were the puppet-masters. The ones who pulled the strings that made him move.

Back in their camp, a trapper pressed a flask of cognac to Drum's lips, held his nose and forced him to swallow.

But although the fiery liquor spread heat through his belly, it did nothing to thaw the ice around his heart—or to make him forget.

Nothing could.

"Time, she is a great healer, *mon ami*," one trapper observed, taking a swig from the brandy flask himself. "Aaah." He wiped his lips on the back of his hand. "One day, you will put this tragedy behind you, *non?* And then—?" He shrugged eloquently. "Only *le bon Dieu* knows what you will make of your life then, eh?"

"Have you eaten today, *mon frère?*" asked another. "Come, you should eat something. A man needs his strength at such a time. In the morning, we will take you with us to Fort Charles. Perhaps you have friends there, yes?"

Instead of answering the man, Drum drew the dirk from his boot.

With a distant look in his eyes, he slashed the sharp blade across his palm. Blood welled from the deep cut. Dipping his finger in it, he painted himself for war, as his Gaelic ancestors had once painted their faces with blue woad before riding into battle.

Moments later, he unfastened his hair and stripped off his fringed buckskin shirt. Bare-chested, he threw himself astride his horse.

Ignoring the trappers, who crossed themselves and muttered that *l'Ecosse* had gone quite insane, he rode off into the darkening wilderness.

He had been denied vengeance once.

This time it would be different.

Chapter Twenty-eight

He lost the tracks in the snow when another light snowfall erased them soon after daybreak of the following day. It was only by a stroke of luck that at midday he stumbled across a snow-covered Indian cornfield on the banks of a river.

If there was a cornfield, a village could not be far away.

He followed the cleared fields for almost two miles until he found a sprawling Huron village, perched on a high bluff that rose over the banks of a vast lake. Ice gleamed like a looking glass under a wintry sun.

The village boasted numerous bark long-houses, surrounded by a palisade of sharpened posts. Outside the palisade lay a broad, cleared area of several yards across which an enemy could not advance without being spotted. On the wooden walkway behind the palisade, sentries wrapped in robes of fur kept sharp lookout.

Drummond saw no defenses. Nor did he see the vigilant guards. Blinded by rage, half mad with grief and hunger, he uttered a blood-curdling whoop and galloped his horse straight into the very heart of the village, as he had once ridden into the hell that was Culloden.

His wild black hair streamed behind him. His gray eyes blazed in his blood-smeared face. His mount's flying hooves scattered savages and village dogs alike as he rode them down, brandishing his flintlock over his head like a club and howling Gaelic war cries.

The horse, terrified by the reek of smoke, the smell of bear-grease and the scent of its rider's blood, snorted and reared up, dancing on it hindquarters.

"Bluidy cowards! Woman-killers!" Drum roared. His features contorted with grief as his mount reared up, its forelegs pawing air. "Come out! Come out from your dens and face me. Fight me like men, if ye dare, ye skulking, yellow-bellied cowards. God rot the lot of ye. I'll cut out your bluidy hearts!"

Swinging the flintlock by its barrel muzzle like a war club, he wheeled the gelding's head around, kicked its flanks and galloped it straight at a group of braves who had just emerged from a sweat-lodge.

Shouting in alarm, they scattered like nine-pins. With a wild whoop of glee, Drum charged through them and beyond, before wheeling his horse around.

How many deaths would it take to avenge Rosamund's murder and erase his grief? A hundred? A thousand? More? However many it took, he would do it, he vowed!

The horse thundered forward again, its mouth open in a scream, its withers flecked with foam. As he leaned forward over its neck, the nail on the cord at his chest flew up. Its sharp point gouged his cheek, drawing blood.

In that single, searing instant of pain, all that the nail had come to symbolize was brought home to him. His guilt that his brother and their clansmen had marched off to war, then lost their lives without him. Remorse that he had stolen an innocent woman away from her home and family. Shame that he had loved her, desired her, wanted a life with her, when his kinsmen were dead and gone.

He had tried to avenge their deaths. To find ease from his sorrow in the killing of others. He had sworn to do the same to avenge his beloved wife's murder. But what purpose did vengeance truly serve?

None. None whatsoever.

Did it restore life to the dead? Did it bring back the lost loved ones?

Never. Nothing could.

Like a plunge into an icy stream, a slap to the face, the deep scratch sobered him. Brought him to his senses not a moment too soon.

Shaking his head to clear it, he saw a little Indian maiden standing in the path of his galloping horse.

She was a small, pretty child with long, glossy black hair and enormous dark eyes. She wore a tiny deerskin dress sewn with dyed quills and embroidered moose-hair flower designs.

Every stitch of the embroidery was crystal clear in that moment.

Her brown eyes widened in terror when she saw his massive horse, bearing down on her. But, frozen in place by terror, she could not move.

She was just an innocent child. Would he slaughter an innocent, helpless little girl in his thirst for vengeance?

His muscles popping, Drum wrenched the gelding's head around. Gripping with powerful arms and thighs, he physically forced the beast to change its direction. To thunder harmlessly past the little girl, who was sitting in the dirt now, crying but—mercifully—quite unharmed.

He would have ridden on and lost himself in the woods like a wild beast if one of the village's young warriors had not leaped for his horse's bridle. Another brave hung on to its cheek-strap until the lathered beast slithered to a halt. Two others dragged Drum down from its back.

Past caring if they tortured or even killed him, Drum let them drag him into the heart of their village without a word or a sound of protest.

Seeming oblivious to the hailstorm of angry blows they rained over his head and upper body, he strode like one of the living dead down the gauntlet of whooping, jeering Huron warriors, his black head held high, his gray eyes fixed on some distant point that only he could see. He looked neither to left nor to right as he walked.

When he reached the last of the jeering braves, an old man stepped forward to meet him.

Picking up the horseshoe nail that hung about Drummond's neck, he looked at it, then into his eyes.

"You are the husband of Make Clouds Woman, neh? My daughter's husband says your heart lies on the ground. That your spirit is filled with sorrow for your woman, who was taken from your lodge."

Something flickered in Drummond's eyes. For the first time, he looked at the Huron grandfather as if he truly saw him standing there.

"Aye, old man. Taken and killed by your braves," he rasped hoarsely, glowering at the old one. "Why? Can ye tell me that? Why did your people kill my woman? What did my wee Rose ever do t' hurt ye or your people? Tell me, damn ye!"

The old man's face darkened. "My village does not take the path of war against our white brothers. Nor do our warriors steal your women or your little ones. The people of this village are Christians. The black-robe fathers live in our village. They teach us of the Christ, who died for our sins. Hear me, *Ecosse*. Your woman is here—unharmed."

"My wife's father speaks the truth. You will not weep for your woman at the Feast of the Dead, my brother, for her soul has not fled to the spirit world," a younger man added softly in French. *"Votre femme est ici.* Make Clouds Woman, she is here, in my longhouse, with my wife and the women of our village. We found her lying in the snow before your lodge and brought her here, to our midwives, to be cared for."

Drum stared deep into the man's eyes. A tingle of recognition shimmied down his spine.

The tall brave with the shaved head and the braided pony tails was Black Elk, the father of the infant Rosamund had plucked from the river months ago.

He frowned as Black Elk's words sunk in. "What did you say?" he demanded hoarsely.

"Votre femme. Et votre bébé. Vous avez un fils très forte, Ecosse. Your wife. And your baby. You have a very strong son, Scotsman. His voice is very loud. The mother of our village has given

him a strong name. She has called him Thunder Talking."

Drum stared at Black Elk, afraid to hope, not daring to believe.

"Surely ye're lying. Ye must be. My baby is dead. I saw the grave—and I saw her! My wife was murdered by your people. Ye killed her and lifted her scalp!"

"*Non*," corrected Two Bears, the old man at Black Elk's side. "Make Clouds Woman is safe. The fire-haired woman with the grass eyes, she and her man were killed by our enemy, the Mohawk. A band of renegades who will not listen to the counsel of their elders, but want only to kill the white man and drink his whisk-ee. It is they who burned your lodge, after we had taken your woman away. Come. I will show you. She is unharmed."

They led him through the village to one of the birch-bark longhouses.

There they halted. Black Elk held aside a flap of animal skin. Drummond ducked his head and followed Two Bears through the doorway.

Inside, the longhouse was dark and windowless. Several small fires burned at intervals along the center of the ground. The smoke from them escaped through several smoke-holes cut in the roof above them. On the farthest wall was painted a crest that showed a great grizzly bear.

"It is the crest of my wife's bear clan," Two Bears explained. "She is the mother of our village. Come, *Ecosse*. Your woman is here."

Drummond followed the old man down the longhouse. There were low platforms built against the walls on either side, like benches, which were obviously used for sleeping. Over them were thrown fur pelts and red trade blankets. From the wooden walls hung braids of corn and squash, iron kettles, pots and weapons, as well as other household goods.

Two Bears halted before a curtain of skins which partitioned off an area within the longhouse for privacy. He drew the curtain aside and spoke to the old woman within.

Kneeling beside her, Drummond saw, was the younger woman whose baby Rosamund had saved from the river. She was holding the child, who lifted his head from her breast to regard the white man with shining dark eyes. The laddie was, Drummond noticed, much larger than he had been.

"My wife welcomes you and bids you enter, *Ecosse*. She says that your son has been waiting for two suns to greet his father," Two Bears explained, smiling and beckoning to him. "Come. Come inside."

Nothing that followed this moment could ever come close to the enormous joy that swelled up in his breast when he saw that Rosamund was alive.

She lay on one of the low platforms. All but

her pale face and golden-brown hair was covered in soft bear and wolf pelts.

"Drummond!" she cried out.

"Sweetheart," he whispered.

Tears spilled down his cheeks as he dropped to his knees beside her.

"Are ye all right?"

She nodded through her tears of happiness. "Yes—thanks to Two Bears' wife and daughter. Black Elk and some other men found me in the snow when they were hunting. I—I was bleeding and unconscious, so they carried me here. But what about you? You're hurt. What happened to you?" Rose exclaimed, touching his bloodied cheek. There was concern in her violet eyes.

"It's nothing. A wee cut," he said dismissing the matter. He stared at her, unable to believe his eyes. He reached out to cup her cheek, feeling the warmth of her flesh beneath his fingers. She was so warm. So alive. Closing his eyes, he pressed his lips to hers. A shudder of emotion moved through him as he felt the pressure of his mouth returned. He could taste the salt of her tears on his lips.

"I love ye, Rosamund McLeod," he said fiercely, framing her face between his hands. "I love ye more than anything or anyone in this world."

"Drum? What happened? What's wrong?" He looked exhausted, gray and desperate. And why was he telling her that he loved her now, after all these months without saying it? What had happened to change him?

"Sssh, dinna stop me, lassie. It's something I should have told ye months ago. God knows, I felt it! Lassie, I love ye. It has naught to do with bairns t' carry on my family line, nor with guilt for stealing ye away from England. I love ye wi' all my heart and soul for the woman ye are. God help me, I always will."

With that impassioned declaration, he drew her into his arms and kissed her hungrily, pouring all his grief and fear for her into the joy of that long, deep kiss.

As he held her, reluctant to let her go, a loud, protesting wail rose from the furs between them.

He pulled away and stared at Rose in shock as she drew down the wolf pelt to reveal a pink bundle cuddled to her breast.

"McLeod, I'd like you to meet your son," she said, smiling with pride. She placed a red-faced, dark-haired, heavily swaddled, screaming infant in his arms. "Laird Drummond, this is Cameron James McLeod, Eighth Earl of Dunmor, Scotland—and the first Earl of New Dunmor."

A look she'd never seen before spread across his face. It was, she realized, an expression of wonder.

"Ye named him for Cameron. For my brother."

"Yes. That was what we agreed, was it not? Do you like it?"

"Aye, love. I like it fine.

She smiled impishly. "Because if not, the mother of the village has given him a Huron name. I cannot pronounce it, but the Jesuit priest explained that it means 'Thunder Talking.'"

Drummond grinned. "I dinna wonder at it. Ye're verra loud, my laddie," he crooned. "Aye, that ye are, my wean." Adding a Gaelic endearment of his own, he kissed the infant's brow.

The eighth earl of Dunmor stopped crying. He stared curiously up at his father from murky dark eyes as Drummond looked down at him, a father's love for his firstborn shining in his gray eyes.

"Whist but he's a bonnie lad," Drummond breathed. "Takes after his mother, aye."

"Hmm. He could do worse than to look like you, McLeod," she said teasingly. "Did you come to take us home?"

"By and by. I thought we'd go t' the settlement when the weather breaks. We'll see how Andy's doing—he's marrit his Kirsty now, ye ken?"

"He didn't!" she exclaimed, laughing.

"Oh, yes, he did. And perhaps we'll stay with Maddy until the spring. She's breeding hersel', aye?"

"It's a miracle. She and Hamish have been waiting for a child for so long. Thanks be."

Drummond nodded. "I fancy she'd like having our bairn about t' cosset." He forced himself to sound casual, knowing how deeply the cabin's loss would affect her.

"I expect you're right, but. . . . I'd much rather go home. To New Dunmor."

"I know. But we canna, lass, not yet. The cabin's gone. A Mohawk war party burned it t' the ground."

"Aah." She swallowed. "Then we'll stay with Maddy until we can build a better one," she agreed simply, squeezing his hand. "Houses aren't what matter anyway, are they? Neither is the land. I've spent half my lifetime looking for a home to call my own, Drum. It's taken me until now to realize that a home can be wherever we want to make it. We can be happy anywhere, if we're with the ones we love."

He swallowed. "Under the trees, there was a grave—"

She nodded and bit her lip. Tears filled her eyes. "It was Scamp's. He died just before the baby started to come. Poor little thing. He never recovered from what Tom did to him, that vicious brute."

Lifting his son, she put him to her swollen breast, touching his cheek to guide his hungry rosebud mouth to the milky nipple.

As he watched his son nursing, Drummond said a silent prayer of thanks that he'd been wrong about the identity of the murdered woman on the riverbank. Arabella had already paid the ultimate price for her sins. Tom's fate at the hands of the Mohawk raiders—infamous for their skill in torturing their unfortunate captives—had surely been even less kind.

"We'll have to start over, Drum. The fire took everything we had that was of any value."

"Nay, not everything, my love," he murmured as he embraced her and the baby. "Everything I value is right here, in my arms."

Chapter Twenty-nine

1752, New Dunmor, Five Years Later

Drummond stared at the length of fringed tartan cloth in his arms, shaking his head in disbelief.

The dark-blue and dark-green wool squares were bordered in black, quartered in both directions by thin, alternating stripes of red and yellow. His hands shook. It was the hunting plaid of the clan McLeod. The tartan that the Act of Proscription, five years before, had forbidden Highlanders to wear on pain of imprisonment or deportation.

If he closed his eyes, he remembered as if it were yesterday how he and Andy had been run like hunted hares through the Highlands, forced to throw their tartan breachans down a well as they fled south, into enemy England, that fateful April. . . .

"Where did ye find this, lassie?"

"Where did I *find* it? The cheek of you, Mc-Leod! I'll have you know I wove this length of plaid myself—with wool that was shorn from New Dunmor sheep, and spun by my own two hands," she confessed proudly.

"You wove this?"

Rose laughed in delight at his stupefied expression. "Aye," she told him, gently mocking his Scots burr. "I had Andrew send to Dunvegan and Skye for the sett. Your Auntie Sheilagh McLeod was delighted to hear you'd survived Culloden, and to be of help. She sent me a most gracious letter, describing the colors and the correct number of threads to use in the weaving. She enclosed another letter for you. Here it is. Happy birthday, my love. Come, Cameron, let your Papa read his letter in peace, there's a good boy. Trelawney McLeod, you naughty girl! Get down off that bench before you fall and break your neck!"

"He was on it," Trelawney retorted, glaring at her older brother.

"That's because I can climb whatever I want. I can climb a tree or a mountain or anything. I'm older than you. So there," Cameron told her, his fists planted arrogantly on his hips. His black curls were Drummond's, but his eyes were a deep lavender gray, halfway between his Da's and his Mam's.

"Aye. But I'm faster. Faster's better than older." With that, Trelawney punched her brother on the arm and then ran off like the wind, her long black curls streaming behind her. Her skirts were hitched up, and her pudgy little legs were pumping furiously. Her squeals of naughty laughter turned her father's head.

"Och, she's in for it now, the wicked wee besom," he observed fondly.

"Perhaps. But first, Cameron has to catch her," his wife said, laughing as she linked her arm through his. "He's older and stronger, true, but 'Lawney climbs like a monkey, swims like a fish and runs like a deer." She frowned. "I don't think he's going to win this time."

"Would ye care to wager on that, madam?"

"Indeed I would. But not with coin, sir. Land is what I want." Her violet eyes sparkled. "I'll take that river meadow you've been keeping from me."

"If you win, you mean," he teased.

"Oh, I'll win, all right," she said confidently, looking very much like her daughter in that moment.

"Dinna be so sure about that," he observed, nodding. " 'Lawney's coming back."

"Why, so she is," Rosamund exclaimed, shading her eyes. "And she has a man in tow."

"I sorely doubt he'll be the last, poor divil,"

Drum said, laughing. His wee daughter showed every indication of being a beauty, like her mam. He watched his wife's face expectantly as she shaded her eyes against the sun to see who it was Trelawney was escorting up to the fine stone house they'd built upon the bluff overlooking the valley.

Pleasure filled his eyes when she frowned and murmured. "Dear Lord. I must have had too much sun. For a moment, I could have sworn the man was—"

"Aye? Sworn what, my love?" He cocked a dark eyebrow and eyed her expectantly.

"That the man with 'Lawney is. . . . Well, of course, it can't really be him, but he does walk exactly like my—"

"Who, love? Tell me. Someone you knew?" he asked innocently.

Rosamund nodded, still so shaken, she could hardly speak. "Ye-es."

As the man strode beneath the rose trellis into the sunlight and the garden proper, he removed his tricorn and wiped his forehead, before putting his hat back on. One of his sleeves was empty, pinned tidily out of the way.

Their daughter skipped alongside him, chattering like a little magpie. Then suddenly, 'Lawney broke away from the man and ran toward her mother.

"Mama, look! There's a man come. He says

he's my Uncle James, and he's only got one arm. Is he my uncle, Mama?"

"*James!*" Rosamund's hand flew to her heart. "Oh, dear God!" She was so stunned, for once she couldn't speak. "It can't be. It just can't."

But it was.

As the man stopped in front of her, he removed his hat. His deep blue eyes shone. "It's been a long time, Rosie."

"Jim!" She threw herself into his arms. He picked her up and twirled her around, her skirts flying up to show the layers of petticoats beneath them. Tears spilled down Rose's cheeks as she hugged and kissed her brother.

"However did you manage to find me? How is it you're not dead?" she cried, hanging on to his hand as if she feared to let him go.

"One question at a time, love." Jim Trelawney grinned as he looked across at Drummond. "You'll be Lord Drummond, I'm thinking."

"Aye," Drum admitted.

" 'Tis a pleasure to meet you, sir."

"And you, James." He warmly shook the hand James offered. "Please, call me Drum. You're my brother-in-law, after all, and we're not sae fancy here at New Dunmor, are we, lass?"

"Drummond it is then," Jim agreed. "Well, two years ago, his lordship—Drummond—sent a solicitor to find me," he told Rose. "But I left the Golden Swan and London soon after you disappeared. Tom thought I'd double-crossed him, you see, and I was afraid he would come back and finish me off. To be honest, I'd given up all hopes of ever seeing you alive again, sis. So, I went back down to Cornwall and that's where Mr. Dawson—the solicitor—found me."

Rose shot an accusing look at Drummond. She punched his arm. "You rogue! You never said a word about it."

"I didna dare, lass. I thought it was worth trying t' find him, but I didna want ye to be disappointed if your brother was really dead. Tom Wainwright lied to ye, did he no', lassie? He couldna take the time to go back and kill your brother. He had t' keep after ye before the scent o' your trail grew cold. But I've no doubt he wanted to, aye?"

"Thank you, my love," Rose murmured, going up on tiptoe to kiss her husband's cheek. "Thank you from the bottom of my heart."

Drummond smiled. "I love ye, Rosamund."

"I love you, too, McLeod."

"Let's walk up to the house, shall we, Uncle James?" Trelawney said with a disgusted expression on her pretty little face. She trustingly tucked her hand into her uncle's. "Mama and Papa are kissing. *Again*. I'm never going to get married. Never ever."

"No? And why is that?" Jim asked solemnly.

"Because then, you have to kiss *boys*. Horrid ones like Ross McKinnon and Alec Lewis," Trelawney confided in a loud whisper. "They put a t-toad down my neck, Uncle James. Uncle Andy said they were truly, truly sorry, and Uncle Hamish said he'd warm Alec's bottom for it, but I still hate them." She scowled, her bottom lip protruding.

Jim laughed. "That's what your mother used to say when she was a little girl. That she hated boys and would never marry one."

"My mama said that?" Trelawney asked.

"Aye, poppet, she did."

Trelawney halted. She turned around and shaded her eyes to look down the hill, to where her parents were still kissing in the gazebo.

A heavy, disgusted sigh escaped her.

"Do ye see her, Uncle James?" Trelawney dropped her voice to a loud yet conspiratorial whisper, cupped her hands on either side of her mouth and said, *"Mama lied."*

James threw back his head, and roared with laughter.

KEEPER OF MY Heart

PENELOPE NERI

Morgan St. James is by far the most virile man Miranda Tallant has ever seen and she realizes at once that this man is no ordinary lighthouse keeper. But while she does not know if he has come to investigate her family's smuggling or if he truly has been disinherited, one glance at his emerald-dark eyes promises her untold nights of desire. Bent on discovering the blackguards responsible for his friend's death, Morgan doesn't expect to be caught up in the stormy sea of Miranda Tallant's turquoise eyes. The lovely widow consumes his every waking thought and his every dream with an all-encompassing passion. For while he cannot abandon his duty to his friend and his family, he knows that he can not rest until Miranda's heart is his.

___4647-4 $5.99 US/$6.99 CAN

SCANDALS

PENELOPE NERI

Marked by unwarranted rumor, Victoria's dance card was blank but for one handsome suitor: Steede Warring, eighth earl of Blackstone. Known behind his back as the Brute, he vows to have Victoria for his bride. Little does she suspect that Steede will uncover her body's hidden pleasures, and show her that only faith and trust can cast aside the bitter pain of scandals.

___4470-6 $5.99 US/$6.99 CAN

Dorchester Publishing Co., Inc.
P.O. Box 6640
Wayne, PA 19087-8640

Please add $1.75 for shipping and handling for the first book and $.50 for each book thereafter. NY, NYC, and PA residents, please add appropriate sales tax. No cash, stamps, or C.O.D.s. All orders shipped within 6 weeks via postal service book rate. Canadian orders require $2.00 extra postage and must be paid in U.S. dollars through a U.S. banking facility.

Name_____
Address_____
City_____State_____Zip_____
I have enclosed $_____ in payment for the checked book(s).
Payment <u>must</u> accompany all orders. ☐ Please send a free catalog.
    CHECK OUT OUR WEBSITE! www.dorchesterpub.com

Seduction By CHOCOLATE

Nina Bangs, ♥ Lisa Cach, Thea Devine, ♥ Penelope Neri

Sweet Anticipation . . . More alluring than Aphrodite, more irresistible than Romeo, the power of this sensuous seductress is renowned. It teases the senses, tempting even the most staid; it inspires wantonness, demanding surrender. Whether savored or devoured, one languishes under its tantalizing spell. To sample it is to crave it. To taste it is to yearn for it. Habit-forming, mouth-watering, sinfully decadent, what promises to sate the hungers of the flesh more? Four couples whet their appetites to discover that seduction by chocolate feeds a growing desire and leads to only one conclusion: Nothing is more delectable than love.

___4667-9 $5.50 US/$6.50 CAN

Moonshadow

PENELOPE NERI

"Lillies-of-the-valley," he murmurs, "the sweet scent of innocence." Yet his kisses are anything but innocent as he feeds her deepest desires while honeysuckle and wild roses perfume the languid air.

"Steyning Hall. It is a cold place. And melancholy," he warns, "almost as if it is . . .waiting for someone. Perhaps your coming will change all that."

Wedded mere hours, Madeleine gazes up at the windows of the mansion, stained the color of blood by the dying sun. In the shifting moonshadows she hears voices calling, an infant wailing, and knows not whether to flee for her life or offer up her heart.

___52416-3 $5.99 US/$6.99 CAN

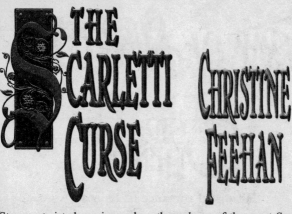

THE SCARLETTI CURSE — CHRISTINE FEEHAN

Strange, twisted carvings adorn the *palazzo* of the great Scarletti family. But a still more fearful secret lurks within its storm-tossed turrets. For every bride who enters its forbidding walls is doomed to leave in a casket. Mystical and unfettered, Nicoletta has no terror of ancient curses and no fear of marriage . . . until she looks into the dark, mesmerizing eyes of *Don* Scarletti. She has sworn no man will command her, thinks her gift of healing sets her apart, but his is the right to choose among his people. And he has chosen her. Compelled by duty, drawn by desire, she gives her body into his keeping, and prays the powerful, tormented *don* will be her heart's destiny, and not her soul's demise.

___52421-X $5.99 US/$6.99 CAN

Dorchester Publishing Co., Inc.
P.O. Box 6640
Wayne, PA 19087-8640

Please add $2.50 for shipping and handling for the first book and $.75 for each book thereafter. NY, NYC, and PA residents, please add appropriate sales tax. No cash, stamps, or C.O.D.s. All orders shipped within 6 weeks via postal service book rate. Canadian orders require $2.50 extra postage and must be paid in U.S. dollars through a U.S. banking facility.

Name _____
Address_____
City_____ State _____ Zip _____
I have enclosed $ _____ in payment for the checked book(s).
Payment <u>must</u> accompany all orders. ❑ Please send a free catalog.
    CHECK OUT OUR WEBSITE! www.dorchesterpub.com

> "A sparkling jewel in the romantic adventure world of books!"
> —*Affaire de Coeur*

Emily Maitland doesn't wish to rush into a match with one of the insipid fops she has met in London. But since her parents insist she choose a suitor immediately, she gives her hand to Major Sheridan Blake. The gallant officer is everything Emily desires in a man: He is charming, dashing—and completely imaginary. Happy to be married to a fictitious husband, Emily certainly never expects a counterfeit Major Blake to appear in the flesh and claim her as his bride. Determined to expose the handsome rogue without revealing her own masquerade, Emily doesn't count on being swept up in the most fascinating intrigue of all: passionate love.

___3894-3 $5.50 US/$7.50 CAN

NOBLE AND IVY
CAROLE HOWEY
Bestselling Author of *Sheik's Glory*

Ivy is comfortable being a schoolteacher in the town of Pleasant, Wyoming. She has long since given up dreams of marrying her childhood beau, and bravely bore the secret sorrow that haunted her past. But then Stephen, her cocksure brother, ran off with his youthful sweetheart—and a fortune in gold—and Ivy has to make sure that he doesn't wind up gutshot by gunmen or strung up by his beloved's angry brother.

Noble—just speaking his name still makes her tremble. Years before, his strong arms stoked her fires hotter than a summer day—before the tragedy that left a season of silence in its wake. Now, as the two reunite in a quest to save their siblings, Ivy burns to coax the embers to life and melt in the passion she swears they once shared. But before that can happen, Noble and Ivy will have to reconcile their past and learn that noble intentions mean nothing without everlasting love.

_4118-9 $5.50 US/$6.50 CAN